VIOLATION

AN ADAM BLACK THRILLER

KARL HILL

Print ISBN 978-1-913419-87-5

ALSO BY KARL HILL

Unleashed

PROLOGUE

1960. Torburn House. Residential Children's Home, Dundee.

The building was old. A rambling Victorian school built of stone the colour of mud. Peaked grey slate roof. A place dark and sombre. Great high ceilings. Bare white walls. Windows which were never opened. Lighting from glass sconces positioned high up. They flickered sometimes, when there was a storm.

The two boys, who seemed inseparable, were always cold. They were given matching blue pullovers, but the cloth was thin and itched the skin. All the boys wore the same. Blue pullovers, blue shorts, blue socks. Two hundred uniforms. Twenty beds in each dormitory. Ten dormitories.

They were playing together, just the two of them. They had been told to stay behind. They played on the wooden floorboards, cross-legged, facing each other. They could feel the draught against their bare knees. One was ten, the other eight.

Between them were toy soldiers. Medieval warriors, with white armour, clutching tiny swords and shields. And a little wooden catapult contraption. They played quietly, knocking soldiers down, picking them up, arranging them in a careful display, whispering to each other. Communication was always by a whisper. They were too frightened to talk any louder. Fear dominated every second of their existence.

Suddenly, the door at the end of the room opened. The boys' heads jerked round, then back to the floor. If you didn't look at them, didn't make eye contact, then you weren't chosen. Sometimes.

Three men approached. Footsteps creaked on the wooden floor. Heavy black shoes, polished and gleaming in the half light. Neither boy looked up. The three men stood over them. Nothing was said. Eventually one spoke, a rich, deep voice. A voice they knew well.

"Hello, boys."

The boys did not reply.

"Shy."

Laughter.

Another man got down on his knees, so he was almost level. "These look fantastic." He picked up one of the toy soldiers. "Marvellous detail." He raised it up to show the other men. "Do you know what these soldiers are?"

Neither boy lifted his head.

"You can tell by the red cross on their chests. They were called Crusaders. They fought for God."

He replaced the soldier back carefully to where he'd found it.

"I love your battle formations," he continued. "Wouldn't like to meet either of you in a fight, for sure."

He turned to one of them, the younger one. "Have you got a favourite?"

The boy reached over, and picked one up.

"Can I see?"

He handed it to him.

The man held it up, turning it delicately in his fingers, admiring it in the amber glow of the lighting above.

"Now he is special. He must be a Lord or a King. He looks very *regal*. He's wearing a fancy robe. He must be their leader. Does he have a name?"

The boy looked up at the man, eyes wide. He darted a glance to one of the other men, the one who had spoken initially, seeking approval. The man gave a nod – *yes, you're allowed to talk*.

"The Grey Prince." His voice was small in that vast place.

"I like it. The Grey Prince. Suits him." He gave it back, then stood.

Both boys sat, heads bowed, eyes fixed on the bare wooden floor, staring at nothing. Waiting.

"We'll play our game, shall we," spoke the one with the rich, deep voice.

"Eeny, meeny, miney, moe..." The voice continued, on and on, smooth and flowing, until it reached the end of the rhyme.

"Well, well," said the other man who had spoken. "Looks like our little Grey Prince is the lucky winner."

Laughter again, three deep voices echoing up into the high ceiling.

"Stand up, please, Grey Prince."

The boy got to his feet, head down, eyes never leaving the floor.

One of the men took the boy by the hand, and led him from the room, followed by the other two. The boy remaining didn't move until they'd left. His shoulders trembled, as he started to cry small, soft tears. He had no choice but to cry quietly, in case his worst dread was realised. That they return.

He studied the array of toy soldiers on the floor before him. He picked up his friend's favourite, and put it in his trouser pocket. He hadn't realised it had a name. Now he knew.

The Grey Prince.

1

Life is not designed to be fair. It's designed to be shit. Fucking shit, to put it politely. Treat this as fact. Once acknowledged, and accepted, killing becomes easier to endure.

Observation raised by Staff Sergeant to recruits of the 22nd Regiment of the Special Air Service

Present Day

Business was slow. Adam Black couldn't have cared less. It was what he wanted.

Needed.

If asked, he would describe it as a shift in priorities. After the trauma of his family being murdered, and the carnage which followed that unspeakable act, he thought he would never return to the law.

But he did. To fill the gaps. To give a modicum of purpose to his life. He had no other profession to fall back on. Unless killing could be counted. And in that department, he had proved more than skilful.

Gone were the long hours, the busy case load, the impossible deadlines. Downsizing, downgrading. His wife and daughter were dead. Black had acquired a new perspective. What had seemed important before was now trivial. Put simply, he no longer chased the buck. If he didn't like the look of a client, then the rule was easy. He didn't act. And few clients complained – at six-two, and with a physique carved from granite, Black got the final say. He turned away more business than he accepted, and the cases he did accept were special. Ones he could give a damn about, involving real people, real problems.

He employed a single secretary, who answered the phone, made the coffee, typed, did just about everything. His office was not noticeable. Nothing showy, above a hot food shop and a vacant beauty salon on the first floor of a tenement block in an area in the south side of Glasgow called Shawlands. Once prosperous, now semi-abandoned, with streets decorated with "To Let" and "For Sale" signs. Those businesses which did remain were charity shops, bookies, American nail bars, corner groceries. Which suited Black fine. No more video conferences and client meetings under high ceilings in oak-panelled rooms. The gloss and glitz were gone. Black was back to basics.

Which was exactly where he wanted to be.

But one legacy of his former life, and one which he had not relinquished, was coffee. Constant. Ten mugs a day, easy. He'd tried decaffeinated stuff, hated it. It had to be real, full roast. If he didn't have a coffee in his hand, then it didn't feel right. And it was halfway through his fifth, at 11.30 in the morning, when his secretary, Tricia, knocked on his office door. Which was unusual. She didn't normally knock. She normally just blustered straight through. There was little, if any, formality in Adam Black's law office.

Which meant a new client. Black braced himself for the usual reaction. Not that he gave a damn. The problem was usually dress code. Or lack of. He'd given up wearing standard uniform – the type of clothing one expected a lawyer to wear. Gone were the dark suits, crisp white shirts, discreet ties, the cufflinks, the polished-up shoes. Instead jeans, casual open-necked shirts, white running shoes. Sometimes even a T-shirt. A million miles from convention. If you didn't like it, then you could get the hell out. And a lot of clients couldn't get it.

When Tricia knocked on his door at 11.30 that morning, and introduced a brand-new client, Black assumed his image would, at the very least, cause some bemusement. At most, a derisory laugh, and a retreat back out the door.

But when Black saw her, hovering in the doorway like a frightened mouse, he knew in that instant she wouldn't give a damn how he looked. It was Black who was bemused. More than that.

Shocked.

2

"This is Mrs Diane Reith," said Tricia. "She doesn't have an appointment, but I assured her this wouldn't be a problem." Tricia gave a look, which Black understood – *she needs help.*

Black stood. "Of course not. Please, come in."

He beckoned her to a chair on the opposite side of his desk. His office could be described as spartan, which was being charitable. It was clean and functional. No frills. The walls were bare of pictures. In a corner was a solitary filing cabinet. His desk was clear, with the exception of a pad of paper, a stapler, a telephone, and a mug utilised as a pen holder.

The only item hinting of a past life was a framed photograph of his wife and daughter, laughing, clutching ice-cream cones. Taken on a July day, under a warm sun, on a beach in the north of Scotland. Both dead.

No laptop, no keypad. Black preferred taking notes longhand, and had made a conscious decision to dispense with emails. If you needed him, you either telephoned or wrote. Or met him face to face. Like the old days. An almost medieval approach to modern business.

But Black didn't give a shit. Back to basics.

Diane Reith entered, head down, managing a half-hearted smile. She sat. Her movements were stiff, awkward. She stared at her lap. She didn't speak. She was maybe about fifty, though difficult to tell, dressed in an unflattering baggy sweat top and pale cream jogging trousers, flat sandals. Her hair was short and blonde. She wore sunglasses big enough to cover half her face, in an effort to hide her injuries. But they were easy to spot. Lips swollen and bruised; cheeks puffed. A gash across her chin, maybe caused by a ring. She moved as if she'd suffered whiplash. Either she'd been in a car crash, or someone had worked her over pretty good. Black knew where he'd put his money.

"I'm sorry I don't have an appoint–" she started.

"Don't worry about it," cut in Black. He essayed an easy smile. "As you can see, we're not overrun. It's no problem."

She looked up. With the sunglasses, it was impossible to see her eyes. Obviously she wasn't wearing them to keep out the sun.

"I need a lawyer." Her voice was quiet, tentative. But she was well-spoken. From a nice neighbourhood, Black reckoned.

Black nodded, but remained silent.

"I have problems." She began fiddling her fingers, playing with a ring. A wedding ring. Chunky. Expensive looking.

"My husband and I, we no longer get on." She bowed her head again. "We very much *don't* get on. You see, he has a temper."

Black waited.

"He's got a very important job. Sometimes it gets to him. The pressure, I mean. I can understand." She looked up suddenly. "I really can."

"What can you understand?" asked Black gently.

"Why he beats me."

Black did not reply. *She blames herself.*

9

"But I don't have the strength anymore," she continued, voice faltering. "Last night was... particularly bad. I packed a suitcase this morning. He doesn't know I've left. I've got a room in a hotel. I don't know what he's going to do."

"What he's going to do?"

"When he finds I've gone. I've never done this before. He's a powerful man."

"Who is your husband?"

"George Reith. Lord Reith. You may have heard of him."

Black knew him. Knew of him. Lord Reith. Prominent High Court judge. Dispenser of justice. Upholder of law. Now beater of women.

"You're right," agreed Black. "He's a powerful man."

"Which is why I'm here." Her shoulders trembled. She started to sob – quiet, desperate tears. She opened a handbag on her lap and pulled out paper tissues, which she used to dab her eyes underneath her glasses.

Black regarded her for several seconds, then spoke.

"Why me, Mrs Reith? There are a hundred lawyers out there. Good divorce lawyers, all of them capable. With resources. I'm amazed you could even find my office. I have one part-time secretary, and I don't own a computer. Plus, I work from a shit-hole. So why me?" Black asked the question, but had a fair idea of the answer.

"My husband will make a fearful enemy. Those good divorce lawyers you mention? He knows them all. And they know him. No one's going to take him on. No one would dare. I'm..." She frowned as she searched for the right word. "...toxic."

"You have rights. We have a legal system."

She straightened her back, reached up, removed her glasses. Both eyes were purple, her right eye badly swollen, reduced to a slit, protruding an inch from her face. "He *is* the legal system!"

Black took a deep breath. "You need a lawyer he doesn't know and who has nothing to lose. Is that it?"

She shook her head. She put her sunglasses back on. "I'm sorry if I've wasted your time, Mr Black. Thank you for seeing me. This is no use." She started to rise.

Black remained seated. "I'll help you, Diane. But you have to understand something. There are certain cases where the law is no use, and the courts can't assist. That's when we look for different remedies."

"I don't understand."

"You don't need to. I'll take your case."

He asked questions, making notes with a pencil on a lined notepad. She gave quiet, faltering answers, and gradually her story unfolded – one of woe and dread. Existing from minute to minute, hour to hour. Constant beatings. Constant humiliation. Constant fear. Reith was a serial abuser.

One thing Black knew for sure: the law did not protect the weak. The courts were used as tools for the powerful. Men like George Reith understood only one message.

And Black believed he was the man to deliver it.

Diane got up to go, hesitated.

"Beware, Mr Black. My husband is a monster."

Black nodded, but did not reply.

He was in the habit of dealing with monsters.

3

B lack visited the village of Eaglesham once every month, for one specific purpose. The place conjured up many memories. One memory, above all others. One which was particularly horrific, which plagued Black every hour of every day, the details branded into his mind, clear and stark – the day he arrived home in the middle of a cold March afternoon, to their ivy-clad cottage, to find his wife and daughter lying dead. Voices silenced. Smiles obliterated by pistol shots fired at close range.

Once every month, he came back. To visit the cemetery on the outskirts. Where they were buried. A place set back from the road, half hidden behind silver birch, in the shadow of ancient oak trees, enclosed by low, red sandstone walls.

After Diane Reith left his office, Black had a sudden, strong desire to be there. He decided to go, leaving Tricia in charge. He drove the ten-mile journey. He bought flowers at a corner shop on the road there. He arrived at the cemetery. The day was warm and bright. It seemed to Black, when he came to this place, a stillness settled. Any wind lessened; any rain slackened. The air was tinged with... what? Black often wondered. A bleak melancholy, perhaps. A sadness he was unable to articulate.

He stood by the headstone and laid the flowers. The words on the inscription were simple and true:

Jennifer Black
1971-2010
My love, my heart

Merryn Black
2005-2010
A moonbeam
Lighting up the dark

He gazed at the piece of stone. After serving with the Parachute Regiment, and then the Special Air Service, he had come to the conclusion the world was mad. Mad, but not lost. He'd found Jennifer. They had Merryn. He had a family. Then, the madness returned, his family killed.

He took a long, deep breath, smelling the freshly mown grass, felt the sun on the back of his neck, heard the trill and chirp of birds.

Diane Reith had come to him. She needed help. She was deeply afraid. She had asked for sanctuary.

Black possessed many skills. He had been trained to survive. He had been trained to kill in almost any situation imaginable, by the very best, to become the very best. And most of all, he had nothing to lose, because he had lost everything already.

Diane Reith had set off a spark. Black wanted to give the world back a little of the madness. He felt it owed him. It was something he excelled at. It was something he craved.

"Forgive me," he whispered.

He left. He had preparations to make.

4

Lord Reith. Black did some background checks. Reith sat in the High Court of Justiciary, the supreme criminal court in Scotland. An illustrious career, presiding over head-line grabbing cases. Tipped to be the next Lord Justice General. A man possessing a profound knowledge of the law. A man regarded as wise and fair in his judgements, but robust in his sentencing. A workaholic, committed to his vocation.

He and Diane lived in a house in the heart of the west end of Glasgow, just off Great Western Road. A rambling sandstone structure sitting on an acre of manicured lawns enclosed by Edwardian copper-coloured railings. A house stately and reserved, reeking of money. Old money. Inherited, so rumour had it. On her side. A wealthy heiress. No children. He drove every day to the court building, four miles from his house, in a Jag 4x4. He was sixty-eight – quite young for a judge in his position. He was fit and athletic. Remarkably so. Ran ultra-marathons. President of a local boxing club. Regular squash player. On the Board of Trustees for several well-known charities. A paragon of virtue. A man of the community. At least on the outside.

At any given time, there could be ten cases being heard at the High Court in Glasgow. Lord Reith was presiding over an armed robbery – three men tooled up with shotguns had barged into a high-end jewellery shop in the city centre. A brazen attack in the middle of a Saturday afternoon. They had escaped with diamonds worth over two million. And left a security guard with his head blown off. They were captured within a month. The trial had lasted five weeks. The prosecution was summing up. Another couple of days and it would be over.

Black arrived at the court building. He needed to blend in. For Black, this was simple. He hadn't worn a suit for weeks. He bought one specially for the occasion. Dark pinstripe, white shirt, dark tie. Smart and boring. He still had his court gown, a relic from another age, collecting dust in a wardrobe. Another relic was a red leather briefcase, in which he'd placed a newspaper. When he entered the building at 9.30 on a warm August morning, gown bundled under one arm, clasping his briefcase, he was invisible.

Just another lawyer.

He made his way through the security entrance. A court official patted him down in a cursory manner. Black placed keys, wallet, coins, into a plastic tray. And three pens. They were barely noticed, for which Black was grateful. One he had specially adapted, for use in extreme situations. Usually as a last resort – a small but effective skill acquired long ago, from men paranoid about self-preservation.

He emerged into the main court foyer. He put on his court gown. The transition was complete. He was similar to fifty other individuals milling about, murmuring to clients, sipping coffee from polystyrene cups, studying files, huddled together swapping stories, reminiscing, debating points of law.

He bought himself a strong coffee from a cafeteria, and sat at a table.

After serving in the army for over twenty years, and fighting with the 22nd regiment of the Special Air Service in some of the most inhospitable places in the world, he always imagined that if he returned to civilian life, he would prefer being a criminal court lawyer. He tried it briefly. And hated it. The cut and thrust of the courtroom was a game of lies and tricks. The aim was to hide the truth in a web of accusation, confusion, deceit. Cheap victories. It was shallow. It meant nothing. He had killed men in the arena of war. With bullets, knives, with his bare hands. He had seen guts spill, blood flow. He'd listened to their death screams as they begged and pleaded for help. It was truth. It was real. No bullshit. The lawyers who paraded up and down the court, bullying and badgering, coaxing and manipulating, wouldn't have lasted a minute in a battle zone. Black saw through them, and saw the process for the game it was. And he didn't want any of it.

He sipped his coffee, and waited.

Reith was at Court No. 3. A woman's voice spoke through a crackly intercom. Court was convening in fifteen minutes.

The place started to thin out. Black left his seat and meandered through a maze of corridors, looking at ease in his surroundings. He smiled at court officers, who smiled back. Security was non-existent. He made his way to the rear of Court No. 3, past witness rooms, toilets, staff doors, and then past the most important door of them all, the lettering plain and unequivocal – *Lord Reith's Chambers*.

Black returned to the foyer, bought another coffee and got out his newspaper. It would be a long day.

But worth it.

5
____

The court finished just after 4pm.

Lord Reith left the courtroom by way of a private exit, directly into a rear corridor. He made his way to his offices. Black followed ten paces behind. Dressed in court gown, carrying a briefcase, he did not arouse suspicion. Reith, wearing judicial dark red robes and long court wig, stopped at a door, produced a key, unlocked it. He entered his chambers.

Black loomed in behind him, putting one foot forward.

"What the hell...!"

"Five minutes of your time, Lord Reith," said Black. "Please." He pushed him inside. Reith recoiled, his face a fleeting image of surprise, transforming to outrage.

"What is this?"

Black pulled the key from the door, closed it, locked it from the inside, turned to face him.

They were about the same height. Reith was slimmer. A runner's build. Long, angular face; narrow forehead; sharp, pale-blue eyes. A chin tapering to a point. His court wig had tilted over to one side. Black was easily forty-five pounds heavier. With no excess fat.

"Your wife passes on her regards."

Reith raised himself up, face reddening, lip curled in anger. "This is a disgrace! You have no right to be here. I'm calling the police. Get out of my way!"

"Sit down, Reith. Otherwise I'll break your fucking neck."

Reith opened his mouth to speak, then clamped it shut. Black gave him a measured stare.

He knows I'm not fucking about.

Black pointed to a desk at the far end of the room.

"Sit."

Reith took a deep, shuddering breath, swallowed, turned slowly.

"This is an outrage," he said through gritted teeth. "You'll pay dearly."

"Shut up."

The office was long, rectangular. The walls on each side were shelved and filled neatly with rows of books. A miniature library. A walnut desk squatted at the far end beneath a circular window. Sunlight streamed through. It was neat, uncluttered, reflecting a honey-gold hue. In one corner was a drinks cabinet with crystal glasses and decanters and an array of bottles of whisky. They sparkled in the sun, like treasure. Reith removed his wig, made his way to a leather chair behind his desk. Black followed.

Reith sat. Black sat on a chair opposite. He smiled. Lord Reith did not smile back. Black stretched over and yanked the telephone off the desk, the line snapping. He placed it back on the polished wood.

"For privacy, you understand."

Reith regarded him with a leaden stare. *If looks could kill,* thought Black.

"Who are you?" asked Reith.

"My name is Adam Black. I'm a lawyer. I represent your wife."

Reith straightened, fixing him with a cold stare.

"Mr Black. I am a judge of the High Court of Justiciary. Do you understand what this means? You have illegally barged your way into..."

Black lifted the telephone and smashed it hard on to the desktop. It disintegrated into pieces. Reith gasped.

"It seems violence is the only way to get your attention," said Black, his voice matter-of-fact. "It got your wife's attention. You may have blinded her in her left eye, if you're interested."

Reith licked his lips, spoke in a careful voice. "Where is she?"

"Far away. When I mentioned earlier that she passes on her regards, she doesn't really. I was lying. She's terrified of you. But I'm not. Far from it. Your position as a High Court judge is irrelevant, because the way I see it, you're just another piece of scum shit."

Now, an edge in Reith's voice when he replied. "I think, Mr Black, we can be reasonable about this. Whatever my wife told you is grossly exaggerated."

"Of course. Nevertheless, she's tired of the broken bones and the disfigurement and all those hospital appointments. And she's too scared to go to court, when men like you can manipulate the system to your advantage. So, I've recommended to her that we take a different approach. We remove all the legal shenanigans, and cut straight to the chase. You okay with that?"

"I don't know what you're getting at."

"I know you don't. It's a novel approach. A faster route to justice."

Black smiled, opened his jacket, took out one of the pens he had been carrying in his inside pocket. He pulled off the cap. The ball point had been removed, the metal shaft sharpened to a point.

Reith watched him, frowning. He spoke, a quiver in his voice, "What are you going to do?"

"Your wife mentioned that one Christmas Eve she was wrapping presents. On the kitchen table, I think she said. Three years ago. You remember? Maybe you don't. You're a busy man, after all. You weren't happy with the way she was doing it. Careless, you said. Your exact word, I believe. Or maybe *careless bitch*. You told her to remove all the wrapping paper and start again. You watched her repeat the process. But you must have made her nervous, because she couldn't get it right. Butter fingers. Then I suppose you got frustrated at her inability to wrap them to your high standard. Do you remember the punishment?"

The blood had drained from Reith's face. His lips worked, but his response was a mumble.

"Let me remind you, Lord Reith," said Black, still smiling.

Reith had one hand flat on the desktop. Black rammed the pen down, through skin, blood, cartilage, into the walnut veneer, to stand vertical, embedded in the timber. Clean through. Reith shrieked. Black slapped him hard across the face.

"Shut up!"

Reith stared at the fixture. Blood bloomed out across the papers on his desk.

Black lowered his voice, his smile gone. "Your wife wants free of you. You will give her what she asks. She will be seeking a divorce, which you will not contest. Whatever she wants, she'll get. Let's call it compensation. For criminal injuries. For years of unremitting abuse. The process will be clean and simple. You will never go near her again. If you do, then listen carefully, Lord Reith."

Black leaned forward. "I will rip your fucking throat out. You understand? And should you mention this little meeting, then it's your word against mine. I know where you live. I know where you play squash. I know the car you drive, and the route you take to work. I know where you go for your morning jog. I know when you go for your morning fucking shit. If you feel compelled to take this further, then that's fine by me, because I'm your man. I will take enormous satisfaction in snapping your spine."

Black's voice lowered to barely above a whisper. "You will never know when, or where. You will spend the rest of your life looking over your shoulder. Do you understand me, judge?"

Reith nodded. His bottom lip trembled. His face seemed suddenly drawn, his eyes sunk deep in their sockets.

Black wrenched the pen free. Reith clasped his hand. Blood poured from the wound, on to his robes.

Black had a cloth handkerchief in his pocket, which he used to wipe the pen clean. He tossed it over to Reith.

"It was a pleasure, Lord Reith. I hope the case goes well."

Black turned, and left.

It had been a productive day.

He left the court building, and headed back to his car. It was 4.30 in the afternoon, the sun still bright in a blue sky. For the first time in months, Black felt good about life.

Until his mobile phone buzzed. It was Tricia.

"Bad news, Adam," she said.

"What?"

"Got a call from some Edinburgh law firm. Your friend Gilbert Bartholomew is dead."

Black didn't respond.

Who the hell's Gilbert Bartholomew?

6

When Black arrived back at the office, he telephoned the firm of Raeburn Collins and Co. He checked them first in the Law Directory. A medium-sized firm located in Drumsheugh Gardens in the centre of Edinburgh. Twenty partners. Conveyancing, wills, estates. Mostly chamber practice, but high-end. Based in the money-side of the city, populated with lawyers, accountants, surveyors, insurance agents, mortgage brokers, merchant banks. All tucked away behind two-hundred-year-old townhouses of brown and blond sandstone, gleaming balustrades, marble steps, high peaked slate roofs.

He got through to the lawyer who had telephoned – Fiona Jackson. Miss Jackson. She sounded young. Maybe an assistant. Or associate.

"You phoned my office. My name is Adam Black."

"Thanks for coming back to me. It's about Gilbert Bartholomew. First of all, please accept my condolences. It must have come as a shock. It certainly came as a shock to me."

"And me."

"I only saw him a couple of weeks ago, to prepare his will. Now he's passed away." Her voice faltered. "It's very sudden."

"I'll bet. And here we are. Listen, Miss Jackson. I think you have the wrong person. I have no idea who this man is. And it's not an instantly forgettable name. Gilbert Bartholomew doesn't spring to my mind."

A short silence followed.

"That's very strange. He said you were old friends. He said he hadn't spoken to you for some time. He'd forgotten where you lived, but he knew where you worked. Hence the phone call."

"And you met this man?"

"Of course. He made an appointment. I took his instructions."

"Doesn't he have next of kin? A wife? Kids?"

A pause on the phone, then, "He has no one, so far as he told us. No family. And he was most specific. You've been named as his sole beneficiary. He's also made you his executor."

"This is crazy. I honestly have no idea who he is."

"It's not the only thing that's crazy. The will itself is... bizarre."

Black was intrigued. "Bizarre? An interesting word to describe a will."

"But accurate. It's not something I can discuss on the telephone. Can we arrange a meeting at our offices?"

"When?"

"How about tomorrow, three o'clock?"

"Suits me fine."

"You know where we are?"

"I'll find you."

Black hung up.

Strange times.

7

B lack decided he would travel by train. Minimum fuss, straight into Edinburgh centre. The train left every half hour, from Glasgow Queen Street station to Edinburgh Waverley. Regular as clockwork. The journey took about an hour on average. It passed without incident, the train pulling into Waverley Station at the allocated time.

Black disembarked, made his way to the offices of Raeburn Collins and Co., a ten-minute walk away. A short distance from bustling Princes Street. It was a Wednesday afternoon, hot, and the place was packed. Black veered off the main thoroughfare, emerging into a quieter section; cobbled streets, elegant Georgian townhouses, pockets of miniature public gardens, all bright flowers and manicured lawns and shiny blue park benches.

He arrived at the main entrance. A nondescript glass door, no different from a hundred others. A small silver plaque fixed on the wall was the only advertising feature. This was an old firm, with old wealth for sustenance, not relying on gimmicks or sales pitches – clients, descendants of clients, word of mouth referral. A hundred years of legal services, and after a while, maybe thirty years or so, the client bank took care of itself, becoming a source of self-perpetuating business.

Black entered a foyer. Two young women sat behind a reception desk. He announced himself. He was gestured to a waiting room. High ceiling, smooth white walls. In a corner, a complicated looking coffee machine. Black sat on a sumptuous leather couch. He picked up a magazine, *Country Living*, and flicked through the pages.

Within five minutes a woman entered.

"Mr Black?"

She was maybe approaching thirty – twenty years younger than Black – dressed in a pale-blue suit, hair tied back. Severely so. Clasped in one hand was a manila folder. She was all business. She gave Black a weary smile. An associate, he thought. Trying to get that elusive partnership. Probably working a seventy-hour week. Permanently exhausted. Black felt a momentary twinge of pity. Back-breaking work without gratitude and a pay bordering on derisory. It wasn't worth it. But it was a choice you made.

Black smiled back, nodded. They shook hands. The handshake was firm, reassuring.

"Hi. I'm Pamela Thompson. I'll be taking care of you, Mr Black."

"Taking care of me?"

"Just a manner of speaking."

"Where's Fiona. Fiona Jackson? She phoned me yesterday." Black smiled. "Shouldn't she be taking care of me?"

The woman who had introduced herself as Pamela Thompson reacted with a slight twitch of her shoulders.

"Follow me, please."

She led him out of the waiting room, past the reception desk, and up a flight of wide carpeted stairs to the first floor, to a hallway with doors on either side. She took him into an impressive room, long and wide. An entire wall was devoted to rows of law books, from floor to ceiling. Two sets of bay windows allowed the sunshine to stream through. The carpet felt thick underfoot. In the centre was a rectangular desk, polished dark wood, a coffee pot and white porcelain cups sitting in the centre on a silver tray. Around it, at least twenty chairs.

At the far end of the table, sitting solitary, was a man sipping coffee. On a chair nearer to the door sat another man, who immediately stood when they entered. Pamela introduced him. "Mr Black. This is Donald Rutherford, our new Estates partner."

Rutherford stood. A big man, the same height as Black, but could have done with losing thirty pounds. A full head of luxuriant blond hair, swept back off his forehead. His face was deeply tanned and baby smooth. Heavy chin. Sleek jowls. Lots of fine wine and fine dining, thought Black. The air was scented with his cologne. He wore a £2000 navy-blue three-piece suit, bespoke. The light glinted on a gold, bloodstone signet ring on his right index finger. A vague tingle of recollection pricked Black's memory. He had seen something like it before. As a package, the man reeked of success, and had no trouble showing it. He oozed money. He regarded Black with clever blue eyes. His face creased into a well-practised smile. He gave Black a strong, confident handshake.

"Mr Black. I hope you don't mind me sitting in on this meeting. I'm new here. Still trying to find my way. But when I heard about this will, I was... well, to be honest, fascinated. Coffee?"

"Thank you."

Pamela gestured to the man at the far end of the conference table. "This is Mr Max Lavelle. Our senior partner."

Black nodded towards the man. The man did not get up. He nodded back. He regarded Black with a clear, almost disconcerting, intensity. His face was round, owlish, his skin pale and waxy. He wore a suit of sombre grey, matching the colour of his hair, which was slicked over one side. He provided Black with the briefest of smiles, but did not speak.

Black sat at the table. Rutherford was sitting opposite. Pamela sat next to him, placing the folder on the table. Rutherford poured him a coffee.

"It must be an unusual case to bring out the big guns," said Black. "I'm flattered." He sipped some coffee. "I think the word 'bizarre' was used when I got the call. Talking of which, I thought Fiona Jackson was dealing with this."

"We've never seen anything quite like it," replied Pamela. She skilfully avoided answering, Black noted.

"How did he die?"

"Very sad situation," said Rutherford. "It seems Mr Bartholomew took his own life. Depression, maybe. Isn't that right, Pamela? We may never know."

"Emergency services found him," explained Pamela. "A neighbour heard what sounded like a gunshot. She called the police. When Mr Bartholomew didn't answer his door, they broke it down." She shifted uncomfortably in her chair. A tremor passed through her voice. "He'd shot himself, so we've been told. I'm sorry to have to tell you this, Mr Black. The whole thing is awful."

"Shot himself? That's not a common method of suicide."

"You have experience of this sort of thing?" asked Rutherford, an edge of condescension to his voice.

"Some. He would need to have access to a gun. It's not that easy. Unless he was a member of a gun club. Or was ex-military, perhaps. Most people don't have that resource. Just a passing thought. What do I know, after all?"

"You didn't know Mr Bartholomew?"

It was Rutherford who asked the question.

"No, I didn't."

Pamela opened the file, and removed a single A4 sheaf of paper.

"This is his last will and testament. Do you want to read it?"

"Tell me what it says."

Pamela flicked a glance at Rutherford, who remained focused on Black. She cleared her throat.

"He made it very simple. Though this doesn't make it any less strange."

Black waited.

"You are his appointed executor. And you are the sole beneficiary. He's bequeathed his entire estate to you." She paused, studying the words on the page before her. She looked up at Black. "But we're not sure what his estate is."

Black frowned. "I don't understand."

"Nor do we," she replied. "It says you must look for what you need." She gave a tremulous smile. "And it says, what you need is located at the bottom of Bastard Rock."

8

Black asked to see the document. She was right. It was short. Barely half a page. And mystifying. He glanced at the signature at the foot of the page. An undecipherable scrawl. Witnessed by the young woman who had spoken to him on the telephone yesterday, Fiona Jackson.

"Does it mean anything to you, Mr Black?" asked Rutherford.

"Not a damn thing. It's crazy. Did you meet the man? Personally?"

"Sadly not. He came in about a fortnight ago, asked for us to prepare the will which we duly did, and he came in the next day to sign it. End of."

"But Fiona Jackson met him. She might give us some more info. Where is she?"

Rutherford gave Black a steady stare.

"Miss Jackson no longer works for us."

Black held his stare. "She resigned?"

"She was let go. It's an internal matter. You understand that, I'm sure. There are some things we cannot discuss. Needless to say, Pamela will look after you."

Black digested this information. "Very sudden," he said. "Given I was speaking to her less than twenty-four hours ago."

Rutherford shrugged. "It's not your concern."

Black moved on. "He must have other assets. A house. A bank account. Anything."

"The address he gave us is rented," replied Pamela. "He had some cash in the flat – three hundred pounds. And a funeral bond. His stuff, his furnishings, are worthless. He had nothing. We've established he claimed benefits. He was not working, as far as we know."

"When is his funeral?"

"When the coroner releases the body. Maybe three weeks."

"It's odd that you don't know this man," interrupted Rutherford. "He seems to have no family. No children. Does the name mean anything to you at all?"

"No, it doesn't. But my name meant something to him."

"And where, or what, is Bastard Rock?"

Black shook his head.

"Perhaps this is something you would rather forget all about," continued Rutherford, his voice slow and measured, the voice of reason. "A penniless man you've never heard of leaves you nothing but a stupid riddle. We'll take care of this nonsense for you. You're a lawyer? You'll have a busy practice to run. You don't want the aggravation of dealing with what I can only describe as the rantings of someone quite possibly with an addiction problem. You agree?"

He stretched over to pick up the will.

Black also stretched over, and rested his hand over Rutherford's. "Not quite. That's my property. I think I'll take care of Mr Bartholomew's will. As his executor."

Rutherford resumed his easy smile, and sat back.

"As is your right."

"As is my right," repeated Black. "How did you know I was a lawyer?"

"Maybe Fiona Jackson mentioned it. Is that important?"

"Not to me. It was you who brought it up."

He picked up the will, and put it in the inside pocket of his leather jacket. "Thank you for your help. I'll take it from here."

He stood, and turned to leave.

Rutherford also stood. "I wish you well, Mr Black. I just hope you're not being sent on some wild goose chase. Pamela will see you out."

He stretched out his hand. Black shook it, and said, "A stranger made it his business to instruct lawyers to prepare a will nominating me his sole beneficiary. His estate is shrouded in mystery. Within two weeks, the man is dead. Let's say, it's aroused my interest. Hasn't it yours?"

"I've more important business to attend to."

"I guess you're busier than me."

Suddenly the man at the far end of the table spoke. Max Lavelle. Senior partner. His voice was low, gravelly. Not loud, yet it cut the air.

"Good luck, Mr Black. A strange set of circumstances, don't you think?"

Black fixed his gaze on the man.

"As strange as it gets."

Black left the conference room, Pamela leading the way. He followed her back down the stairs, past the front reception area. He turned to thank her. She pressed something in his hand. She gave him a tight, strained smile.

"My card, Mr Black."

Before he could respond, she turned and disappeared back into the bowels of Raeburn Collins and Co.

He watched her go. He studied the card. On one side, in embossed black lettering, her name and the name and telephone number of the firm. On the other, handwritten in blue biro were the words:

Fiona Jackson
31 Brereton Place
Help her!

9

Extract of the transcript of evidence given during the subsequent Court Appearance of SAS soldiers, relating to their actions in the Iranian Embassy Siege, 1980 –

Crown – You were part of Red Team?
Sergeant A – Correct, sir.
Crown – You entered through the balcony?
Sergeant A – Yes, sir.
Crown – Upon entering the room, what happened?
Sergeant A – The room was empty. I ran out, to the foot of some stairs.
Crown – What happened then?
Sergeant A – I encountered a terrorist.
Crown – How did you know he was a terrorist?
Sergeant A – He was holding a grenade, sir.
Crown – What did you do?
Sergeant A – I fired my weapon.
Crown – What type of weapon were you carrying?
Sergeant A – A Heckler & Koch MP5 Sub-machine gun.
Crown – Do you know how many bullets you fired?
Sergeant A – Difficult to say. It has a 30-round capacity.

Crown – If I said the man had sixteen bullet wounds, would that be accurate?

Sergeant A – That makes sense.

Crown – That makes sense? Why the need to fire sixteen bullets into one man?

Sergeant A – I don't believe in half measures, sir.

B lack was in no particular hurry to return to Glasgow. He decided he would pay Fiona Jackson a visit. He made his way back to Princes Street, and bought a map from a tourist shop. He could have brought up directions on his mobile phone, but Black preferred to do things the old-fashioned way. Brereton Place was close, set in the heart of the west end, maybe only a mile from where he was. A trendy place to live, he thought. Not inexpensive.

It was a glorious afternoon. He would walk. Dressed in blue jeans, a pair of old running shoes, and a plain white shirt, he blended in with a million other tourists that day. He slung his leather jacket over his shoulder, and set off at pace to his destination.

Edinburgh city centre was packed tight with people. Cars in the centre had more or less been eradicated, replaced by buses and trams. Overlooking everything, sprawled on a hilltop, were the grey stone battlements and towers of Edinburgh Castle, replete with fluttering flags and glossy black cannons, gleaming in the sunshine.

Black headed back to Drumsheugh Gardens, and kept walking. The crowds thinned, dissipating to nothing. The buildings were old and grand, the streets and avenues wide. Fifteen minutes later, he arrived at Brereton Place, and to a block of new-build flats, looking incongruous in their surroundings of vintage architecture. He wondered how the hell they'd got planning permission. No doubt bribes were paid, palms were greased. Edinburgh, the seat of the Scottish Government, was no different from any other place. Where human beings existed, corruption was never far away, as Black well knew.

Number 31 was communal for a block of ten flats – five levels, including the ground floor, two flats on each level. Black inspected the list of names by the front door, a press-button by each name.

F Jackson. Flat 3/2.

He pressed the buzzer. Several seconds passed. A voice responded. It was impossible to make out, static interference rendering it incomprehensible.

"Fiona Jackson?"

The voice responded, several staccato sounds, sounding more machine than human. Black had to guess.

"My name is Adam Black. We spoke yesterday on the phone. I've been to your office. Your friend Pamela gave me her card. Can we talk?"

A silence followed, another few seconds. The communal lock buzzed. Black pushed the door open, went inside. The hall was clean and functional and modern. Pale-blue tiles on the wall, clean tiled floor. A bicycle was parked by a door. Black made his way up.

Her flat was on the third floor. Her door had a small gold nameplate.

The door was open.

Had she opened it for him? Unusual. Not the normal reaction to a stranger. Suddenly, he was alert. Something, call it instinct, told him this was wrong. Alarm bells rang. One thing the Special Services had taught him – trust your instinct. Tried and tested. It had saved his life many times.

He knocked gently. No sound from inside. Silence. He

shifted his position, standing pressed against the wall, and with one arm, pushed the door wide open. He waited, expecting to hear something, at the very least the routine sound of human activity. No such sound.

He had a choice. He could walk away. Or he could keep moving. Black was not the type to walk away.

He inched round. He was facing a hallway. A mirror hung on the far wall opposite. Black glimpsed his own reflection. Dark wood flooring, walls painted warm brick-red. A narrow glass table along one side, on top of which should have been a telephone. Instead, it was lying in pieces on the floor, cable pulled from its socket.

Trouble, thought Black. He was unarmed and thus disadvantaged.

A sound disturbed the silence. The creak of weight being shifted, somewhere in the interior.

Muscles tensed, he eased himself along the corridor, which was a dog-leg, his senses alert for the slightest sound, the shift of movement. He passed a door to his left, opened it a fraction – a hall cupboard containing domestic stuff: ironing board; clothes rack; towels on shelves. Other oddments. On the wooden flooring before him, a scattering of broken glass. He turned the corner. Three doors, one facing him, one to his right, one to his left. The one facing was half open, and looked like the entrance to the living room. He took a deep breath, entered.

And plunged into a nightmare.

10

The living room was a mess. Television toppled on the floor, screen smashed. Shards of glass strewn across the wooden flooring. Jagged remains of wine bottles; broken ornaments; torn cushions; the window blinds ripped and hanging askew. The room was large, open-plan, stretching into the kitchen. Taking up a good proportion was a black leather corner suite. The black leather had almost disappeared under a new coat of a very different colour. Blood. Everywhere. On the furniture, on the floor, spattered on the walls. Lying sprawled on the suite was the naked body of a young woman. Her torso, neck and groin were a mass of stab wounds. Her clothes were scattered on the floor, saturated in blood. Her eyes stared at the ceiling, empty and dead.

Black held his breath. A noise behind him. He turned slowly. A man stood in the doorway. He was dressed from head to foot in the papery plastic outfit worn by crime scene investigators. In one gloved hand he held a semi-automatic pistol. Black recognised the issue – a Glock G22. Equipped with silencer. The man had narrow features, jutting chin, nervous eyes set under a beetling brow.

Black heard the front door close. Another man, similarly garbed, entered the living room via the kitchen. In one hand, a long steel-handled butchers' knife, smeared in blood.

Easy to guess what it had been used for.

The man held the Glock in a two-handed grip, the barrel only four feet from Black's face.

"You're here," he said. "You couldn't let it go."

"Let what go?" asked Black, ignoring the pistol, keeping eyes locked on the man's face. The man with the knife stopped an arm's length from him, hovering. Waiting for instructions, Black surmised.

"Our lucky day. This is how this plays out. You had drinks. Things got out of hand. You wanted to fuck. She said no. You're not the type of man who takes no for an answer. You had your way. You stabbed her. Stabbed her, and kept going. Using the knife as your dick. Classic sex crime. But she caught you in the neck. A single flick of the blade. Caught you in the carotid artery. You'll bleed out on the floor, beside your girlfriend. Your fingerprints all over the knife. Hook, line and sinker. The police won't look beyond the end of their nose. Case closed. As I said, lucky day."

"You should have been in amateur dramatics. Shooting me with that fancy Glock isn't going to help your little stage setting."

"Shut up. Kneel down, Mr Black, or I will blow your fucking brains out. I kid you not."

"I assume the dead girl is Fiona Jackson."

"Shut up. Kneel."

"No."

The man took a step closer, licking his lips with a small darting tongue. His voice rose.

"I swear I'll blow your fucking head off!"

Black answered in a measured voice. "I have no doubt. But whether I kneel or not, I'm a dead man. Either shot, or stabbed by your friend. I don't like my choices." He gave a cold grin. "So, I guess I want to fuck things right up for you. I'd rather have a bullet in the head and the cops asking lots of questions, than giving you a gift-wrapped crime scene. So be my guest. Pull the trigger."

Black held the man's stare. He heard a sound in his head – the drum of his heart. He was playing a dangerous bluff. The man looked nervous. A millimetre twitch of the finger, and Black had a bullet in the head. He focused, nerves stretched. A second passed, two seconds. The man gave a delicate, almost imperceptible shrug, flicking a glance at the man with the knife. But Black saw it. And Black knew exactly what it meant. It was what he was hoping for. The last thing they wanted was to shoot him.

The other man knew as well. He jerked forward, slicing the knife towards Black's neck. Black wheeled round to face him, stepped in, raised a forearm, blocked, jerked up his elbow, slamming it under the man's chin. He heard teeth crack. The top of the man's tongue flew out, a pink lump of moist gristle, bitten clean through. The move was performed in two seconds. The man was stunned, staggered back.

Black wasn't finished. He caught the man's wrist, pulled him in, twisted. A bone snapped. The man shrieked in pain. The knife clattered onto the wooden floor. He was off-balance. Using his momentum, still gripping his arm, Black whirled him into the man holding the Glock.

A further two seconds of confusion followed. The man with the Glock shoved his friend out of the way. Too late for niceties. He would kill Black any way he could. Gunshot or knife wound, it was past time for caring. He pointed the Glock. Black was on him, slapping the pistol to one side. It fired, the silencer reducing the shot into a sound like a muffled cough. The man who'd carried the knife grunted, as a bullet punched through his chest, shredding organs and spine. He collapsed onto the broken television, and lay still.

Black was in close. The man tried to bring up the pistol, manoeuvring it with his hand to shoot Black at close range. Black seized his wrist, holding it away. The man hacked at Black's neck. Black shifted his body, absorbing the blow, but it was expertly executed, crunching the nerves. Black experienced sharp, mind-jarring pain. He head-butted the man once, twice, slamming forehead into nose, mouth. The man's hold on the pistol loosened. He brought his knee up, catching Black on the groin, and hacked at his neck again. Black grasped the knee, pushed forward, using his weight to propel the man back through the living room entrance and into the hall. They both fell with a clatter. The pistol spun away. Black was on top. He punched the man hard on his throat, crushing the larynx. The man made a strangled gurgling sound, suddenly disorientated. Black struck again, bringing another fearful blow down on the man's throat. The man convulsed. Black caught his head in an arm lock, jerked hard to one side. The neck snapped.

Black lay back, panting.

In less than thirty seconds, he had dispatched two men.

He got to his feet. His neck and shoulder ached. He made his way back to the living room, past the man with the hole in his chest, past the young woman still bleeding out from countless stab wounds. It was a place of death. Black went to the kitchen, found a dish cloth in the sink, made his way back to the dead man in the hall. Wrapping the cloth round his hand, avoiding fingerprints, he unfastened the man's outer garment. Beneath he was wearing collar, tie, jacket. Someone who like to be smart when he killed, thought Black grimly. He reached into his inside pocket, retrieving a mobile phone. There was nothing else. No identification. The man was experienced.

Black turned his attention to the other dead man. His blue

overalls were soaked. The bullet had ripped through, his back yawning open, blood and tissue spilling on to the floor, mingling with the blood of the young woman.

A fucking horror scene, Black thought. He took a deep breath, steeled himself, repeated the procedure, checking for ID, but the man was carrying nothing save a packet of chewing gum and some loose change.

Black stood back, surveying his surroundings. He would telephone the police from a phone box a half mile away.

Suddenly, the mobile he was holding buzzed in his hand. Black looked at the screen, which revealed a number, but no name. Black answered.

A voice immediately spoke. Deep, brassy. Unnatural. Modified. The other person was using a voice modulator.

"Is it done?"

"Yes," said Black.

A pause.

"Who is this?"

"Adam Black. The man you tried to kill. Who are you?"

Another short silence.

"You're a dead man, Black."

"Apparently not. But there are two dead men here. We weren't introduced."

Breathing. The voice spoke.

"You have no idea who you're dealing with. You'd better run, Mr Black. This is your new life. Running. Until we find you."

"My running days are over. You've crossed the wrong man, friend. I swear to Jesus Christ it's me who will find you. And when I do, I'll rip your fucking lungs out."

Black hung up. Let them sweat.

He closed his eyes, trying to stay calm, manage his thoughts, keep the tremble from his hands.

The prestigious and established firm of Raeburn Collins and

Co. had tried to lure him to his death. Two men had killed a young woman, and tried to kill him. People were dying – all because of a man called Gilbert Bartholomew. And his last will and testament.

To unlock the riddle, Black had to find a key.

What the hell was Bastard Rock?

But maybe, just maybe, he had the beginnings of an answer. And if he was correct, then the riddle only deepened.

11

Black left the building. His skin prickled. Others would come. He felt considerably more conspicuous leaving than he did arriving. If people noticed him, what would they say? A big guy in jeans and a leather jacket. Not much of a description. Should the police come knocking on his door, then he would deal with that problem when it arrived.

He walked the mile back to the city centre, taking a different route. He phoned the office from his mobile. Tricia answered immediately. "Where are you?"

Black cleared his throat, kept his voice as neutral as possible. "Enjoying the sights. How's things?"

"Quiet."

"Good. Take a week off. Make it two."

Silence.

"What?"

Black attempted flippancy. "I'm going on a holiday. Spur of the moment. I need the break. And being out in this weather has given me the urge. I can pick up my messages on the answering machine."

Tricia hesitated. "You sure? This is very sudden, Adam."

"Nothing wrong with a bit of spontaneity."

"You never seemed to me the spontaneous sort."

"You have a holiday home in Millport, don't you? Use the time. Enjoy the summer weather." He attempted humour, hoping it didn't ring false. "Get out on that bicycle of yours. Isn't that what Millport's famous for?"

She laughed. "I don't own a bike. The thought appals me. Are you sure?"

"Positive. Two weeks."

He hung up. It was fair to assume that his office was on his enemies' radar. As such, no one was safe.

He ditched the mobile phone he had retrieved from his attacker, tossing it into a public waste bin. He found a phone booth on Princes Street, and made a call to the cops. *Commotion at 31 Brereton Place. Flat 3/2. Men with knives. Better get there quick.* He hung up.

He didn't get the train. He grabbed a taxi, a black cab he hailed on the street, and headed straight to Glasgow. Expensive. But Black had no desire to stay longer than required.

Black rented an apartment in a part of Glasgow known as Mount Florida, a two-bedroomed flat in a tenement block in the south side, a half mile from his office, adjacent to a sprawling park where Black ran four miles every morning before work.

Black arrived back early evening. There was a strong possibility his address was targeted. He watched the building from a coffee shop for an hour. Everything seemed normal. It meant nothing. If he was under surveillance, and properly done, he would never know. Nerves tingling, he made his way to the front communal entrance, expecting a car door to open, a looming figure, a motion, the scrape of movement. He entered without incident. He was one level up.

He reached his front door. It seemed perfectly normal. Again, if the lock had been tampered with, he might never know.

With the right tools, a professional burglar would enter and leave without any trace. Black turned the key, opened the door, waited, straining to detect the slightest sound. With held breath, he entered.

Everything was normal. Nothing had been touched. No one had been there.

He locked the door behind him and went immediately to his bedroom. He opened a wardrobe and started unloading cardboard boxes onto the bed. Stuff he'd taken from his house a lifetime ago and had never bothered unpacking. Stuff he wanted to forget, but for some reason didn't have the courage to destroy. Books, journals, photograph albums. He flitted through pages of photographs. Pictures of his wife and daughter. Holidays, moments in time, smiles captured, mannerisms caught forever. He swallowed back a wave of sudden bitter sadness.

But Black had to go back further. He still had photos of his old life, the life in the army. He came across a folder containing loose pictures, documents, papers.

There it was – a faded photograph. On the back, scribbled in pencil, a date. 1998. He tucked it into his jeans pocket.

Black went through to the kitchen. Like every other room, it was minimalistic, clean, uncluttered. Black had never enjoyed cooking, but he refused to live on take-outs, and he knew the truth about food and health. You could be the fittest human being on the planet, but you could never outrun a bad diet. An electric juicer sat on the kitchen worktop. Twice a day, morning and evening, he used it – spinach, kale, a banana, an apple, ice, plus a half pint of orange juice. Blended. The end product was green and mildly disgusting. But it was his concession to five a day. He tried to cut out sugar, and went easy on the salt. Other than that, he didn't give a damn what he ate. When he was on tour, deep in enemy territory, he ate stuff that would make a dog puke.

But it wasn't the blender he chose. He opened a cupboard, and pulled out a bottle of single malt whisky – Glenfiddich – and a glass. He poured himself a generous quantity. Rough day.

He went back through to the living room. Black did not believe in clutter. He had never got round to decorating, or kitting the place out with excessive furniture. The room had a bookcase, crammed with books. A low coffee table. Black did not own a television. On a shelf was a CD player and a couple of small speakers. He pressed play. Some old Rolling Stones music. His wife loved them. He sat on a faded red cloth armchair. Other than a small couch and the coffee table, there was nothing else in the room. No paintings on the walls. No ornaments, no memorabilia, no framed pictures. His past was a time of death. He chose not to be reminded of it.

But yet it had found a way to surface. He took out the photo, gazed at it, sipping the whisky.

Three men wearing combat fatigues. Smiling. Exhausted. Taken at the top of a hill. Forty-pound Bergen rucksacks dumped at their feet. He was the man in the middle. He barely recognised the face which stared back. All SAS, serving with the 22nd Regiment. He had just been promoted to captain, as he recalled. The men on either side were both dead. Sergeant Peter Welsh, shot in the head by a sniper in Afghanistan. Sergeant William Kent, cancer of the throat. Behind them, some way off and at the top of a further incline, a large rock, about the size and approximate shape of a double-decker bus.

He thought back. This was taken in a place called Cape Wrath. The most north-westerly point in mainland Britain. Difficult to get to. Most of it owned by the Ministry of Defence. An uncompromising, brutal landscape, exposed to the elements, with severe frosts in the winter, and winds that could whip a man off his feet. Perfect for training. Perfect for SAS training.

He studied the photograph. He remembered the circuit.

Running up the hill, full gear, rifle, ammunition. Touching the rock at the top, then back down. Then again, until the lungs felt they would burst, the muscles screamed in revolt. But you kept going.

To the top.

To Bastard Rock.

12

Who Dares Wins – Official Motto of the SAS
Who Cares Who Wins – Unofficial Motto

Black felt the need to move quickly. The clock was ticking. He had enemies. People – unpleasant people – were aware of his existence. They'd tried to kill him, for reasons unfathomable. Black had little doubt in his mind they would try again. Whoever wanted him dead would regard this as priority. Keep moving, thought Black. If he stayed in his flat any longer than he had to, he'd wind up dead, of that he was sure. He had to make assumptions – that they knew where he lived; that if they didn't strike here, they would follow him, and strike elsewhere. He closed the blinds in his front bay window, glancing outside. Everything seemed normal. He would have been surprised if it were otherwise. There was little he could do. It was something he had to accept, if he wanted answers. The trick was to stay alive. Keep moving.

Cape Wrath was not the easiest place to reach. Roughly a

six-hour drive from Glasgow to Durness, the closest village. From there, a passenger ferry across a stretch of water called the Kyle of Durness. Then a thirty-minute journey in a minibus along a track barely resembling a road. The rock – Bastard Rock – was about a mile from the lighthouse, as Black recollected. Stuck in the middle of brutal, windswept moorland, as close to nature as you could get, devoid of human habitation. Impossible to reach by car. Difficult on foot for the average tourist.

But Black was no tourist.

He would travel light. He would drive up, leaving at dawn. He daren't risk driving in the dark. In daylight, he would at least see his enemies. He would take a holdall, packing mountain boots, waterproof trousers, fleece top, woollen hat, gloves. Also, a light rucksack. In the Scottish Highlands, the weather could change in the blink of an eye. Sunshine one second, blizzard conditions the next. Volatile and deadly. One reason the army trained their combat troops in such conditions – confront and cope with the unpredictable.

Also, he would equip himself with a fixed blade Ka-Bar Marine Hunter knife, kept in a leather sheath strapped to the belt of his trousers. Razor sharp, serrated edge. And two switch-blades, one in an inside pocket, the other he would strap to his calf under his sock. Black had a strong intuition he would need them.

Black fell into a light, fitful sleep, on his chair, one ear open for the quiet click of his lock being picked, the creak of footfall.

He awoke to a grey, listless dawn. Rolling clouds heralded rain. He got ready, slipped out. His car was parked on the public street outside. He opened the main entrance door. The air felt heavy, tinged with cold. It was late August, though it felt like autumn had arrived. Summer was dying. Black surveyed the street, the place illuminated by the sickly yellow glow of street-lights. It looked deserted. He drove a Mini Cooper. He made his way to the driver's door, unlocked it, got in, senses heightened. Nothing untoward.

Black drove off, heading north, on the long road to Cape Wrath.

The journey was uneventful. He stopped at Inverness, for a coffee, in a nameless roadside café, senses alert for anything unusual. A glance, a stare too intense, contrived movements, anything suspicious. He was aware that a good surveillance team would be invisible, almost impossible to detect. He sipped the hot liquid from a paper cup. It was too public to strike, if indeed he was being followed.

Two and a half hours later, he arrived at the village of Durness. He enquired about the ferry times; one was leaving at noon from a jetty at East Keoldale. He had time to kill. Durness was sparse, a cluster of bleak buildings clinging to the land, the brisk Atlantic winds whistling. He changed into his mountain boots and took his rucksack, loaded with a litre bottle of mineral water, and ordered a late breakfast at the only restaurant – sausage, eggs, bacon, a round of toast, a pot of strong coffee. He sat by the window. The clouds had cleared a little, allowing some pale sunshine to filter through. The air felt damp, the breeze bringing a misty rain from the sea and over the cliffs. A young couple entered, laughing, talking loudly, and sat two tables up from Black. Their accents were English, maybe from London. They seemed oblivious their conversation could be heard by those around them. Tourists. Light ruck-sacks slung across their backs, which they dumped at their feet. Talking about nothing. Black switched off, thoughts inward.

He had killed two men. A young woman was dead. He had listened to the news on the drive up, but there was no mention. Too early? Perhaps. But the deaths combined were both brutal and unusual – a man shot, the other with a broken neck, a woman with at least twenty stab wounds. All in the one location. Three different styles of attack. That was easily front-page news. He had called the police. They would have arrived, confronting carnage. And then what? If it had been covered up, then that involved considerable influence. Influence emanating from the very top, reflected Black with a chill.

Death followed him. He had a knack for violence. He had been trained to endure, to cope, to kill without compunction. *A lifetime of blood.* His mind drifted inevitably to other moments in his life. His wife and daughter had died because he had killed certain men. He had been attacked randomly by a psychopath one winter's evening, and reacted exactly as he had been trained – with extreme violence. And the consequences were devastating, his family murdered. It was on him. His hands dripped with their blood. Black knew why he sought danger, why he sought the destruction of evil men.

Penance. And something more fundamental. Something he craved.

Death.

He gazed out at the scenery before him – the open sky, the endless stretch of sea beyond the cliffs. He took a deep, reflective breath. So be it. If people tried to kill him, he would take great enjoyment in returning the compliment.

And Black was a hard man to kill.

13

The passenger boat held a maximum of twelve people. Black stepped aboard, sitting on one of four wooden benches running starboard to port, exposed to the elements. The interior was not designed for comfort. A wind had whipped up. The rain was suddenly heavy. The waters were choppy; the boat rocked back and forth. Black held on to a side railing. The skipper, a small man, lean as a whippet, wearing an oversized black donkey jacket and black woollen hat pulled past his ears, smiled a toothy smile. Black smiled back.

"Thunderstorm," said the man.

Black nodded. "Looks like it."

Two other passengers boarded. The young couple from the restaurant. Black watched them. Both athletic, clean-limbed, clutching their rucksacks. The young woman waved at Black. She was dark-haired, tanned skin, flashing a brilliant white smile. Black gave a half-smile in response. The couple sat together, started chattering.

The skipper waited another five minutes. The engine rumbled into life. The little boat pulled away from the jetty. The journey was short. Ten minutes. In the space of that time, the rain turned to sudden hailstones. Above, rolling black clouds covered the sun, the daylight rendered to a dreary grey. Black pulled the hood of his mountain waterproof over his head, and watched the sea.

The boat docked at a makeshift wooden pier. The three passengers disembarked. A minibus waited for them. Every hour, so the timetable said. They got in. They were met by a cheery driver, dressed in a blue uniform and blue cap. The cost was five pounds, there and back. He would drop them off at the lighthouse, then pick them up. He immediately launched into a history of the area, shouting above the grind of the engine. Black gave a wintry grin. It was no use talking the place up. It spoke for itself. Remote, desolate, brutal. Nothing else. You loved it, or hated it.

The road was a single track stretching up and skirting the cliff edge. The weather did not improve. The bus bounced and lurched over a range of potholes. The road weaved its way around the cliffs. Sixty feet below, the sea boomed as it crashed against the rocks. Black could see it was shaping up to be a wild day.

A half hour later, the bus stopped, a hundred yards from Cape Wrath lighthouse. They trooped out, all three passengers. The couple immediately set off for the obvious tourist attraction, which was the lighthouse itself. Black had other thoughts.

"I'll be back in an hour," said the driver. Black acknowledged by a wave of his hand.

He set off in the opposite direction, away from the cliff edge. A route unfrequented by tourists. Across moorland. An inhospitable place, impossible for vehicles to traverse. An area of land comprising little more than low rolling hills coated in cotton-grass, wild bracken, gorse, sticky bogs. One hill, however, stood out in the landscape. Even as Black set off, he could see it, a mile distant. Noticeable because of the lump of rock sitting on top, protruding on the horizon like a dark wart. Memories resurfaced for Black. All of them painful. Training for those elite soldiers handpicked to serve for the Special Air Service.

Black headed across the wild lands of Scotland, towards Bastard Rock.

14

The hike across the moorland was a slog. Black was undeterred. He had experienced landscapes much worse. In particular the mountain range of the Hindu Kush, in the north of Afghanistan, hunting Taliban at night on steep, hazardous slopes in blizzard conditions. Sometimes being hunted. Walking for miles in darkness so deep, it was easy to think you'd gone blind, nerves stretched, waiting for the impact of a bullet. Or being caught in a trap, and then the ultimate nightmare. Capture.

A walk in the rain during daylight hours on Scottish moorland did not faze Black.

He made good pace. The rain slackened. Nothing seemed untoward. Yet something niggled Black. He turned back. No one was following him. The scenery was unblemished by human presence, at least as far as he could tell. If a sniper was lying flat, covered by the vegetation, then that was it. Game over. Black would take a bullet in the head, and his problems were gone. It would be sudden. Instant oblivion. His body wouldn't be found for weeks, maybe months. Maybe never. He had to take his chances. No one would miss him, he thought ruefully. Maybe

Tricia, his secretary. A few would perhaps uncork champagne, to celebrate.

Time passed. Fifteen minutes later, Black stood at the foot of a steep hill, which flattened into a plateau after about sixty feet, then rose again, maybe another sixty feet. At the top was the rock each soldier was required to kiss, then immediately turn and scramble back down. Over twenty years ago. Not easy with a full, forty-pound Bergen pack strapped to your back, clutching a standard issue C8 assault rifle. Again and again. Until you dropped. And then you dragged yourself up and carried on, staff screaming abuse in your ears. Part of SAS selection training. A very small part, but enough for seasoned soldiers to fling in the towel, there and then, and tell their instructors to fuck the hell off.

Black climbed up the hill. He reached the plateau, and surveyed the land from his new vantage. To the west, the lighthouse. Beyond that, the grey expanse of the Atlantic. In all other directions, the monotonous spread of moorland, rising and falling like the gentle swells of a great green ocean. The rain had stopped. A brief respite. Brittle sunlight glinted through gaps in the cloud.

Black continued. He wondered if he could still run up with a pack on his back. He reckoned he could. Black had made it his business to stay supremely fit.

He got to the top. There it was, five feet from him. Bastard Rock, as it had been affectionately nicknamed by the regiment. Twenty feet high, thirty feet wide. Unchanged. Black looked up. A big square monolith of pale grey sandstone. An ugly piece of rock, providing Black and many other soldiers with unpleasant memories.

According to the will of the late Gilbert Bartholomew, Black had to look for what he needed. And what he needed was at the foot of Bastard Rock. A cryptic message. He slowly made his way round, searching for something, anything. He squinted in its shadow. There! A small arrow in grey paint, barely detectable, at the base of the rock, pointing downwards.

Black was mystified. He scanned the ground to where the arrow was pointing. A patch of grass. Nothing to make it stand out. Nothing had been disturbed. Black had an idea. He unzipped his jacket, reached round and unclipped the top of the sheath attached to his belt, and drew out his Ka-Bar knife. He thrust it into the ground. The grass was moist. It entered easily. He dug up the soil, using the blade like a trowel. He continued for five minutes, creating a hole about a foot deep. The tip of his knife struck something. Something solid. Something flat. He dug round the object, gently, teasing away the dirt. It was metal and square. He lifted out a white box, roughly the size and shape of a cigar box. It was light, the lid held shut by a single nickel-plated draw bolt latch. Black scrutinised it for a second, shaking it slightly. Something rattled inside. Black put it in his rucksack, stood, and looked back the way he had come.

And saw them approach.

15

The fundamental component of a Special Forces operator is aggression. And a touch of fucking madness.

Observation by Staff Sergeant to new recruits of 22nd Special Air Service Regiment

Taking roughly the same path as Black, the young couple approached. They were maybe a hundred and fifty yards distant. The female waved up at him. Black was easily visible from where he stood, at the pinnacle of the hill, at the foot of the rock. It was impossible for him not to be noticed. Black waved back. He watched them carefully, their movements, their mannerisms, the way they walked, the way they regarded their surroundings. Every little detail was important. They weren't making any effort to conceal themselves. He couldn't hear them, but they looked as if they were chatting to each other, unconcerned, enjoying the ramble. The picture of innocence.

The only way down the hill was the way he had climbed up.

The other side of the hill was steep, verging on vertical. The type of descent that could lead to a broken neck.

Black made his way down, zigzagging to prevent strain on the ankles. He got to the plateau. Flat, and about the size of a tennis court. Short, wild grass, and clusters of small rocks. He sat on the edge, took out the bottle of water from his rucksack, took a sip, and waited. The rain started again, a sudden drizzle. The sun was gone, hidden by clouds the colour of old bruising. The air felt heavy. The skipper was right. Black sensed thunder looming.

The couple reached the foot of the hill, in plain sight. They looked up.

"Ahoy there!" shouted the man, raising an arm, his manner careless, unconcerned. To Black's mind, he was maybe thirty. Perhaps younger. Clean-shaven. Brown hair cropped short. Regular, forgettable features. Maybe six feet. Lean and muscular. "Is it worth the climb up?"

Black responded, smiling. "Depends what you're looking for."

"Is it just a big rock?" shouted the woman. She too was about thirty, strong and fit. Athletic. Black noted that neither seemed out of breath after the mile hike through the moors. "We thought it was some sort of monument!"

"No monument! A big chunk of sandstone!"

She looked at her partner. They exchanged glances. They didn't move. Hesitation, thought Black. The man gave the slightest shake of his head.

"We'll not bother!" shouted the woman, her laughter ringing up through the rain. "Seems too much like hard work! If you're coming down, we'll walk you back!"

Black nodded grimly. Of course you will. They had reacted as he would have done. Climbing up the hill was disadvantageous, with Black looking directly down at them, perched as he was at the edge of the plateau. You don't attack an enemy uphill. Too many variables, and essentially, the other side always has momentum. And momentum can make all the difference. Basic rule of combat. And more obviously, if they'd walked all the way to get here, they would have climbed anyway. Perhaps he was being paranoid. But Black had learned that in his world, paranoia was essential for self-preservation. And when Black thought something didn't add up, he was usually dead right.

Black stood. He had to follow this through. Play act.

"Sure! Why not!"

He started the descent, keeping one eye on his footing, one eye on the couple. They had separated, unnaturally so. Classic positioning. Soldiers were taught in Special Services to function in small groups, and never in close proximity with each other, making them difficult targets in the event of attack.

Black made his way down gradually, nerves taut, thinking. The conversation between the pair had stopped, both intent on Black's descent. The rain got suddenly heavier. Thunder rumbled.

Black was six feet from the bottom.

"Some weather," he said, casually. He stopped, leaning back against the incline of the hill, and stooped down, as if adjusting the lacing on his boot. The woman was closer to him, standing directly beneath him. The man was fifteen feet to her left, standing further back. Black watched her out the corner of his eye.

Maintaining a cheerful smile, as if in slow motion, she pulled a pistol from a side pocket of her rain jacket.

Black didn't hesitate. He leapt, using the hillside as an improvised springboard, Ka-Bar knife in one hand. The woman took a step back, shocked. Not what she was expecting. She raised the pistol, but too late. Black cannoned into her, hard. They both tumbled on to the long grass. Black thrust the knife up and through her throat. Blood arced into the air, a sudden red rainbow. She spasmed. Her hand jerked open, releasing the pistol. Black retrieved it, rolled her on top. Just in time. Gunshots. He felt her body reverberate as it absorbed the impact of four bullets. Her male companion approached, firing two more. The woman's head exploded, Black momentarily blinded with segments of bone and brain. He lifted his hand, fired, more in hope than accuracy. The man recoiled, clutching his shoulder, dropping on his backside. Black pushed the dead woman away, stood, aiming the pistol at the man, who was sitting up, head bowed, taking short, sharp breaths, the top of his shoulder blown off. The man tried to aim his pistol, but his arm was wavering, uncoordinated. Black kicked it out of his hand. The man groaned.

Black loomed over him.

"Who are you?"

The man raised his head, staring fixedly at Black. His shoulder was a ruin, blood pumping in small, short bursts from shredded veins.

"Finish it," said the man, his voice a dry croak.

Black pressed his foot against the man's chest, pushing him flat to the ground, keeping his weight on him.

"Who are you?" he repeated.

The man gave a ghastly smile. "Fuck you," he mumbled.

Black adjusted his footing, pressing on the man's shoulder. The man screamed. Almost in symphony, the sky rumbled. Black waited five seconds. The man took a deep, ragged breath.

"I can do this all day," said Black. "Until your blood runs out. No one can hear you."

"I need to get to a hospital."

Black nodded. "I agree." He pressed down again. The man inhaled sharply, releasing a low moan. "Talk."

"I don't know anything. We were given instructions. All

verbal. We followed you from Glasgow. We were to find out what you were doing, then kill you, and report back."

"That's not very sociable. Report to who?"

"I don't know."

Black made a movement, about to put his weight again on the man's wound.

"No, please! The contact didn't give us his name. Not his real name. But we know him as something else."

"What?"

"The Grey Prince."

"Colourful. How do you contact him?"

The man coughed, his lungs bringing up phlegm and speckles of blood. "Please. I need to get to a hospital."

"How do you contact him?"

"Mobile number. That's all I have. When the job's done, I call him. He knows my voice. He doesn't call us. Please."

"Please what?"

"Please help."

"Of course."

Black shot him in the head.

He had something. A name – the Grey Prince. It meant nothing to Black. But it was a start. Plus, he had the estate of the late Gilbert Bartholomew in his rucksack, whatever the hell that was.

Black left them where they lay. They wouldn't be found for a good while. Let the wildlife feast.

16

The Arizona climate was a dry heat which suited Boyd Falconer perfectly. He had developed asthma as a young child, his mother was a chronic smoker, and then his aunt, after his mother died. In all the places in the world he had visited, and he had visited many, this was the easiest on his lungs. He rarely used his inhaler here. When he'd made his first $10 million, he decided to build a ranch deep in the Sonoran Desert, two hundred miles south of Phoenix. Two hundred and fifty acres of nothing much. Miles from anywhere. Privacy was high on Falconer's list of priorities.

Now $10 million was loose change. Human trafficking had proved highly lucrative for Boyd Falconer. But it was just the start. Over the years, Falconer had honed his skills, perfected his expertise. Now he offered a very specialised, niche market product to the wealthy and powerful. And it was a global demand.

Falconer sat in the middle of a large, sprawling, semicircular cream suede couch, in the living room of the main house. The room was huge. The oiled Georgian oak wood flooring was dotted with plush Bokhara and Kilims rugs.

Falconer had them imported from Uzbekistan and Iran. Bespoke Italian furniture; exquisite white marble table lamps. The ceiling was a cluster of rippled cupolas, and from each, suspended Venetian crystal chandeliers. One side of the room was a series of large windows framed in aluminium extrusions, offering a view of the front courtyard. Triple strength bullet-proof glass. Afternoon sunshine streamed through. Facing the couch, set in a column of pale-blue quartz, was a television the size of a small cinema. Falconer was watching horse racing. A man in his late sixties. Deeply tanned. Hair swept back, dyed deep black. Lean, ropy muscle. His face oddly stretched and tight – a consequence of cosmetic surgery and chemical peels. He was dressed in jogging trousers, T-shirt, running shoes. He was soaked in sweat. He had just come from his state-of-the-art gymnasium, an annex to the main house. He'd completed a ten-mile run on the treadmill. He did this every day. A slap in the face to his asthma.

His assistant, Norman Sands, sat at one end of the couch. He was dressed casually – blue jeans, white tennis shoes, open-necked shirt. A spindle-shanked, middle-aged man, a tousle of receding dark hair, skin unnaturally pale for the climate he was in, silver-rimmed spectacles. Born and bred in Wichita, Kansas. He was a chartered accountant by profession, and looked every bit of it. He lived at the ranch in a separate outbuilding. He had worked for Boyd Falconer for ten years, and knew him better than anyone. Which was not a lot. He had a laptop sitting on his knees. He waited for the race to finish.

Falconer switched off the television, using a remote. His horse had come in first. He'd won about $200,000, but he displayed little emotion. He had other things on his mind. "Speak," he said.

"Your friend is anxious. Two men have already been killed. The couple he arranged to… take care of things, haven't communicated. He's getting nervous. He's asked that you intervene. He's... what's the expression? He's reached out."

"Where the fuck does he get these people," muttered Falconer. "Incompetents. Now I have to clean up after him."

Sands cleared his throat.

"What the hell is it that you're trying to say?" snapped Falconer.

"With respect, I don't think they were incompetent. He would have picked them specially for this job. It may be he underestimated the target."

"Perhaps. Now it becomes our problem. Which means it becomes your problem. He should have been taken care of at the girl's flat. Who the fuck is this guy?"

"A nobody. An inconsequential. It will be taken care of."

Boyd turned to meet Sands with a glittering gaze. "Well, this *inconsequential* is becoming a pain in my arse. So, Norman, put a fucking lid on this, or I swear to Christ I'll put a fucking lid on you. If we can't resolve this, we'll lose a fortune. And you know how I feel about losing money. So, if anyone's *reaching out*, it will be me. With an iron fist."

Sands fidgeted on the leather couch. "We have a more pressing problem."

Falconer had picked up a newspaper from a low mosaic-topped coffee table constructed cleverly in brass, steel and bronze, and was skimming through the sports pages.

"What."

"The doctor was called this morning."

"So?"

"It looks like No. 4 might have measles."

Falconer looked up from the paper, stared into some indeterminate space before him.

"Are you kidding me?"

He tossed the newspaper away, picked up the remote,

pressed five digits. The image of the racecourse vanished, to be replaced by a chart on the television screen. There were names, locations, figures.

"No. 4 is due out next week. We have $16 million riding on that one." He turned back to his assistant. "How bad is it?"

"She has a rash."

"A rash?"

"It's over most of her body."

"Shit. We've got clients who've paid their money and are expecting quality goods. Good clients. Japan. People we can't let down. Is it infectious?"

"By the nature of the disease, yes. But we're okay. The others haven't been infected, and No. 4 has been quarantined. Lampton's on it."

"He'd better be. Monitor the situation. I'll speak to the clients. This'll need the personal touch. I'll tell them there'll be a slight delay. We'll chuck in another one for free."

He studied the screen.

"No. 9. Too old. It's not worth much. $1,000,000. Maybe less. We can write that one off."

Sands tapped the keyboard of his computer, inputting fresh data.

"About the other situation," continued Falconer. "The *inconsequential*. This has to be dealt with. Get it done. The Grey Prince has asked for help, so we do what we do, and give him the assistance he needs. Speak to Mr Lincoln." Falconer chuckled. "He'll break his fucking balls."

"It'll cost. Mr Lincoln is not cheap."

"Do I look as if I give a fucking shit." His mood shifted abruptly. Sands had learned this of his employer. Unpredictability. Violent mood swings. "We can't have some fucking idiot fishing about our business. If our clients hear even a whisper, then it spreads like an infection. Like the fucking measles.

Before we know it, this *inconsequential* becomes a nightmare. So deal with it. What's his name?"

Sands checked his computer, running through a variety of secure emails he'd received from Glasgow.

"His name is Adam Black."

"Then Adam fucking inconsequential Black needs to be destroyed. Him, and everything about him. *Man that is born of woman is of few days*. Especially when he fucks with me. Do it."

Falconer switched the television back to the sports channel. Sands was dismissed. He nodded and left the room. He had an important message to send. To a man regarded as the best in his field.

Mr Lincoln.

17

Black returned in time to catch the hourly bus.

"Where's the other two?" asked the driver.

Black shrugged. "Probably enjoying the view."

The journey back went without incident. Black had searched both his assailants to discover nothing much. Him – a wallet containing £300, a set of car keys, a mobile phone, loose change. Her – nothing except a mobile phone. Both phones required passwords. Black had tossed them and the keys. If they had a car, and it was parked locally, then eventually its abandonment would spark interest. Black doubted if anyone, including the police, would find much. Probably rented, under assumed names. Though it would initiate a search of the area. Black was unperturbed. He would be long gone. He kept the money. Waste not, want not. No use on a corpse.

Each rucksack contained ammunition and weapons. High-powered hand cannons – Desert Eagles .50 calibre. As powerful as a semi-automatic gets. Expensive equipment. Not for the faint-hearted. Black was grateful the man who'd fired into his female friend had used a KelTec model. Probably because of its low recoil and light weight. Easily carried in the pocket of a rain jacket. If he'd used the Desert Eagle, it would have cut through the woman's body like warm butter, and sliced Black in half. Unlucky for them. Lucky for Black. Black loaded the weapons into his rucksack.

Whoever wanted him dead wanted it bad.

When he arrived back at Durness, he went straight to his car, changed, and drove off. He reckoned the couple would have been instructed to check in. When they didn't, possibly at a pre-arranged time, somewhere alarm bells would start to ring. His flat would be watched, for sure. And on the assumption they had informed their masters that he had travelled north, to Cape Wrath, others might follow. And maybe the road down to Glasgow was being watched, if they were well organised. Which they were. Plan for the worst. As such, Black could not go back. Not yet.

He headed in the opposite direction. The coastal route around the very north of Scotland. Part of the so-called North Coast 500. Five hundred miles of Highland wilderness along narrow, meandering roads. Black headed for the town of Thurso. His wife had been born and brought up there, in a rambling old country house on the outskirts, by a small stream near a wood full of Scots pine and slender silver birch. Black remembered it well, from when they visited. A million years ago. A different time. The house now belonged to someone else, to strangers, sold when his wife's mother had died, her frail heart broken at the loss of her only child and grandchild. Black thought about them every day. The sadness did not lessen. Nor the rage. Nor the guilt.

He needed somewhere to stay, somewhere his presence would not attract attention. Thurso was big enough for him to disappear for a day, perhaps two. The drive was uneventful. Black hardly noticed the scenery, the clear white sands of the shoreline and endless choppy expanse of the North Atlantic to his left, sweeping green hills of grass and gorse to his right. The rain fell harder again. Clouds gathered. He passed places no bigger than hamlets with quaint and eccentric names. Places he knew little about – Tongue; Bettyhill; Melvich; Scrabster. He reached Thurso. The rain now was a downpour. It had been about two years since he had last visited. The place hadn't changed. Being perched on practically the northern most part of the British Isles had given it a rugged, windswept appearance. The streets and lanes looked the same – robust stone-built houses, grey and brown; a scattering of shops. No frills. Simple, straightforward.

Black booked into the Royal Oak, a hotel close to the centre and a hundred yards from St Peter's Church, a ruin over a thousand years old. He made sure to park his car a distance from the hotel, in a secluded back street, where it wasn't noticeable. But if they were dedicated enough, they would find it eventually. Black would ensure his time in Thurso was brief.

The first thing he did was to get something to eat. The hotel dining room wasn't yet open. He ate haddock and chips in a nearby fish restaurant, and had a cup of tea. He sat at a table well back from the front window. He was the only customer. He took time to reflect.

He had disposed of a man and a woman less than three hours earlier. They had been armed with pistols and had tried to murder him on the Scottish moorlands. Black had returned the compliment, erasing their existence. His training had kicked in. Second nature. He had to accept the fact that he was adept at killing people. A thought flitted through his mind. One he tried to shut out, but which obstinately refused to leave – that when he killed, it was more than instinct. Something else. Something dreadful. Enjoyment? The word brought a chill.

Which was why maybe he had volunteered and was gladly accepted in such a fighting force as the SAS, who embraced young, maladjusted men with a penchant for violence. Men who thrived on conflict. Men who liked to kill. He lifted the cup of tea. His hand trembled, the slightest tremor.

Killing still wasn't easy. No matter how used one was to the theatre of war, there was always aftershock. Reaction. Black took a deep breath, tried to rein in his emotions, focus on the present, just as he had been trained. But after an act of extreme violence, it could still prove difficult. He sat, calmed himself. The waitress smiled at him. Black smiled back. He finished off his tea, paid the bill, and went back to the hotel and straight to his room.

He opened his rucksack and removed the box he had unearthed beneath *Bastard Rock*. Gilbert Bartholomew's legacy. Black drew the curtains, and placed the box on the bed.

He clicked open the latch, and lifted the lid.

18

Boyd Falconer gave his explanations to Koboyashi Kaito via video link.

Falconer was sitting in the living room of his ranch. He had dressed for the meeting – he knew exactly what his Japanese clients liked – order, neatness, correct behaviour. Structure. For the occasion, he wore a light powder-blue cotton suit, white shirt, navy tie, black brogues. Image was everything. It was three in the afternoon, Arizona time. Hot. Way too hot for what he was wearing. Cotton was breathable and smart. He'd increased the air con.

Kaito listened, his expression inscrutable. If he felt anything, he chose not to reflect it in any facial mannerisms. He remained rigidly still. He was currently on a short holiday in a town called Karuizawa, an hour from Tokyo, where he kept a forest lodge. Kaito had homes dotted all over the world, as would befit a shipping billionaire.

Falconer continued, unflustered by Kaito's lack of reaction. Falconer had dealt with difficult situations before. This was just one more, a hazard of the profession he was in. He could afford to be confident. He had products which few others could provide.

He explained that due to unforeseen circumstances, there would be a delay of maybe two, possibly three weeks, before the product could be transferred.

"But an agreement was reached," replied Kaito in perfect English, his tone the embodiment of reason. "You have my money. A date was set."

"Quite right, Mr Kaito. The funds were transferred exactly as requested. You kept your side of the bargain with the integrity and honour I would expect from a man such as yourself. It is I who has failed in his obligations. I hope and pray that this doesn't sour our future relationship."

Kaito gave the slightest of nods. Almost undetectable. It didn't escape Falconers attention.

"And as a mark of respect, I would like to offer you a gift. The photograph and details are being sent to you now."

Kaito didn't move. Thirty seconds later he was handed a document. He examined its contents. He turned his attention back to Falconer. "A gift?"

"Yes, indeed. To be delivered simultaneously with the main acquisition."

"I accept this gracious gift," said Kaito. "But no delivery."

Falconer frowned. "I'm not quite sure I understand, Mr Kaito."

Kaito regarded Falconer for several seconds.

"I will come to you. As a guest. You said two or three weeks? I shall visit in three weeks. That way there are no further delays. It will... what is the expression? Help to concentrate the mind? Then I can pick it... sorry, *them*... directly. No hiccups."

Falconer hadn't expected this. He'd never had a client stay at the ranch. Still, $15 million was a lot of money. And Kaito was a man he'd made a lot of money from over the years. But there was protocol.

Falconer sighed, raising both hands in placation. "That isn't our standard policy, Mr Kaito. The transfer takes place through intermediaries, as you know. This ensures our preservation. Our protection. The whole basis of these transfers should be arm's length. That way, we can continue to prosper."

"Sometimes, exceptions must be made." Suddenly Kaito's face broke into a wide smile, flashing white teeth. "To ensure continued prosperity. For both of us, Mr Falconer. I don't want to be disappointed."

Falconer returned the smile, though strained. "Very well, Mr Kaito. If this is what you want."

"Thank you. A little flexibility makes all the difference, don't you agree? But Mr Falconer, you haven't explained the reason for the delay. I'm curious, you understand, given you have $15,000,000 of my money."

Falconer responded in his silkiest voice.

"Nothing to concern yourself with, I promise. I felt the merchandise needed a little more training. When we sell goods to our most trusted clients, we have to be sure those goods are premium quality. The one you've chosen needs a little more time. To press out the wrinkles. Squeeze out the remnants of rebellion. You will thank me for this, I promise, Mr Kaito. You will thank me."

"But the package will still be fresh?"

"Of course."

"Very well. Three weeks, Mr Falconer."

The screen went blank. Falconer turned to Sands, who had been standing quietly to one side.

"You heard him. Three weeks. He's coming here."

"It'll be fine."

"It had better be."

"Regarding the other matter. I've made contact with Mr Lincoln. He's already in the UK. I've given him the details of the target." Sands hesitated.

"What is it?"

"I've done some digging. Mr Lincoln wanted to know as much as possible about Adam Black."

"So? I'd expect nothing less. He'd be a fool otherwise. And Mr Lincoln is no one's fool."

"When he got the details, his price doubled."

Falconer gave Sands a long stare. "Why would he do that?"

"Because it wasn't incompetence. The people hired by the Grey Prince were good. It's just that Adam Black was better."

"Stop talking riddles. What the fuck are you trying to tell me?"

"Adam Black is ex-special services. He's trained. He's a killer. Maybe we should be worried."

19

B lack opened the box.

It contained two items. A sealed envelope, wrapped in a transparent polythene bag. And a matchbox. Black slid it open. Inside was a memory stick.

Black removed the envelope from the bag. Handwritten in black biro, on the front, and in clear block capitals, was his name. More specifically, CAPTAIN ADAM BLACK. Little doubt as to who it was meant for, he mused. He opened the envelope, pulled out the letter inside. The contents were similarly handwritten – neat, precise. Black went over to a chair by the window, sat, and read.

Captain Black,

If you're reading this then you've fulfilled the instructions in my will, and I'm dead. You're probably a hunted man. My deepest apologies. But the truth is, of all the people I've met in my life, I believe you are the best equipped to deal with the situation. Which is why I chose you, Captain Black.

An avenging angel.

You'll not remember me. I served briefly in the 22nd Regiment under your command in Afghanistan, 2001. Helmand Province. I was there for less than a month. An IED caught the Snatch Land Rover I was driving, flipping it right over. You'll recall how useless these vehicles were. Two of my friends died instantly, and I was trapped, both legs smashed. I survived. Because of you, Captain Black, and what you did that day.

I never returned to active service, and left the army six months later with a disability pension. But I followed your career. You were something of a legend. You probably still are. And I saw, first hand, what you're capable of.

Which is why I think you're the only person who can see this to its rightful end.

Six months ago, my daughter was taken. She is five years old. Her name is Natalie. She was stolen from her bed during the night. It was planned. She was targeted. She hasn't been found. The police believe she was abducted and murdered. They've given up on her. I think they're wrong. I think she's alive. My wife didn't. She overdosed. She took her own life because she thought our little girl might be lonely in heaven. As I write this down, my heart is breaking.

I haven't given up. I never will. But time's running out. I'm being watched. I'm being followed. This is not paranoia. Hence this letter. Hence the will.

I've researched paedophiles, paedophile groups. Their patterns of behaviour, their characteristics, their modus operandi. I've trawled the dark web. I've borne witness to the most depraved things. Things that make the skin crawl, and the stomach heave. But I think I'm onto something massive. A ring of individuals deeply involved in child abuse. They're secretive, they're clever. And they're very powerful.

I stumbled across a video of one of their "parties". I think this video can help me find Natalie. I know there's a connection.

But I've been careless. I've been asking too many questions, and been too open about it. I am under no illusion that my life is in danger. The fact you're reading this bears out my prediction.

These people need to be destroyed. Like vermin. I can't do it. I believe you can.

Following your career, having seen what you can do, I know something about you, that perhaps you don't see yourself. You're more than a soldier. Much more.

You are a man of war, Captain.

A warrior.

I need a warrior now. These children need a warrior. Kill these fuckers. Find my daughter.

Godspeed, Captain Black,

Gilbert Bartholomew

Black read the letter twice, then let it rest on his lap. There was a photo of a little girl stapled at the bottom. Tousled yellowy blonde hair, blue eyes, looking at the camera from under a Christmas tree, face alive with joy. He gazed out the window. The view was of a small back court with industrial-sized rubbish carts, and beyond, the brick gable end of a house. Black cast his gaze inward. To a desert scene fifteen years ago. In the Afghan badlands, where life was cheaper than a bullet. Another world, another time. Black remembered, memories caught in the smoke of the bomb, the hazy swirl of the desert sand, the smell of diesel...

The Snatch Land Rover turned a half somersault, only thirty yards from Black, who was driving the vehicle next in line. The explosion was short and powerful. Black felt the ground shake. Like a tremor. Then, a hail of bullets from a cluster of stones imbedded in the sand, fifty yards from the road. Perfect camouflage. Their target was the fallen Land Rover. Black saw the glint of weaponry. Looked like AK-

47s. The Taliban's rifle of choice. A legacy of the Russian invasion two decades before.

Normal protocol — stop the vehicle, get out, take cover, evaluate, respond. Fairly obvious. But the soldiers in the Snatch were under fire, and there was no time. If they weren't dead already, they would be soon. Either by gunshot or exploding fuel tank.

Black hit the gas pedal. The Snatch Land Rover was built to be quick in rough terrain. He headed off-road, direct to where the Taliban had dug in. Suddenly, the direction of the fight changed. The windscreen exploded into a million pieces. The front chassis shuddered, absorbing round after round of Taliban bullets, the armour-plated shielding doing its job. Black kept on.

Five seconds later, screams of consternation as he drove the vehicle across the stones and on top of their heads. Maybe eight assailants. Four crushed on impact. Black leapt from the vehicle, already aiming, firing once, twice. Another two down. A man came from nowhere, leaping on his back, knife poised to slit his throat. Black hurled him over his shoulder, fired a bullet in his head, close range. A man scrambled across the sand to get away. Black calmly shot him in the back. Eight dead men.

He sprinted back to the flipped over Land Rover. Clock was ticking. The sounds of gunfire could attract a hundred more insurgents in minutes. Black reached in.

"Got to get you out of here and to a hospital."

Black pulled the driver from the wreckage, delicately. His legs were twisted. Other men had now arrived to help.

The driver held Black's hand for a second longer.

"Thank you."

And that was the one and only conversation Black had with the man he would come to know as Gilbert Bartholomew.

20

Mr Lincoln was in Oxford when he was given the contract on Adam Black's life. "The City of Dreaming Spires" as it is known, and how he preferred to call it.

He visited every year, at about the same time, for a week. He was a man of routine. This was, for him, a short holiday. He made it his business to visit the Bodleian Library. Books fascinated him. Literature. Poetry mesmerised him. He had acquired a collection of rare first editions, which he kept secure in his home in a little fishing village called Monnickendam, a fifteen-minute drive from Amsterdam, a place few people knew about.

He wasn't Dutch. Far from it. He was American. The name he was using currently, and the name he liked his American friends to use, was Jonathan Lincoln. He worked under several assumed names, had several passports. He spoke without accent, always in a soft, well-modulated voice, which was rarely raised. He spoke several languages. Fluently. Self-taught. He kept supremely fit, running five miles every day. He was skilled in hand-to-hand combat, and competent with knife and sword. He was an expert marksman, particularly the pistol. He was patient and precise. He planned to the point of obsession. There was nothing in his demeanour to stand him out from the crowd, which suited him perfectly. Forgettable. Average height, lean, medium-length hair. A very slight scar above his left eyebrow. He dressed casually. Never formal, unless he had to. At first glance, he seemed like any other tourist, completely at ease in his surroundings. Which he was, when he visited Oxford.

Mr Lincoln. A one hundred per cent kill rate. Hitman for the super wealthy.

His holiday had been interrupted by the urgent email from Norman Sands. Normally, he would have ignored such an intrusion. But Sands represented people who paid generously.

When he got the details of the target, he knew, instinctively, the task would represent a challenge. More challenging than the average kill. Perhaps the most challenging he'd been asked to face. He could refuse. But the prospect intrigued him. Compelled him. And of course, there was the money.

He was sitting in the Bodleian Library, as he re-read the résumé of the man he was to kill. The résumé was thorough and meticulous, every aspect of his life captured and condensed. It seemed the man Captain Adam Black had led an interesting life.

Mr Lincoln had asked for double his usual fee, given the urgency, and got it instantly. Which told him they wanted him silenced very badly. It wouldn't be easy. Far from it. The man had spent a good chunk of his adult life in Special Forces, had won the Military Cross. Plus, he was already aware he was being hunted, so the element of surprise was reduced. To complicate things, he had no family, so there was no leverage. He had already killed, possibly four people. He was not scared to spill blood. In fact, pondered Lincoln, he might enjoy it.

Lincoln deliberated, alone and in the tranquil ambience of the Bodleian, where silence was the absolute rule. He had an almost intuitive sense about his intended victims, piecing together the facts of their lives, creating a picture of their psyche, behaviour patterns, habits, determining what they would do, their next move, their fears, their desires. In Adam Black's case, Lincoln saw something he had never seen, and thought he never would. He saw something of himself. A killer. A man used to death, who wasn't scared of it.

He would catch a flight to Glasgow that evening, and book himself into a hotel. The instruction was clear. Black had to be expunged quickly. And discreetly. Lincoln already had a half-plan formulated. Despite his apparent invulnerability, Lincoln saw an angle – the chink in Black's armour.

For the first time for as long as he could remember, he felt his heart race with excitement. He would have taken on this job for nothing, for the sheer thrill of killing a man like Captain Adam Black.

A trophy kill.

21

The trick is to stay alive. How do you accomplish this? Simple. Kill every bastard in the room.

Advice given by Staff Sergeant to recruits of the 22nd Regiment of the Special Air Service

B lack toyed with the memory stick. He had killed men, with guns, knives, his bare hands, had faced death many times. Yet now, at this moment, he was truly scared. The memory stick held material that might open a window to dark and terrible places. Places he definitely did not want to visit. He could turn back. It wasn't too late. He could shut up shop, lose himself in another country, never be found. Eventually, his trail would run cold, and those hunting him would give up. Maybe.

But if he looked through that window, even a glimpse, to the dark beyond, then a line was crossed. Perhaps no going back. He studied the photograph of the laughing girl, Natalie. The essence of innocence. He read the letter again. He thought of the bastards who'd tried to kill him, the bastards who'd undoubtedly murdered Gilbert Bartholomew, who'd stabbed Fiona Jackson to death and left her naked in her flat to rot. This had to stop.

He had £300 cash in his pocket. Courtesy of one dead assassin lying in the bleak, windswept Highland moors. Black left his hotel bedroom, wandered into the town centre, found a computer repair shop, where he bought a second-hand laptop. He returned to his room. On the way back he'd bought a bottle of whisky – Glenfiddich. He suspected he might need it. He poured himself a large glass, neat, and took a hefty gulp.

He powered up the laptop, plugged in the memory stick.

Black gazed at the screen, watched the events unfold. Every second of a ten-minute video. He paused it halfway through, poured himself another large whisky, downed it in one, went through to the en-suite bathroom and retched. He returned, then stuck it to the end. He kept the volume low, but the screams of the little girl, and the laughter of the men, was a melody like no other, twisting into his brain like an infection.

The video finished. Black took a deep, faltering breath. He felt disgusted, sickened, appalled. Violated. A whole range of powerful emotions.

But despite the outrage, something he saw sparked a flicker of recognition. A tiny fragment. Another large swig of neat whisky. Black started again, from the beginning, taking more care to absorb the details. The quality was good, the images sharp, heightening the horror. This had been taken for subsequent viewing, he presumed.

The child was led into a large room, filled with chairs, divans, couches, positioned round a wide, impressive black marble hearth. A fire crackled. This was not a typical front living room. More like an upmarket hotel lounge, or the sumptuous smoking den of a private club. There was an intimacy about the place. It was opulent – plush red carpets, dark glossy oak-panelled walls. Heavy velvet curtains drawn shut. Large paintings in gold gilt-edged frames. On one wall, a tapestry, glinting gold and silver in the firelight. The illumination was soft, muted. Men sat, scattered about the room, in no particular order, maybe ten. All wearing identical dark robes, except one, whose robe was pale grey. Hoods drawn over their heads, each wearing a white face mask. They were naked underneath. Three men stood at a far wall, black suits. Also masked. Guards? Possibly.

She was no older than five, and terrified, squirming in the arms of two of the robed figures. Wearing a simple white dress. When she cried, the men laughed. When she screamed, the men screamed with her, imitating her, their voices shrill.

Behold the embodiment of true evil. A living, gasping nightmare. They passed her about, the little girl, one to another, like a sack of soft meat.

There! Black paused the video. A man had his hands on her shoulders. Black concentrated. He rewound, paused again. He was not mistaken. What he saw was distinctive. He had seen it before, twice in the last week. He watched again, to the finish, the video ending as her screams escalated to a heart-freezing pitch.

What happened afterwards, he did not wish to conjecture. But he did. More pain, maybe even death.

Black removed the memory stick from the laptop, snapped it in two. He wrapped the pieces in paper tissue and flushed it down the toilet. He put the laptop on the floor and smashed it with the heel of his shoe.

He poured another large whisky, and drank it in one, trying to contain the tremble in his hand.

He gazed out the window, at the unspectacular view of the back of a building.

He knew himself. He knew this was how it would be after

watching the video. Pandora's box was opened. People had tried to kill him. He had killed right back – a reflex, almost. Survival instinct.

This was way beyond that.

He turned away, opened the wardrobe door, stared at his reflection in a full-length mirror. The reflection staring back was a man moulded by others, their sole purpose to create a fighting machine capable of inflicting maximum damage. Who did that little girl have in her hour of need? She had screamed, desperate and terrified, and her screams had gone unheeded. He seethed with a dark, consuming rage – if his daughter were alive, she'd be about the same age.

Avenging angel. Warrior. Black thought hard on those words.

Time now for this killing machine to give a little back. He had nothing to lose, after all, except his life, which he would gladly give. The die was cast, a decision made.

He would do exactly as Gilbert Bartholomew requested. He would try to find his daughter, little Natalie.

And if need be, kill every last one of the fuckers involved.

With pleasure.

22

The ranch had been built initially as exactly that. A cluster of buildings, luxury living accommodation, barns, outbuildings. But as the years progressed, and Boyd Falconer's business interests expanded, he adapted his home to accommodate his line of work. Very special adaptations, several million dollars' worth of changes. Money, however, was not an obstacle.

Another level was created. A sub-level. The few that knew of its existence gave it a chilling nickname – the *Dungeon*. An area about quarter of an acre in dimension. Comprising one broad corridor, with rooms off either side. Each room was spacious, comfortable, with single beds, toilets, showers, no windows, for obvious reasons. The colours were bright, gaudy. Pink or blue wallpaper, spotted with yellow love hearts, glittering rainbows, smiling teddies. Coloured cushions on chairs, beanbags to sit on. Hanging from the corridor ceiling were large silver and gold rotating globes, which made the walls sparkle, as if gold dust was being sprinkled.

Each room was locked. Hidden video cameras monitored those inside.

At one end of the corridor was a room occupied by the individual responsible for those confined in the locked rooms. Stanley Lampton. He kept check. If need be, he was empowered to administer penalties, in case of disobedience. Sometimes he had to make an example of one, to create the desired subservience in the group. Though he was not allowed to maim or disfigure, or draw blood. Occasionally, if Falconer felt magnanimous, he granted him one as a gift, to do with as he pleased.

The man who lived in that room was feared by those in the dungeon. Like the sub-level he inhabited, he also had a nickname – the *Dungeon Master*. Lampton was a man with a past. He'd spent a good portion of his adult life in the state penitentiary for child molestation. Lampton had been an early starter. He'd raped his first minor when he was sixteen, and had never looked back. Those who had suffered at his hands would describe him as a monster. Lampton had many victims in many states.

Which was exactly the type of man Falconer needed to keep order in the dungeon. A man who enjoyed his work.

It was Lampton who had called the doctor about the measles, and it was Lampton who ensured a strict quarantine was in place.

"This had better be under fucking control," said Falconer. He and Sands were in Lampton's room at the end of the hall. It was large, of regular dimensions, and scrupulously clean. It was devoid of anything personal. No pictures on the wall, no needless furniture, no ornaments or memorabilia. No family photographs – Stanley Lampton's family had disowned him years ago. Lampton sat directly opposite the two men on a small leather swivel chair. He was spindle thin, his back rigid, his pale, long-fingered hands resting on his lap, like two monstrous albino spiders. He liked to dress in blue hospital scrubs, the type a surgeon might wear.

He regarded the two before him with dark eyes set deep in a skull face. Sharp cheekbones, narrow jaw. Lank black hair sat like a flat rag on his scalp, trailing over his ears. Sands was reminded of a moving cadaver when he had a conversation with Lampton. He liked to keep the meetings short. The man creeped him out.

"I couldn't do anything about the measles," replied Lampton, his voice soft, reasonable, respectful. "She'll be fine. She's in isolation. The doctor's seen her."

"I repeat..." said Falconer, "it had better be under fucking control. Do you know how much the doctor costs, just for one visit? Humour me, Lampton."

"I imagine it's expensive."

"Imagine all you want. Let me tell you. One hundred and fifty thousand dollars. Do you know why it's so expensive?"

Lampton remained expressionless.

"Because," continued Falconer, "I have to buy the doctor's silence. Every time someone here gets a cut or an infection, or a fucking summer cold, I pay a thousand times more than the going rate. Thus, for reasons of economy, I depend on you to keep these episodes to an absolute minimum."

"I understand completely."

"You'd better. She needs to be ready in three weeks. Make sure she is."

"She'll be ready," said Lampton. "Count on it."

23

Black had a lead. He'd spotted something in the video, and it was enough to plan. He would set off early in the morning.

He lay in bed, staring at the ceiling. He finished the bottle. It was 9pm. Thoughts drifted in and out of his head. The images he'd witnessed recurred, rearing up, uninvited, casting grotesque shadows in his mind. He thought of his own dead daughter. Black fought back a wave of nausea.

He needed space to breathe. He needed perspective. He decided he'd venture downstairs, to the hotel bar for a nightcap, some friendly faces. Anything to chase away the shadows.

The bar was like any hotel bar anywhere. The Royal Oak was not the largest hotel in Thurso, but the bar was big enough to attract a crowd. Several booths, rectangular wooden tables with short stools and chairs. Tall bay windows with darkened glass looked on to the street outside. The walls had been reduced back to rough bare brick and stone – a popular feature in trendy pubs, apparently. Black had never cottoned on to the idea. In a corner, a real fire smoked and crackled beneath a copper-coloured hood. Quaint. *Olde Worlde.*

Black sat on a high stool at the bar and ordered a Glenfiddich. Double. The gantry was built on to a frosted mirror, holding rows of obscure whiskies. Black studied his reflection. The face looking back was tanned, chiselled, handsome in a hard-bitten way, dark hair cut short, dark eyes. Eyes which had witnessed death in all its forms. And outrages. He had witnessed friends tortured in Iraq, arms and legs blown off in makeshift roadside bombs built from scrap in basements; witnessed executions by terrorists, some as young as twelve. Beheadings. Mutilations. Black had seen all aspects of evil. But nothing compared to the video of the little girl. His soul felt numb. His insides felt hollow.

He took a large gulp of his whisky.

A group of four young men sat round a table in a corner. They were necking down shorts, ordering them up as soon as they were finished. Their conversation was loud, and within half an hour, took on an edge of menace. The atmosphere got uncomfortable. People began to leave.

The man sitting on the stool next to Black shook his head, smiling, and spoke to Black out of the corner of his mouth.

"Fishermen from Orkney, I reckon," he muttered. "Over for a long weekend. A bit of skirt and a bit of drink. Wish I had the energy."

Black nodded, but didn't say anything. He sensed trouble. He knew he should politely retire to his room, and stay out of everyone's radar. Low profile. But Black had no such inclination. Not this night.

A glass suddenly smashed. One of the men had flung a pint tumbler against the wall. Beer sprayed on the table, on the floor.

The barmaid who had served Black lifted a section of the bar, opened the half door, and approached the group.

"I think you've had enough," she said, laughing. Trying to play down the situation. Keeping it jovial. Diffuse.

"I think you should fuck off," one of them shouted. The biggest one. Even sitting, Black could tell he was massive. Wide shoulders, bull-necked, the T-shirt he was wearing stretched tight over rolling biceps. Forearms like slabs. Hands like shovels. He looked up at the barmaid, his expression slack, eyes glazed. The others laughed loudly. One of them leaned over and tried to put his hand up her skirt. She took a sudden step back, slapping him away.

"That's enough," she said, all remnants of laughter gone. Things were getting out of control. "I need to ask you to leave, or I'll call the manager."

This caused another eruption of laughter. From all of them, except the big one, whose gaze flickered on the barmaid.

"Call the fucking manager," he said. "I dare you."

The man who'd tried to grope her, tried it again. He lurched forward, and caught the end of her skirt. She kicked out. The movement unbalanced him. His chair toppled, and he fell onto the stone tiles. He remained motionless for a second, on his hands and knees, then got to his feet. He was small, wiry. Thin-faced, with two days' stubble. He wore black jeans, blue collared polo shirt. Shaved head, displaying an old scar. Lean muscle, but not built like his friend. He glared at the barmaid, face contorted in a snarl.

"Fucking slut fuck!" he shouted.

The man sitting next to Black leaned over and whispered in his ear. "Trouble."

"Definitely," Black whispered back.

A man appeared, probably from the restaurant section next door. He was in his fifties, overweight, dressed in a pale-blue suit which had seen better days, collar, tie. Thick dark-rimmed spectacles. The manager. When he saw the situation, and the four men, he baulked. This situation was way above his pay grade. Nevertheless, he had a job to do. Black was mildly impressed.

"Come on, lads," he said, his voice low and calm. "I think the fun's over. Let's call it a night. What do you say?"

The man standing turned slowly round to face him. He was two inches shorter, but had three friends as back up.

"What do I say?" He took a step forward, now six inches from the manager's face. "I say, why don't you go and fuck right off, and let me deal with that fucking slut!" He pointed at the barmaid, who had retreated, standing with her back to the bar. Black saw in her face an emotion he had seen a million times. Fear. Both she and the manager were suddenly thrust into a new world. Danger, violence. Black's world.

"Please," stammered the manager. "Let's all calm down."

Black eased himself off his high stool, and walked calmly up to stand at the manager's shoulder.

"You heard what the man said. He would like you to calm it down."

Black, at six-two, was four inches taller than the manager, in peak condition, and looked it.

"Who the fuck are you?"

Black reacted with a thin-lipped smile, but the steel glint did not leave his eyes, and the smaller man saw it. He flicked a glance at the big man sitting at the table, who ponderously got to his feet. Six-four, easy.

"He asked you a question, fuckwit," said the big man.

Black gently ushered the manager to one side, and stepped forward, so he was close to the thin-faced man. He spoke, his voice calm, unruffled.

"I'm the guy who's here to ensure you keep your appointment."

Thin Face looked uncertain. Again, another darting glance towards his friend.

"What fucking appointment?"

"Intensive care."

A silence fell in the pub. No one spoke. Tension was wire tight. Everyone in the place was fully focused on the scene unfolding.

"Are you having a fucking laugh?" slurred the big man. He clambered his way round the table, staggering slightly, to stand next to his friend. Bodybuilder. Big and clumsy. Drunk, maybe high on drugs. Joints probably crippled by steroids. Black had met his type before. Bravado, posturing. Usually without substance.

Black shook his head, shrugging slightly.

"No laughs here." He fixed his attention on the thin-faced man. "I'm going to break your arm. More specifically your ulna and your humerus. I might wrench your shoulder out of its socket for good measure. And you'll lose some teeth. Plus, you'll be spending a bit of money on facial reconstruction."

He turned his attention to the big man. "You're muscular, but slow. You're clumsy. You've been drinking all day, so you have no reflexes. I'm going to snap your spine. The lumbar region. You'll never walk again. Your pals can cart you round in a wheelchair next time you're out, until they get fed up." He faced them, eyes glittering. "This is where we are, my friends."

Black took a half step forward.

"So why don't we play this out, right fucking now."

The remaining two at the table watched, open mouthed. Peripherals, thought Black. Any trouble, and they would vanish.

Black stared at the big man. Black was ready. More than ready. His body tingled for action. And they knew it.

Thin Face licked his lips, took a deep breath. He tapped his friend on the elbow. "Fuck it. Let's get the hell out of here."

The big man stood, wavering on his feet. The eyes were vacant, the face slack. Suddenly, a glimmer of understanding. Through the alcohol, something penetrated. That this was a fight he might not win.

Nothing more was said. The two shuffled past, taking care to walk round him. The two at the table followed suit, keeping their eyes averted from Black. They sloped out, into the night. Black returned to his high stool, and his drink, and finished his glass.

"Thanks for that," breathed the manager. "The next one's on the house."

Black nodded. The barmaid fixed him another Glenfiddich, regarding him with a new appreciation.

The man sitting next to his side scrutinised him for several long seconds. Black turned, smiling.

"Looks like they didn't have the energy after all."

24

The dining room opened at 7am for breakfast, and Black got something light. He had little appetite. A coffee and buttered croissant. The day looked as if it would be a repeat performance of the day before. Grey, rolling clouds, the breeze bringing a touch of rain from the sea, the sunlight wan and dreary.

Black did not see either the manager or the barmaid, and was glad of it. The last thing he wanted was attention. He chided himself for getting involved the previous evening. He should have left it. He needed to be invisible. Damage done. He had to move on.

Black ate his breakfast, went back up to his room, packed his holdall. Time to go.

He walked the quarter mile to his car. On the way, he deposited the smashed laptop in a public waste bin.

He got to the car. Nothing seemed out of place. His flat would be under surveillance, of that he was sure. But there was nothing there to require him back. His next stop was Edinburgh. They would be expecting him, no doubt. But he had questions

to ask, scores to settle. A certain legal firm was in the frame –
Raeburn, Collins and Co.

Time to pay another visit. Though this time, a little less
civilised.

25

The offices of Raeburn, Collins and Co. were closed for the evening. At least to the public. It was during the evening hours when the real work was carried out. No interruptions – zero client contact, which meant no meetings, appointments, phone calls. Things got done.

Most, if not all, of the partners had left. Those who remained were assistants, associates, paralegals. Working a ten-hour day. Maybe more. Crippling workloads with little thanks. Complain, and the door was shown. For every vacant position in a law office, fifty desperate solicitors were there to fill it. The law was a shrinking market. And as brutal as any other industry.

Donald Rutherford had left. Black had watched him leave the building at 6pm.

Black had arrived back in Edinburgh that afternoon, driving from Thurso, allowing only one stop in a roadside café on the outskirts of Aberdeen. He'd booked into a cheap hotel in Edinburgh's Old Town, and decided against parking in the hotel car park. Instead he found a space in a side street five hundred yards from the hotel and walked. No point in advertising his presence, if he could help it.

A hundred yards diagonally opposite the lawyer's offices was a quaint little coffee shop. The Blue Willow. All bright colours and trailing flowers from hanging baskets. He sat at the window with a newspaper, sipping a flat white, and watched. He'd been there for over two hours. The view was good. A clear visual on people entering, leaving. The place was busy. With twenty partners and another maybe fifty ancillary staff, it ought to be, he thought. He was virtually undetectable where he sat. Unless he had been followed, in which case they knew exactly where he was, and they would be watching him.

Black drank his coffee, considered his options. He had little choice in the matter. If they came for him, then fair enough. Unlikely in such a public place, though a drive-by shooting wouldn't be far-fetched. A motorcyclist whizzing by, peppering the coffee shop window with bullets, uncaring who they hit, as long as they got Black.

Black had to bring it to them. Attack. Mobilise. If he stayed still, he was a dead man. Keep moving. Something the SAS had drummed into their recruits. A man compelled to move was a man who tended not to dwell on the harshness of his situation. Such was the philosophy of the Special Air Service. His enemies would assume that Black would target the firm. More specifically the individuals at their original meeting – Donald Rutherford, Max Lavelle, or the young lawyer, Pamela Thompson. They were the last people he'd spoken to before the incident at Fiona Jackson's flat. It wasn't rocket science to assume they would expect a visit from Black. Because now they knew he wasn't the type of man to back down.

He wouldn't have it any other way, he mused.

He watched. Time ticked on. Black had learned patience throughout his years in the army. Surveillance in extreme situations, sometimes lasting days, even weeks. Confined to one spot. Shitting in paper bags, then burying the bags. No sound. Body crawling with insects, skin itching under the heat, the sweat. Waiting for the enemy, exactly as he was doing now. The difference was, here in civilian street, Black was unsure who his enemy was. Shadows and smoke.

The door opened, a bell tinkling. Black looked up. A skinny young man entered clutching a laptop, no older than twenty-one, faded jeans, Motorhead T-shirt, a long unruly beard, which seemed to be the trend for young men. A tattoo running up the side of his neck. Another trend, which Black thought hideous. A student? Possibly. Black stayed alert, nerves stretched. The young man sat, opened his laptop, ordered a coffee.

He saw the unmistakable figure of Rutherford leave at 6pm. Striking blond hair; tanned skin. Escorted by two men. Both tall, lean, dressed in sharp close-fitting suits. Tough-looking. They walked by his side, no conversation. Rutherford wasn't taking any chances. He noticed the slight creasing on one side of their jackets. Probably gun holsters, fitted over the shoulder and under the arm.

They walked twenty yards to a pale-blue 7 series BMW parked on the main street. The alarm bleeped, the three got in, one of the men driving, Rutherford sitting in the rear with the other. The car drove off.

Black waited. The coffee shop closed at 7pm. It was 6.45. Black ordered another coffee, his fourth. The waitress who served him took his order, reminding him they closed soon. Black acknowledged the information with a polite smile, but ordered anyway.

Five minutes later, he spied a young woman leave the building. He recognised her instantly, her manner brisk and sharp. No guarded escorts for her.

"Forget the coffee," said Black.

He left the shop and followed.

He stayed on his side of the road. She turned a corner, up a narrow street. Black crossed the road, and followed twenty yards behind. She got to a Fiat 500, ivory with a red roof, parked half on the pavement. She pressed her key alarm, opened the driver's door, got in.

Black opened the passenger door, and sat in beside her. "Remember me?"

Pamela Thompson gasped, eyes wide.

Black produced his Ka-Bar knife, pressing it into her ribcage.

"Sure you do," he continued, his voice low. "You gave me your card. Nice message. Some might have described it as a death sentence. Thanks for that. Time to talk."

Pamela Thompson stared for several seconds. "Is she dead?"

"Who? Fiona Jackson? Of course she's dead. Now start talking."

Tears welled up in Pamela's eyes. Her shoulders shook. Her face crumpled. She began to cry soft, silent tears.

"She's dead," she said, barely a whisper. Suddenly her face hardened; her look turned to defiance.

"Do what you want, Mr Black. I don't care. They killed her."

Black leant closer. "Talk to me!"

She held his stare. Her voice trembled when she spoke. "Fiona Jackson was my sister!"

26

Jonathan Lincoln had arrived at Glasgow airport at 8.15pm the previous evening. He met his contact at the restaurant at "Arrivals". He was to recognise him by a lime-green briefcase placed upon a table. Lincoln spotted him almost immediately. The man sitting at the table was thin, balding, ruffs of hair above his ears. A dark grey dapper suit, grey silk tie. He had a cup of tea placed on a table in front of him.

Lincoln approached. He'd dressed casually, but smart. Circumstances dictated he wear a coat, incongruous for the summer heat. But he had no choice. The pockets were adapted to hold very specific equipment. He had no luggage, save a carry-all hanging from his shoulder, containing a change of clothing for three days. He wasn't expecting to be in Scotland any longer.

"Mr Lincoln?" The man stood, offering a handshake. Lincoln ignored it, sat opposite.

The man sat back down.

"We've fixed a room up for you," he said. "A nice one. At the Hilton. Should hopefully come up to scratch."

"No, thank you," said Lincoln. "I've organised my own hotel."

The man raised an eyebrow. "Really? Anywhere in particular?"

"Nowhere in particular."

"Well, it's up to you. We've arranged a car hire. It's waiting in the car park. Jaguar. I'll take you to it. I think you'll be impressed."

"Again, no thanks. Car hire's no good. I'll make my own arrangements." *They must be mad*, he thought. *Or stupid. Or just a bunch of fucking amateurs.* Car rental meant paper trail. Something to be avoided at all costs.

"I'll take a taxi."

The man regarded Lincoln for several seconds.

"We're trying to help. This has come from the top. We're to assist in any way we can."

Lincoln responded in a measured tone. "Then doing as little as possible would be beneficial for both of us. To be candid, I'd rather not be talking to you. But you have information I need. Do you have it?"

The man reached into his inside jacket pocket and produced a folded piece of paper, which he placed on the table and pushed across with one finger. Lincoln took it, unfolded it, read it, placed it in his pocket. Two addresses. Two names. A man and a woman.

"He's expendable?"

"Of course. He's expecting £3,000. Enough to buy his silence. He'll not be missed. Not for a while anyway. By which time you'll be long gone."

"And the woman?"

"What about her?"

"Her circumstances remain the same, I assume. No partner, still lives alone?"

"Correct. She lives on her own. We've checked."

"Let's hope so. Thank you for your time."

Lincoln got up to go.

The man stood. "You have my number, if you need assistance. Please remember, Mr Lincoln, I represent very important people. If you need any help, then all you have to do is call. This is a sensitive matter, you understand."

Lincoln inspected the man before him, then spoke in a soft voice. "I don't require the help of your friends. I prefer to work on my own. And usually when I'm asked to carry out a little spring cleaning, it's a sensitive matter. Tell your friends not to worry. All will be well."

The man nodded, raised his hand again to offer a handshake, which again Lincoln ignored.

He left the airport, hailing a black cab, and immediately headed for the first address on the list.

The game had begun.

27

Black told her to drive.

"Where are we going?" Pamela asked. "I have a husband. He's expecting me back. He'll wonder where I am."

"I'm sure he will. I'll give you directions. Just shut up and drive."

She didn't reply. She kept her eyes on the road. Black had the distinct impression she didn't give a damn. The mystery was deepening.

He gave her directions. She drove, eyes fixed on the road before her. If she was scared, she wasn't showing any immediate signs.

He took her back to his hotel, a distance of two miles. Black had some knowledge of Edinburgh streets. He took her by a circuitous route, glancing back every twenty seconds, testing whether they were being followed. It seemed all clear. Cars could swap in an elaborate surveillance. Black had to take his chances. If he worried about every move, he would be rendered paralysed, and end up dead anyway.

"Are you going to kill me?" she said suddenly, her voice flat, listless.

"Keep driving."

They got to the hotel car park.

"We're going up to my room," said Black. "If you try to run, I'll catch you, and cut you with this knife." He held the blade up before her face. It gleamed. "Look at me. Do you believe I will do this?"

She looked directly into his eyes for several long seconds. She nodded.

"If you say anything, or do anything, then we have a problem. Do you understand me?"

She nodded again. They got out of the car, Black watching closely. They both entered the main lobby of the hotel, Black gripping her under one arm. The place was quiet, an elderly man sitting in the foyer sipping tea, reading a newspaper. The receptionist glanced up, busy on the phone. Black acknowledged with a friendly nod. A couple returned from some Edinburgh sightseeing. All sweet in the garden. Such was the image Black hoped to convey.

They got to the elevator. Black pressed level three. The doors closed.

"Are you going to kill me, Mr Black?" she asked again, her voice emotionless. Black was bewildered at her sangfroid.

He said nothing.

The elevator opened. Still holding her by one arm, he guided her along a hallway, to his room door. He used his key card, led her inside.

"Sit please."

She sat on a chair by the single window. She looked up at him, face pale, drawn, dark shadows under hazel-brown eyes. Her auburn hair was tied tightly back. She wore a plain blue business suit – jacket, skirt, white blouse, a blue silk neck-tie.

Black sat on the edge of the bed opposite.

"When we last met, you wanted me to help Fiona Jackson.

You had written down her address on the back of your business card. Remember? I went to her flat, and bumped into two men. They were not admirers. Nor were they collecting for the Red Cross. They tried to kill me. But I killed them. Much to their disappointment, I imagine. You can understand why we're here, talking. Explain, please. I'm on a short fuse, so make it quick."

Pamela swallowed. She took a long, careful breath. *Trying to hold back tears*, thought Black. *Let her squirm*.

"Fiona kept her married name. Her husband died last year. Prostate cancer. I can't believe she's gone."

"Accept it. Keep talking."

"The firm had no idea we were sisters. We never told them. There was no need. It was coincidence we ended up working together. We were thrilled. Working side by side in a place like Raeburn Collins. A blue-chip lawyers' office in the centre of Edinburgh. What's not to like. We thought we were so lucky."

She fixed Black a burning gaze. "How wrong could we be."

"Keep talking."

"Fiona was sacked. Dismissed. Misappropriation of clients' funds. £10,000 was transferred into her personal account. She didn't know the first thing about it, and I believe her. It was what you would describe as a 'fucking stitch up', if you forgive the cliché. She needed to be removed. But I had no idea they would go so far..."

It started – small, shuddering sobs, her shoulders trembling.

Black waited. "Who are *they*?"

"They! Them!" retorted Pamela, fiercely. "How the hell should I know?" She took out a paper tissue from a pocket in her jacket, and dabbed her eyes. "She was scared. As I was. As I am. She told me she'd spoken to you about the will. She believed you could do something. Make a difference. Gilbert had such faith in you."

"Gilbert?"

"There were three of us, Mr Black. I had a sister and a brother. My maiden name, as was Fiona's, was Bartholomew. Gilbert Bartholomew was my brother, our brother. He was murdered. Fiona was murdered. I'm as good as dead. And there's nothing you can do."

28

Lincoln hadn't booked anywhere. It was not his way to book via internet, telephone, or any other medium. He was strictly face to face, cash up front. Safer, cleaner. No trail. He knew there were plenty of hotels in Glasgow with empty rooms. He'd chosen one within a mile from Black's office. A small, somewhat tired building in an area called Govanhill set behind some playing fields. He'd checked out the photographs online. Wedged between a semi-derelict nightclub and a dismal grey block of tenement flats, it was the type of place you'd drive by and not notice. Not for your typical tourists, but ideal for Lincoln.

He didn't head there straight away. He asked the taxi driver to take him instead to the first address on the piece of paper he'd been given at the airport.

Sixteen Glenburn Square. A new-build block of flats in Dennistoun, in the east end of Glasgow, a mile from George Square. His particular destination was a residence on the third floor. Lincoln paid the driver, and surveyed his surroundings. Mostly houses. Not far away was the massive rectangular structure of Parkhead football ground.

He didn't waste time. He went immediately to the main entrance. Despite its newness, it was already showing signs of neglect. The front communal gardens were overgrown, rubbish scattered across the grass. Parts of the front cladding were cracking, some of it crumbled away. The windows on the ground floor were boarded up.

The buzzer system and front lock were broken. Anyone could walk in and out. Lincoln entered, made his way up to the third floor. The stairs and walls were pale jaundice-yellow concrete. He passed an elderly man shuffling along a corridor, aided by a Zimmer frame. He was mumbling to himself, head down, concentrating on putting one step in front of the other. He didn't notice Lincoln passing.

Lincoln got to the third floor, arrived at the address on the note. Flat 1. There was no name on the door. Lincoln knocked gently and took a step back, admiring the spray paint on the walls.

Noise inside. The movement of somebody approaching. The sound of a bolt being loosened. The door opened.

A man stood in the doorway. He was of indeterminate age. Drugs had ravaged his face. He was probably much younger than he looked. Wide eyes regarded him from sunken sockets. His hair was thin and stuck to his scalp like a wet rag. Emaciated body. Stick-thin arms covered in marks. Blue jeans hung from his narrow hips. Bare feet.

Heroin addicts were remarkably reliable in this sort of transaction.

"Mr Chalmers?"

The man smiled, revealing a row of crooked brown teeth. His eyes sparkled. He was wired, desperate for his next fix. He saw Lincoln as the immediate answer to his problem, and Lincoln knew it.

"Yes," said the man. "You're here for the package?"

"I am. May I come in?"

"Of course, sir."

Respectful.

Lincoln followed, closing the door behind him. No carpets, bare floorboards. The carpets probably sold. Bare walls. He passed two closed doors, emerging into a living room, devoid of anything except a couch, two chairs and a table. No curtains on the windows. A plate sat on the floor, full of cigarette butts. Sitting in a chair was a woman, smoking. Skeletal. Neck and arms spotted with needle marks. Wearing a shapeless grey dress, hanging like a sack. No make-up. Long, listless brown hair. Same haggard, drawn skull face. Stretched white skin. Again, impossible to tell her real age. Maybe once, an eternity ago, she might have been attractive. Now, the walking dead.

"The man's here," said Chalmers, waving his arms up and down, agitated. "Get the fucking box."

She stood, almost robotic, and left the room through the door they had entered.

"Do you want a cup of tea?"

"No thank you."

"A smoke?"

"No."

The man licked his lips. "You're a very smart man. Maybe I'll buy myself some nice clothes like yours, when I get paid."

Lincoln nodded. "Sure." But any money he would get would be spent on other things. Though it would never get that far.

"Please, have a seat."

Lincoln sat on the couch. The man remained standing.

"Where is that fucking bitch?" he muttered. "My wife's fucking slow as shit. Sorry about this."

"No problem."

The woman re-emerged. She carried a package – a box, about the same dimensions as an office briefcase. Wrapped in brown paper, tied together by string. She handed it to him, and stepped back. They both watched him. Lincoln was reminded of two scrawny birds fixated on a crumb of bread.

"I hope you haven't tried to have a peek inside," said Lincoln, his tone jovial.

"No way, sir. Wouldn't dare." Their eyes glistened under the single bare light bulb hanging above them, which served as the only illumination in the room.

"I believe you." Lincoln did believe them. It didn't look as if it had been tampered with. And the thought of getting £3,000 hard cash was too much of an incentive to break the deal. Enough money to keep them on hard drugs for a couple of months. Or less, if they overdosed.

He reached into his jacket pocket, and took out an envelope, which he placed on the armrest of the couch.

"This is the money. It's in £20 notes. Three thousand as agreed. All for you. But first I'd like to check everything's what it should be. Okay?"

It wasn't okay. But Chalmers nodded anyway. The woman didn't respond. She kept tapping her hand against her thigh, the heel of her right foot twitching. She was chronic. Desperate for that next fix.

"You didn't introduce me," said Lincoln.

"Sorry. This is Tilly, my wife. Say hello, Tilly."

Tilly stared. No response.

"She's shy."

"That's okay. Why don't you both sit down. You're making me uneasy, standing over me like that."

They sat on the two chairs.

"Thank you."

He untied the string and carefully removed the paper. It was a soft leather case bound by black ribbon.

"It's a box of chocolates," said Chalmers, grinning.

"Maybe."

Lincoln loosened the ribbon, opened the lid.

Inside were various items, each in its own moulded compartment. A pistol, a silencer, two boxes of bullets, two knives.

Lincoln looked at the two opposite. "All seems good."

"I've never seen a gun before," said Chalmers, darting his eyes from the box on Lincoln's lap to the fat envelope on the armrest.

"Really? Let me show you."

Lincoln gently teased the pistol from its compartment, and held it in his hand.

"This is known as a Glock 20. Massive fire power. Good accuracy. Semi-automatic, which means it's self-loading, so I don't need to worry about the next bullet. I just need to keep pulling the trigger, and bam! bam! She's a beauty. And very reliable."

He removed the silencer. A stubby, black cigar-shaped object. "This screws on to the end of the Glock. You'll have seen this in the movies. A silencer. Also known as a sound suppresser. It fits like a glove. Watch."

He carefully attached the silencer on to the end of the barrel.

"You see? Pretty neat, yes?"

"Fucking awesome. Look at that, Tilly. Like one of those spy movies."

Tilly did not reply. Her focus was centred entirely on the envelope.

"Exactly," said Lincoln. "And to make the Glock the weapon that it is, it requires a cartridge. People sometimes get mixed up. They call it a bullet. But in fact, the bullet is a component of the cartridge." He lifted out one of the boxes, opened it, and spilled several into the palm of his hand.

"It's pretty straight forward to load a Glock. You put the cartridges into the magazine tube, and load her up."

He unclipped the magazine and began to feed cartridges in. He slid the magazine back in place.

"These are 10mm cartridges. Pretty potent. Get shot in the head, and the head explodes. Let's try."

He aimed at the woman called Tilly, and fired. The sound which emanated was like a short, stifled cough. Tilly remained seated, but half her face suddenly disappeared, and in its place, tangles of vein, blood, bone. She slumped onto the floor.

"Fuck!" shouted Chalmers. He leapt to his feet.

"There you are," said Lincoln.

He fired again. Chalmers took it full in the chest. He was catapulted off the ground, chunks of flesh erupting from his back, spattering across the bare walls. He landed on the floorboards with a dull thud. Lincoln stood and walked over to his body. The torso was shredded, organs spilling out. Well and truly dead. He fired again, nevertheless. One in the forehead.

A noise, from another room. A child, no older than seven, appeared in the living room doorway. Dressed in a filthy vest and underwear. A little boy. He stared at the scene before him, wide-eyed.

Lincoln aimed, fired a fourth shot. He disconnected the silencer, and placed that and the pistol in his inside coat pocket, adapted to hold a heavy piece of firepower. He picked up the cartridges, knives and envelope, and left the flat.

He was disappointed. They'd not told him he had a wife, a family. He would speak to them about their intelligence. Careless. Three bodies would be discovered more quickly than one. *Definitely fucking amateurs*, he thought ruefully.

Still, he had the Glock, which was the important thing. Job done.

Next, the second person on the list. The woman.

29

"We never got over Natalie. I think about her every hour of every day. We were devastated. My poor dear brother. It crushed him. And when Christine committed suicide, I think his mind snapped."

Black hadn't moved from the edge of the bed. Pamela Thompson spoke in a flat monotone, as if all the life had been sucked out of her voice.

"Christine?"

"His wife. A bottle of aspirin one February night. She took two days to die. Drifted into a coma. Then her organs failed. Yet even after all that, Gilbert wouldn't leave any blame at my door."

"Why would he blame you?"

Pamela took a second to respond, her gaze inward, reliving an old nightmare. "Because I deserved it."

Black said nothing.

She opened her handbag, took out a packet of cigarettes. "Do you mind?"

"No."

She produced a cheap plastic lighter and lit up. She took a deep inhalation, closed her eyes. Then she spoke.

"Natalie went missing when she was five years old. Maybe you remember the case. 'Went missing' is not the way to describe what happened. She was taken. Stolen. From her bed. From our house. She was staying the night with us. My husband and I were to look after her. Gilbert and Christine were out for the night. A fortieth birthday party. They asked if we could look after her. Simple, yes?"

She looked at Black, angry, defiant. "We were to look after her! He trusted us!"

She started to cry again, soft tears.

"I put her to bed. We watched some television. A stupid film. We went to bed at 11.30. I remember all the details, like it happened yesterday. You can understand that."

Black could. He imagined every minute detail of that night would be firebranded into her mind.

"I checked up on her. She was sleeping. She was fine. I swear to Christ she was fine."

She took another deep drag. She was going to finish this and needed every ounce of courage.

"In the morning, I made breakfast. My husband slept on. I fixed up some scrambled egg and toast and juice, and placed it all on a tray, and went to the room where Natalie was sleeping. I opened the door. The bed was empty. I thought she was in the toilet. But she wasn't. I thought she was hiding. I shouted her name. She didn't reply. Then I noticed the window was open. She was gone. I haven't seen her since. And I never will."

She stopped and looked down at the floor.

"I don't remember opening the window," she mumbled. "It was warm. But I swear I didn't leave the window open."

"Gilbert left me a note," said Black. "A letter. He thought I could help."

"Can you?"

"Maybe." Black pondered, running recent events over in his

mind. "I don't think you're in any danger. If they knew about you, you'd be dead by now."

"They killed my sister."

"My guess is, they killed her because they were following Gilbert, and Gilbert went to your sister to prepare his will. They met face to face. They would have no idea what he said to her. And these people don't take chances. Better to kill her. Dead people don't talk. But you're in the clear. You've met me once at the office, and it wasn't a one-to-one meeting. As far as they're aware, that's it. You're not being followed. What's your husband's name?"

"David. David Thompson."

"He's expecting you. You should leave now. Act normal, if you can. Dry your eyes. But first, I need some information."

"What?"

"Tell me about the firm's new head of Estates. Tell me about Donald Rutherford. And your senior partner. Max Lavelle."

30

As he'd expected, Lincoln had no trouble getting a room. The hotel was called The Queens Park Royal. It had seen better days. The foyer needed a lick of paint, a new carpet. Maybe new staff. The single receptionist was surly and ungracious. A somewhat ostentatious candelabra hung from the ceiling, glittering silver and gold.

Lincoln was on the second floor. The lift was out of service, but he didn't mind the climb. His room was functional and clean. It was non-smoking, but smelled of stale cigarettes. Lincoln didn't care. The room had an en-suite bathroom, with complimentary soap and shampoo. Lincoln showered. He could still smell the stink of the flat he'd just come from.

He changed into fresh clothes. Blue jeans, white shirt, dark suede ankle boots. He put his coat back on, and kept the Glock in its inside pocket. Time for a little evening sightseeing.

He had chosen the hotel specifically. It was roughly a mile from Black's office, a mile and a half from where he lived. Reconnaissance was an integral part of Lincoln's timetable. He liked to get a feel for his targets. Experience the things they experienced on a daily basis, look in the shop windows they looked in, hear the sounds of the traffic, smell the food from takeaways and restaurants, saunter past the bars and clubs. He wanted to connect. By sensing the surroundings, Lincoln got some sense of the people he was to kill. Their movements, habits, behaviour.

Lincoln strolled past a park on his left – appropriately named Queens Park – and on to a main thoroughfare. Pollokshaws Road. It led straight to that area called Shawlands where Black had his office. The traffic was quiet. On one side, the darkness of the park, on the other, blocks of sandstone tenement flats, blackened with age and grime. Every hundred yards or so, little coffee shops and bars advertising live music.

Lincoln reached Shawlands. Either side of the main road, more tenement blocks, though an effort had been made to clean them up, sandblasted from black to pale blond. Boarded-up shops, retail units to let, charity shops, Turkish barbers, bookie outlets, tired-looking pubs selling cheap beer. He reached Black's office. First floor premises, with three rather grimy windows looking on to the road, no advertising of any nature. Beneath, a hot food takeaway and an abandoned beauty salon. The entrance was a main communal door. There was nothing to indicate he was a practising lawyer. No plaque screwed on to the wall, nothing with his name on it. Zero.

Adam Black wanted to be invisible. He was here reluctantly. Lincoln had read his résumé. He knew his past, the murder of his wife and child.

Lincoln drew a deep breath. It was late August, and the evening was still and pleasant.

Adam Black was running away. Running from his past. He'd seen death close up, death of his loved ones, a nightmare he was unable to confront. Damaged goods.

Black was fragile. Lincoln knew exactly the buttons to press.

The woman was the key. Once he had her, Black was a dead man.

31

According to Pamela Thompson, Rutherford had been with the firm for all of two weeks. She'd worked with him several days, but he didn't give much away. Like any typical office, rumours, speculation, idle chat were rife. Office gossip.

Word was, he was a hotshot lawyer come back to Scotland from Dubai, where he'd headed up a commercial litigation team for an international law office. High flying stuff. Had enough of the desert heat and the sand and the constant blue sky. Hankered after the clean, crisp Scottish air. Normally, the process of joining a law firm as a fully-fledged solicitor, especially one as prestigious as Raeburn Collins, was a slow, time-consuming process. CVs were checked, double checked. References were verified and taken up. Interviews were held, maybe as many as three. The partners deliberated, held meetings, debated, then decided.

Word was, Rutherford's application was accompanied by a million-pound cheque. He'd bought his way in. Split amongst the partners, that was £50,000 each. For doing nothing. But it was a shotgun offer. To be accepted immediately, failing which, Rutherford would try the next firm up the road. It was accepted.

Within a day of his application. But he had stipulations. He wanted to head up Estates and Wills. Light years from the type of work he was used to. Puzzling, but who cared when a million-pound cheque was part of the package. All happening the very day after Gilbert Bartholomew's meeting with his sister, the doomed Fiona Jackson. Quite a coincidence.

Black did not believe in coincidences. At least not one's like this.

To add further mystery, he hadn't found a place to live, so was staying at the Edinburgh Excelsior. Five-star hotel. Penthouse suite. At around £2,000 per night. The guy had money to burn.

Such was the gossip. But to Black's mind, it was so far-fetched, it carried the bones of truth.

She knew little about Max Lavelle. A private man, who didn't fraternise with his employees. Aloof and unapproachable. Unmarried. Possibly gay, but no one knew for sure. Incredibly wealthy. He lived alone in some big mansion in the heart of the west end of Glasgow, apparently. An expert in company takeovers, mergers. One thing she did know was that he drove a gun-metal grey Bentley Continental. Two hundred grand's worth. She remembered being slightly shocked, and intimidated, when he chose to sit in at their meeting with Black. He hadn't given any explanation, nor did he require to give one. After all, he effectively owned the firm. Why he was there, she couldn't speculate. Possibly because the terms of Gilbert Bartholomew's will were so extraordinary.

Black watched Pamela Thompson drive away from his hotel window, anxious that she wasn't being followed. It seemed all clear. Her story added up, he thought. On the day she had given him the handwritten plea on the back of her business card, she genuinely believed her sister was in danger, and that Black could help. But they'd got to her before Black did. It was just bad timing. Black pondered on the events of that particular after-noon at Fiona Jackson's flat. The two men he'd encountered were as surprised to see him, as he them. Black was never the intended kill.

Though her story made sense, it didn't mean he trusted her. Black didn't trust anyone. Trust was dangerous. In the game he was in, trust killed. He would watch Pamela Jackson. She could still betray him. But he had to move forward. His next stop was the Edinburgh Excelsior. Time to pay the esteemed Mr Ruther-ford a visit. If she phoned to warn him, then Black was walking to his death.

But death was an old friend. Black had seen it in all its forms. And he had one advantage over his enemies – death did not scare him.

32

Boyd Falconer had, over the years, established an elaborate organisation. Child trafficking, primarily for sexual exploitation, was a high-end risky business. The rewards were vast, the penalties severe. Falconer was a careful man. Obsessively so. The process was handled through a variety of intermediaries. From the initial capture to the final deposit. Small fortunes had to be paid to certain officials to look the other way. The closer the child got to their destination at his Arizona ranch, the greater the sums of money involved.

Which was the paradox of the business he was in, reflected Falconer. The initial "grab" was usually carried out by hired thugs, junkies, people desperate for cash. Payments were relatively small. As the child changed hands, the costs rose. Sometimes, there were as many as four or five handovers. Each essential, to create a further layer of confusion for the authorities. Especially when a child was taken overseas.

But once the captive was received, and safely ensconced in the "dungeon", then the auction began. Falconer could name his price. Net profit per product was usually never less than ten million dollars. And the clamour for new flesh never lessened.

They came and went. Rarely was the merchandise kept longer than four weeks. Business was brisk. New arrivals were received every month, usually as many as eight or nine. They came from different backgrounds. Secreted away from orphanages, street kids bundled into the backs of cars, sometimes sold by addict mothers, abducted from leafy suburbs, stolen from the beds of the affluent and rich, whisked away from a busy beach. Falconer didn't care, even if there was press coverage, which there often was. In such cases, Falconer didn't baulk. In fact, the greater the media storm, the greater the profit. In such cases, he could name his price. This was the other paradox – if there was a media storm over a missing child, then the bidding became more frenzied, and the prices sky-rocketed.

But on a rare occasion, an item of merchandise, no matter the profit, had to be sacrificed. For the greater good. But never wasted.

Nothing was wasted in Falconer's world.

A vehicle arrived, cutting its way through the terrain by a road no more than a dirt track. Falconer watched its approach, stirring up plumes of sand. A silver-grey Range Rover, darkened windows, driven by his people.

The electric gates opened, the car swept through, along a wide stamped concrete driveway, to park at the courtyard at the main entrance to the ranch. Doors opened. The driver, a man in the passenger seat, and a man sitting in the back seat, all got out. The one in the back seat was carrying something. At first glance, it could have been a roll of white blanket.

Falconer oversaw the delivery personally. Hovering at his side, as ever, stood Norman Sands.

"Take it downstairs," said Falconer. There were no stairs. There was only an elevator to the basement. But the man understood.

Falconer turned to Sands. "I'll be down shortly."

Sands and the man carrying the package, headed through a main hallway, to the back premises. Another room, with doors on either side. At one door was a keypad. Sands pressed the four-digit code. The door unlocked. Another smaller room, like an ante-chamber. In this room was a man sitting at a desk. On one wall were screens of each room in the house, plus views of the outside. Sands nodded at the man. He was wearing a shirt and slacks. Strapped across his shoulder, in plain sight, was a holster. In the holster was a semi-automatic pistol. They entered, and faced a further door. Another keypad. In their particular industry, security was high on the agenda.

Sands pressed another code. The doors opened automatically. The elevator. The only way in and out to the sub-level.

They got in. The doors closed. Machinery hummed. A brief sensation of movement. Three seconds later, they stopped, the doors opened. Another small room, another man stationed by a desk, holstered.

Opposite, a door. Sands again nodded at the guard, who nodded back. Sands opened the door, the man with the package following silently.

They were in the dungeon. The globe lights above sparkled, the walls bright with teddy bears and rainbows. At the far end of the corridor, at the doorway to his room, stood the skeletal figure of Stanley Lampton, dressed in his blue hospital overalls. Perhaps it was the reflection of the globes, but it seemed to Sands his eyes gleamed.

"Which room?"

Lampton beckoned to a door on his right. "Room seven is vacant."

Lampton unlocked the door. The three men entered. Inside, was a child's single bed, pink wallpaper, deep pink carpet, golden stars on a white ceiling. A rocking horse in one corner. A doll's house in another. A play table and chair. A shelf of books, cuddly toys, games. A toilet and bath in an adjacent room.

The man carrying the package, placed it gently on the bed.

"You can go," said Sands. The man left.

Lampton spoke. "May I?"

Sands nodded.

The package was covered in white sheeting, kept in place by belts tied in the middle and at one end. Carefully, with long, thin fingers, Lampton undid the belts, removed them, and opened out the sheeting.

A child of perhaps six lay before them. Pale and still, in a drugged state. Lampton sucked in his breath.

"Mr Falconer will be here directly," said Sands.

They waited, not speaking.

Two minutes later, Falconer entered the room. He gave the child a cursory glance, then turned his attention to Lampton.

"No. 4. How's she doing?"

"She's fine," replied Lampton.

"Fucking right she's fine. She'd better be, Lampton."

Suddenly his mood changed.

"You like it?"

Lampton stared at the child.

"Perfect," he breathed.

"A gift. For you. Make sure No. 4 is in pristine condition for our Japanese friends when they arrive, and no fucking measles shit. If there's no hiccups, then, and only then, this one's yours, to do as you wish. She's all the way from the United Kingdom. She's been moved about for months, from safe house to safe house. Always under the radar. And now she's here. With you."

"Thank you."

Falconer stepped close.

"But if you fuck up, then I swear to Christ you'll wish you'd never been born, and I will personally nail your fucking liver to one of those damn globes. No. 4 has to be perfect. You understand me?"

Lampton looked as if he was only half listening. "I understand."

"You'd better."

This was the only way to incentivise people like Lampton, and Falconer knew it. They lived for something more than the dollar. Sometimes, for the greater good, merchandise had to be sacrificed. Sometimes, Falconer had to lose money to make money.

Nothing was wasted in Falconer's world.

Everything had a use.

33

The Excelsior. Some would say an iconic structure. A hundred and eighty rooms. The most expensive hotel in Edinburgh. Situated on the eastern side of Princes Street, opposite Princes Street Gardens, beneath the brooding presence of Edinburgh Castle.

A Victorian building, built with all the excesses of Victorian architecture. Broad marble columns, arch-headed stained-glass windows, a central tower housing a clock which was never inaccurate, two lesser conical towers – one at each end of the building – grey granite walls hewn into elaborate decoration.

All in all, one impressive building, thought Black, as he surveyed it from the other side of Princes Street. Way beyond his bank balance. Not beyond Donald Rutherford's. Pamela Thompson had been correct. The office gossip hadn't let her down. Rutherford was occupying a six-room suite on the top floor with a panoramic view of the castle. More specifically the Bothwell Suite.

The information had taken Black five minutes to find. He had merely telephoned the hotel as soon as Pamela Thompson left the hotel car park. The receptionist had been most obliging. He'd asked if Rutherford was staying there, and she confirmed he was, together with the name of the suite he was in.

She was talkative. Without prompting, she explained to Black that if he required a room, then he was out of luck. The place was full. The Edinburgh law faculty dinner was being held that evening. Eight pm. Three hundred guests. The place would be frantic. But he could try The Grand just down the road, if he wished.

Black saw an opportunity.

Without wasting time, he left his room, and went straight to the biggest and nearest department store he could think of – Jenners, on Princes Street. He carried one of the KelTec pistols retrieved from his would-be assassins. It was light and flat and easily concealed. Also, the switchblade he'd brought, strapped to the side of his calf, inside his sock.

The place was still open. He'd gone straight to the men's section. He tried on a dinner suit, tux, black bow tie, black evening shoes. He regarded himself in the mirror. Tall, unobtrusively muscular, dark hair cropped short, dark eyes, hard flat cheekbones.

A mismatch, he thought. He'd killed with his bare hands, with guns, with knives. And doubtless he would kill again – unless he was killed first, he thought grimly. Yet here he was, posing in a dinner suit – the mark of refinement, sophistication. He was the other side of the coin. A blunt instrument. A killer. Which probably should have worried him. But it didn't. The opposite. He was almost joyful. He was about to dispense his own brand of justice. Swift and violent.

He'd kept the dinner suit on, leaving his jeans, boots and shirt in the waiting room, which he told them they could bin. He paid cash. He transferred the pistol to his inside pocket.

Black surveyed the Gothic structure of the Excelsior, dressed in formal dinner wear, impressed by the architecture, as anyone would be. People were streaming in, dressed identically to him. Lawyers. Black joined the procession, blending in perfectly.

Time to have a chat with Donald Rutherford.

34

Everything was relayed through secure email. Lincoln needed solid information fast.

Lincoln – *His office is shut. She's not at the given address. She's gone away.*

Sands – *How do you know? She might turn up.*

Lincoln – *No. I've wasted a day already. You need to pull those strings of yours, and get me what I need.*

Sands – *I'll see what I can come up with.*

Lincoln – *Thank you.*

Twenty minutes later he received another email. Another address. Efficient, he thought. Whoever was feeding Sands his information had influence. Lincoln was under no illusion the people he was working for were powerful. And rich. And incredibly well connected.

He checked the internet. The address was a slightly awkward location, but nothing he couldn't handle. He was mildly irked the job was taking longer than anticipated. Setbacks were to be expected. It did not diminish his excitement. In the end, it would be well worth it.

He checked timetables. If he got a taxi now, he would make the final crossing.

It was early evening, just as Black was meandering his way through the grand main entrance of the Excelsior, when Lincoln set off to capture the bait.

The bait to reel in Adam Black.

35

Black passed two kilted doormen, who nodded politely at those who entered. The main reception hall was elegant and subtle, without being ostentatious. The floor was travertine tiles, coral red. White marble pillars stretched up to a high ceiling of intricate glass construction. Black was impressed. The walls were dark oak, painted glossy black, richly decorated. Silver box lanterns hung suspended from the ceiling. Perhaps a little ostentatious, he decided. Classical music played, just on the periphery of the senses.

The elevators were on one side. Black counted five. On the other, wide sweeping carpeted stairs.

The reception counter was manned by four uniformed women, multi-tasking. Another two kilted stewards were beckoning them through double-sided glass doors, holding trays of flutes of champagne. Black took one, and followed a group of young lawyers, laughing loudly. He laughed with them. Part of the crowd. A short passageway and then through to the Cairngorm Bar. It was already full. More oak panelling, plush carpets, soft lighting from candelabras. Candles flickered from deep shelves and alcoves. Heavy tapestried curtains prevented any evening light. The place was alive with conversation, laughter. People out to enjoy themselves, and get blasted with drink in the process.

Black could hardly blame them. He recognised himself in those smiling faces. His former self. When he was a partner in his old firm. When life made sense. Rubbing shoulders with colleagues, swapping stories, gossiping, drinking at the bar. Laughing. When he was a normal human being.

What had he become? A vigilante. He'd been made, created. His wife and daughter murdered, and as a consequence, the veneer of his humanity ripped away. Maybe he was kidding himself. Perhaps the death of his family had done more. Perhaps it had set him free. That the man he was now was the man he had always been. A stone-cold killer. A chilling thought, which he did not dwell on.

He looked about him, keeping to a shadowy corner. It wasn't inconceivable that someone in the crowds might recognise him. From the old days. But unlikely. He was just another face in a penguin suit. Those around him were immersed in their own worlds. More people were filing in. It was 7.45. The meal would be announced in about fifteen minutes, he reckoned.

Time to move.

The Bothwell Suite was one of two penthouse rooms on the west wing of the top floor. Black left the bar, still holding his untouched champagne glass. He smiled at the stewards, at the girls at the reception. No one noticed him, too preoccupied. Black strolled up the stairs, without a care in the world. People were coming down. Polite nods. More smiles.

He got to the first floor, to a hall. A discreet sign on the wall indicated the gymnasium and saunas to his left. Black turned right, along a broad passageway. The walls were decorated with portraits of people he didn't know. The ceiling was arched with wooden beams, the coving intricate silver filigree.

He arrived at a series of lift doors. He pressed a button. He waited twenty seconds. The doors slid open. It was empty. He got in. Mirrors all around. He pressed the button for the top floor. The penthouse. Ten storeys up.

Black felt an almost imperceptible shift of movement. Lights flashed as he progressed past each level. A soft sound chimed. He'd reached the top. He took a deep breath, focused, calming himself. Fun time. The doors opened.

He arrived at a small carpeted foyer. A sign with an arrow pointing left – the Bothwell Suite, through heavy double wooden doors. It was a gamble. Rutherford might not be in. He might be out for dinner. Or just out. But Black didn't think so. The man he saw leave the offices of Raeburn Collins earlier looked like a man scared. Scared enough to have bodyguards carrying concealed weapons. He'd be lying low until he'd got the message. The message that Black was dead.

Black steadied himself. Suddenly he barged through the double doors, and staggered in, bouncing from one wall to the other. He was in a broad corridor, with only one door at the end. This was an exclusive section of the hotel, offering privacy for the occupants. Which was advantageous. Any commotion wouldn't be instantly noticed, giving Black time.

On either side of the door sat a man, suited. They both jumped up, startled at Black's entrance.

It looked like Rutherford was home.

Black weaved his way towards them, spilling champagne, face slack, one hand on the wall to steady himself.

"Think I'm lost," he slurred. "Where the hell am I?"

One of the men shook his head.

"Wrong place, pal." The man who spoke was tall, as tall as Black. Bulky with muscle, visible through a tight-fitting suit, one hand under his jacket. Head shaved to the bone. Heavy features. Flat, broken nose. Prominent brow. Ex-boxer, thought Black. He looked supremely fit and strong. The other, who had sat back down, was tall, but slimmer. Lean muscle. Black glossy hair tied back into a ponytail. An old scar split his face from his eye to the side of his mouth, causing his lip to raise in a constant sneer. One evil looking fucker.

The Boxer approached him.

"You should be downstairs with the other shitheads, so fuck off."

Suddenly the door to the Bothwell Suite opened. A man appeared, framed in the doorway. He paused to inspect the commotion. Large, full head of blond hair, ruddy red cheeks. Dressed in black bow tie, tuxedo, evening suit. Ready to go downstairs.

Donald Rutherford.

For one frozen moment, their eyes locked. Rutherford recognised Black instantly. He took a step back, eyes wide.

"Black!"

The two men, Scarface on his chair, Boxer standing one foot from Black, turned towards Rutherford, puzzled.

"It's Black!" he roared. "Kill the fucker!"

He darted back into the suite, the door slamming behind him.

The distraction was all Black needed. The Boxer turned back to him, in the process of pulling out a pistol from beneath his jacket. Scarface was rising from his chair, similarly reaching for under his jacket.

Black rugby tackled the Boxer, propelling him backwards into Scarface, the three men toppling onto the hall carpet, like skittles in a bowling alley. Black rolled, got to his feet, pulling out the KelTec. The Boxer was on one knee, aiming a smaller pistol. Possibly a Walther PPK. Black beat him to it. The Boxer's face suddenly exploded with the impact of Black's bullet.

Scarface fired, missed, the flying fragments of the Boxer's

face spoiling his aim, the bullet lodging into a picture on the far wall. Black returned the compliment, fired back, once twice. For the briefest second, Scarface gave Black a look of startled indignation as his throat burst open, then the look was obliterated as the top half of his head spun across the room.

Two down.

Now, the clock was ticking. Black had to move quickly. Despite the seclusion, the noise could still attract people – guests, hotel staff, security, police. A grisly sight awaited them. With two dead bodies on the floor, Black would have a lot of explaining to do. With the distraction of the dinner function going on downstairs, he might have gained a little extra breathing space. Black opted for worst case scenario, and reckoned he had five minutes, maybe ten at a push.

He got to the suite door, fired at the handle. The door bounced open. Black stepped to the side, anticipating gunshots. Which is exactly what happened. Four shots, muffled by a silencer, peppering the corridor wall.

Black had been trained for exactly this scenario. He crouched, dived through the door way, firing randomly as he moved. More shots, above his head. He was in a large, high-ceilinged room. Above, a massive crystal candelabra. A real fire crackled under a stone hearth. A huge television on one wall. Couches, chairs, low coffee tables, an ornate bureau in one corner. In another corner, behind a high-backed chair, a man firing a pistol. No sign of Rutherford. Black took all this in as he dived behind a leather corner suite, offering zero cover. This was not the movies. A bullet would scythe through furniture as easily as a knife through hot butter. Bullets ripped behind him, churning up cushions, fabric, chunks of leather.

Black fired back. His last bullet. A pause. His adversary was reloading. Black had no bullets left. He took his chance. He vaulted over the remains of the corner suite, sprinted across the room, hurdling over a long coffee table in front of the fire. The man was reloading the cartridge sleeve. No time. He flung the pistol at Black, and dodged from behind the high chair, just as Black cannoned into it.

The man produced a knife. Black spun round, produced his own flick-knife. They faced each other. The man was four inches shorter. Wide shoulders. Long arms. He was wearing a loose white shirt. A short neck as wide as his head. Cropped white hair. Stocky, muscular. A slab of a face. He weaved the knife left and right, then a circle, metal glimmering in the firelight.

"Come on, you fucker."

Black made a sudden hard motion. He threw his blade. It flashed through the air, penetrating the man's chest. The man gasped, staring in shock, incredulous at the sudden turn of events. He reached up to pull the blade from his suddenly soaked shirt.

Black stepped in. The man staggered back to avoid him, bumping into a footstool. He pulled out the blade. Black was on him, hacking at his neck, then driving his fist into the man's face. The man grunted, but seemed to absorb the blows, maintaining his stand. He scythed the blade through the air with one massive arm, trying to slice Black's jugular. Black blocked, but the effort sent him off balance. The man lashed out with his other arm, rocking Black with a thunderous blow to the side of the head. It felt like he'd been hit with concrete. Black stepped away, disorientated. They stood, regarding each other, panting.

The man lurched forward, waving the knife, the movement uncoordinated, sluggish. He was losing blood fast, and was dying on his feet. Black moved aside, caught the man's wrist, pressed a pressure point, jerked the wrist round hard, then rammed the palm of his hand against his elbow, feeling the bone snap. The knife fell. The man sucked in his breath, bending over to protect his broken arm. Black grabbed the back of his head, yanking his face down against his knee. Teeth broke.

The man sank to the floor. Black retrieved the knife, and slit his throat. He picked up the man's pistol, a Walther PPK, similar to his dead friend in the hall, loaded the cartridges.

The suite was a series of interconnecting rooms. Time was precious. He made his way through double glass doors, emerging into a long dining room complete with full-size dining table and ten cream leather chairs, and a bar on one side. No sign of Rutherford.

Black went from room to room. The last was the master bedroom. Locked. This was it. If he wasn't here, then he was a fucking magician.

Black fired once. The door cracked open. A large room, all oak cladding, blackened rafters on the ceiling, king size bed. Beside the bed stood Donald Rutherford, hands above his head.

"I'm unarmed!"

Black appraised him. It was almost humorous. Two lawyers dressed for a formal evening. About as civilised as you could get. In Black's case, his crisp white tuxedo stained with the blood of three men. This was a million miles from being civilised.

Black raised the pistol.

"I've called the police," said Rutherford.

"Quite right," replied Black. "But we've still time for a chat. Gilbert Bartholomew got too close for comfort, and you had him killed. Yes?"

"I don't know what you're talking about. The police will be here in five minutes."

His eyes flickered from Black's face to his gun. Black almost admired his bluster. He fired a round into the bed, six inches from Rutherford's leg.

"Jesus Christ!"

"The next one you get in the balls. It won't kill you, but the agony will be fucking unbelievable. Tell me why you're so keen on killing me?"

Rutherford blinked, forehead glistening with sweat. His lower lip trembled.

"I don't know what you're..."

"Fair enough," said Black, aiming.

"No, please!" shrieked Rutherford. He talked, the words staccato, rattling out his mouth like bursts of machine gun fire. "Bartholomew was proving dangerous. Asking too many questions. He needed to be removed. I was told to get into the firm, find out all I could. About why he'd gone there. When I discovered he wanted a will prepared, and mentioned you, we needed to find out more."

"You were told to join the firm?"

"Ordered. These people are fucking powerful. They can do anything."

"But you are one of these people, Rutherford," said Black.

"No! I get orders. If I don't do what they say, they'll kill me. My family."

"Your family?"

Rutherford nodded. The seconds were ticking by. Black took a deep breath, swallowing down his urge to get out fast before any more goons appeared at the door. Or the police, for that matter. But he needed a piece of vital information.

"You're just a foot soldier. Is that it? Innocent. Just following orders."

"That's all I am."

"Gilbert Bartholomew. Fiona Jackson. And only five minutes ago you told your handsome friends to kill me. Who are all dead, by the way."

Rutherford sobbed. "Please. I don't know anything."

"And the little girl?"

Abruptly, Rutherford's face straightened, eyes fixed on Black.

"The little girl?"

"Sure. The one in the video. Though I dare say it's a regular thing, so I might need to be specific. About five years old. Blonde hair. Being passed about. Remember that one?"

Rutherford's lips worked, but managed only a mumble.

"You see, Rutherford, I know what you and your circle of acquaintances indulge in. I know what you're trying to keep quiet. You have a family? Christ knows what you do there."

"I don't know..."

"I saw the video. You were one of them."

Rutherford shook his head.

"You were all wearing masks," continued Black. "But that fancy ring you're wearing gave it away. The type you were all wearing. A token of club membership, yes? You really should be more careful. When is your next gathering? Tell me, or I swear to Jesus Christ Almighty, I will fire a bullet into your fucking eye."

"Three days from now," gasped Rutherford. "Monday evening."

"Where?"

"I don't know. I swear it. No one knows until that morning. We're given a location by email. It could be anywhere in the country."

Suddenly he sank to his knees. "Please, I was forced. These people have their ways."

"The only person forced was that child. Who are these people?"

"I don't know. Government ministers. Police. Corporate executives. Never any names. We get emails. Instructions. Only one person knows who everybody is. He organises things. He chooses where and when."

"Who, Rutherford?"

"He calls himself the Grey Prince. Why the fuck do you care?"

Black regarded him for two seconds. "Two reasons. First, your ring of confederates tried to kill me. You brought it on yourself. Second, you've abused, raped and murdered kids for God knows how long. This has to stop. I'm speaking for them. Let's call it retribution. A reckoning."

Black paused, then asked, "Did the little girl die?"

Rutherford lowered his head to stare at the carpet. "They all die."

"Look at me."

Rutherford lifted his head.

"Do you know her?"

Black showed him the photograph of Gilbert Bartholomew's daughter. Rutherford glanced at it, looked away. Black stepped forward, grabbed him by the hair, jerking his head up to face the picture, his pistol pressed under his chin.

"Do you know her?" he hissed.

Rutherford stared at the girl's face.

"No," he muttered. "They all look the same."

He bowed his head again.

"Of course they do," said Black. "Look at me, Rutherford."

Rutherford looked up.

Black shot him in the face, then again in the chest.

He had information. A date.

And if his hunch was right, then he knew how to find them.

36

Stanley Lampton had never been a victim. He didn't have abusive parents. He hadn't been abused as a child. It was just in him. Borderline psychotic. During his many meetings with prison psychiatrists, the general conclusion was that it all could be boiled down to power. Power over the vulnerable. Power over kids. The complete destruction of their innocence turned him on. The ruination of a young life got him hard. If asked, Lampton would disagree. He would say he loved those kids, and he would say they loved him right back.

The power which his employer Boyd Falconer had granted him was something he could only have dreamed of. In his mind, he had arrived in paradise. He was careful not to overstep his limits. Falconer had made this clear. If he did, then the penalties were severe. He would be taken out to the desert, shot in the back of the head, and left for the vultures to pick. This frightened Lampton, but the rewards overshadowed everything.

He was rarely disturbed in his subterranean kingdom. A wall in his room was devoted to twelve monitors. Each showed him a full of view of each of the other rooms. He would watch. He would listen. They often needed tenderness, a display of affection, especially the very young ones. He was a master of that. To gain their trust. To calm their fears. Sometimes, in case of minor emergencies, a nurse was brought in. To deal with cuts or bruises or common colds. In extreme cases, such as the measles thing, they wheeled in a doctor. Beyond that, Lampton took care of everything. He consoled them, comforted them, humoured them. Loved them. The nurse and the doctor did it for the money. Lampton found such a concept vile. Never would he debase himself in such a way. He did it all for nothing. His was a higher calling.

He loved those kids.

But the rules were strict. He was allowed to read stories. During the day, he could play games. Interact. Keep them occupied. Made sure they brushed their teeth. Bathed them, which was difficult for him. But he kept his discipline. Sometimes, if a child became unruly, or particularly difficult, then he would threaten. Sometimes he would make an example of one in front of all the others. He did this rarely, but when he did, they listened, and any trouble went away.

Lampton accepted all this, because he knew he must. If he didn't, he would die. But the rewards were glorious.

And one such reward awaited him. The little girl from the UK.

She had been drugged when she arrived. With great delicacy, Lampton bathed her and changed her into fresh clothes. When she began to rouse, he fixed a hot chocolate from the little kitchen in his room, and brought it through to her.

He placed it on her bedside table, and sat at the edge of the bed.

She was pale, fragile. A little wisp of life. Perfect.

She stared at him. How incredibly blue her eyes were, he thought. Blue, like the Arizona sky.

"I've made you hot chocolate. Not too hot. With cream on top. And sprinkles. Look – little stars."

She didn't reply.

Lampton smiled. "What's your name?"

Nothing. Lampton expected no more. He was patient, attentive, understanding. These kids had been through a lot.

"You can tell me later. People call me Stanley. Or Stan, if you want. I'm your friend. I'll look after you. Nothing can hurt you now."

He leaned in a little closer, and spoke in a whisper. "And if you eat all your dinner up tonight, I've got a treat for you."

Closer still.

"Ice cream!"

No reaction.

"Everybody likes ice cream. Do you like ice cream?"

She responded with a slight nod, which set Lampton's heart thumping.

"That's good. I think we're going to be close buddies. Now if you need anything, anything at all, you just press this red button at the side of your bed, and Stan will come to help you. Strawberry or vanilla?"

She blinked her eyes, but said nothing.

"Both!" said Lampton. "With more sprinkles. I'll be back soon, and we'll play some games. And remember, if you need the smallest thing, press the button, I'll be right here."

He left her, and returned to his room at the end of the corridor. He watched her in the monitor. He saw her cry into the sheets.

Soon, he thought, the crying will stop, when he gives her love.

37

Black left the hotel without incident. He chose not to take the lift, but rather stairs via the emergency exit. The Bothwell Suite was a secluded section of the hotel, but the gunshots could easily have attracted attention. In the remote possibility the bodies weren't discovered until morning, then the housekeeper was in for a hell of a shock. Rutherford, a minute before his final breath, had said he'd called the police. Black suspected the police would be the last people he'd phone. But he might have called someone.

As Black left the hotel, he remained vigilant. He was hard to spot. Another lawyer in an evening suit. One amongst hundreds. He'd bet a million dollars he was the only one with blood stains on his tux. He kept the front of his jacket buttoned up.

He made his way out of the front entrance. Still more people were streaming in. A car stopped on the road directly outside. A black Lexus. Three men emerged. The car drove off. They hurried up the stairs. Men in dark suits, hard features. Unspeaking, preoccupied in getting to their destination fast. Black turned his back, stood by one of the pillars, pretending to be on his phone. They passed him and disappeared inside. The cavalry. A tad late. But they would know in about five minutes that Rutherford was dead. And they would be careless not to assume Rutherford had given Black information.

Black reflected. Rutherford could only tell him what he knew. Which was not a lot. They would still think their gathering on Monday evening hadn't been compromised. Rutherford said an email would be sent to him that morning. With Rutherford dead, they simply wouldn't send the email. Thus, no reason to abort. Especially if entertainment had been arranged. *The show must go on*, he thought grimly. It was a simple logic, but it was all he had. Plus, a hunch. All he needed was the particular day, which he now had. The rendezvous he would find. If his hunch played out.

He headed for his hotel. He chose back streets, narrow lanes. No one was following him. The man he had killed with the blade had proved a difficult opponent. His head hurt. The side of his face ached. His cheek was swollen. His shoulder felt stiff. Maybe a torn muscle.

He approached the hotel – a man waiting outside, smoking. Big, strong build, well dressed. Black could see the interior of the hotel through the glass entrance. Another two men sitting at a table. Not speaking. Waiting. Probably more men stationed outside his room. All of them waiting.

Waiting for Black.

Only one person knew where he was staying. Pamela Thompson. He cursed his stupidity, allowing her up to his room. She'd talked.

The bitch was working for his enemies.

The bitch would pay.

Black turned back in the direction he'd come, and headed towards his car. No one had spotted him. He hoped. Every few yards, he checked to see if he was being followed, nerves stretched, the hairs on the back of his neck tingling. He was exhausted. He doubted he could handle much more. If he were attacked now, he would be ineffective. He was living on adrenalin, and the tank was running low. He still had the Walther PPK. He held it in his jacket pocket, cradling it in his hand, its presence providing a modicum of reassurance.

He got to the car. The night was quiet. The evening was warm and still. A couple strolled by, chatting, walking a small dog. They smiled at Black. Black smiled back. They seemed innocent enough. He waited until they were past, got into his car.

He'd left nothing of any importance in his hotel room. He would not be going back. He'd kept the rucksack with the Desert Eagles in the boot of his car. A couple of small cannons. More than useful in a firefight.

He drove off. It was suicide to head back to his flat. He was a wanted man. They knew he wouldn't go there but would watch it anyway, just in case.

He made his way out of Edinburgh, relieved he was leaving the city. A place where he'd experienced death close up. But then he tended to experience death close up wherever he went.

He got onto the M8 motorway, the main road between Edinburgh and Glasgow, and took the turn-off to the town of Livingston. He found a Premier Inn. Same routine. He parked his car, found an off-sales, purchased a bottle of Glenfiddich, then checked in. The room was cheap and functional. No frills. He didn't have any change of clothes, but he hardly cared. He showered. He poured himself a generous glass of whisky and drank it in one. Then another, which he mulled over. He suddenly realised he was ravenous. He used his mobile, found a local pizza shop, and ordered a delivery.

Thirty minutes later there was a soft knock on the door. With a pistol in one hand, he opened the door a fraction. The pizza guy. He took the box, paid for the pizza. Wolfed it down.

He was tired. He slipped under the covers, one pistol on the pillow next to him, one on the bedside cabinet, the Walther under the bed.

He fell into a fitful sleep. Images flitted in and out of his mind. His daughter, screaming from the shadows. His wife, lying like a broken rag doll with her face torn to shreds from an assassin's bullet. Strangers pointing at him. Accusing him, blaming him.

A noise, barging its way into his sleep. It persisted, like an insect gnawing in his brain. Black woke to the sound of his mobile phone, on the floor next to the Walther.

He checked the time. 6.30am. He had slept for eight hours. Longer than he expected. He felt mildly refreshed. He sat up, stretched over to his mobile. A number he recognised.

He answered.

"What's up, Tricia?"

A silence.

A chill dread bloomed in his chest.

"Tricia?"

He heard breathing.

Then she spoke.

"He says he's going to kill me." Her voice broke. He heard her sob.

Black's heart rose to his mouth. He waited. A man's voice.

"Mr Black?"

"Yes."

"Your secretary says hi. She's a little distressed right now. She's unable to come to the phone. She has a lovely place here in Millport."

Black waited, time suddenly frozen. He said nothing.

"My name is Mr Lincoln. You know why I'm here. We should meet. Have a chat."

Black waited five seconds before he spoke, then said, "Why bother. You're going to kill her anyway. And then you'll kill me. Get it over with now. Then I can hunt you down and rip your fucking lungs out. Because that's what's going to happen."

"I don't think so, Mr Black." His voice was calm, relaxed, apparently unfazed by Black's response.

"She's alive," he continued. "You've heard proof of life. And while she lives, you'll do what you can to protect her. I know you will, because that's the type of man you are. So don't bullshit. We don't have time for it. Tricia certainly doesn't. The ferry leaves Largs harbour at 8am. Be on it. We can meet for breakfast at the Oyster Café. My treat. 8.40 suit you? You should find it okay. As far as I can gather, there's only one street in Millport. So don't get lost. If you're late, or you try anything remotely heroic, the consequences for Tricia will be... how can I put it? Tragic. Do you understand me, Mr Black?"

"I understand completely, Mr Lincoln. I look forward to meeting you. And one thing you should be clear about."

"Yes?"

"You have no idea of the type of man I am."

"We'll see."

The line went dead.

Black stared at the blank screen of his mobile phone.

Death followed him and spread about him. Like a fucking cancer. So be it.

If death was what they were looking for, they'd come to the right man.

Bring it on, he thought.

Bring it on.

38

Lincoln turned his attention back to Tricia. He'd located her easily enough. The address had been found by his employers in less than twenty minutes. They'd probably bribed someone in the Land Registry. He had to admire their efficiency and their ability to get information quickly. Of course, it had been a gamble. But when it came to gambling, Lincoln had always been lucky.

She owned a second house on the island of Millport, her old family home she'd never sold when her parents had died. So she'd told him. It was an obvious destination. Black's office was well and truly closed, and he wouldn't risk her coming to work. Her main home had also looked unoccupied. Lincoln had assumed Black had told her to stay away for a little while. His assumption had proved to be correct.

Two miles from the centre of Millport, set back two hundred yards from the shore, sitting at the foot of tall white veined cliffs, her house was a remote building built of solid brown stone, red slate roof, bay windows with bright white window frames. A neat front garden bounded by a rough dry-stone wall. An orderly lawn, with flower beds and hanging baskets. Not an unattractive place. Perhaps once a steading of some sort, complete with two outbuildings. One a small shed, the other a low-roofed barn. He was in the barn now, with Tricia.

She was naked, her hands suspended above her head, bound by rope, the rope looping round a ceiling joist. Also rope binding her ankles. He smiled at her, but she wasn't looking at him. Her head drooped, chin resting on her collarbone. She was still crying but not as loudly as before.

Lincoln inspected her. She was fifty and looked as if she kept in shape. Though she wasn't in prime condition at this precise time, Lincoln had to concede. He'd had a little bit of fun. He'd cut her breasts and thighs. Surface wounds. No deep scarring. Not yet. Purely to terrify. Enough to give her the right tone when she spoke to Black. There could be no defiance. Black had to know she was scared.

Lincoln leant in, put his lips close to one ear. "Your knight in shining armour will be here soon," he whispered.

She raised her head a fraction. He'd replaced the gag in her mouth. She gave a soft moan.

"I knew you'd be pleased."

He held up a knife in front of her face, and with one edge, gently brushed back her hair.

"You've had a rough time," he said, voice calm, soothing almost. "Blame Adam Black for that. He's such a nuisance. But it will be over soon. I promise. No more pain."

On a rickety wooden workbench was a variety of old tools – discarded rusting stuff. Hammer, a box of screw drivers, chisel, saw, hacksaw, crowbar. Other equipment, including his Glock 20, complete with silencer. He placed the pistol in his inside coat pocket and sat on a stool he'd brought from the kitchen. He manoeuvred it closer to his captive. Its legs screeched on the stone floor.

"Some lemonade?"

A twitch of movement. A nod.

"Good. I'm going to remove your gag. If you scream or do anything stupid, I'll prise out your eye with this knife. Do you understand this instruction, Tricia?"

Another nod.

"That's good."

He carefully untied the cloth bound across her mouth. She spluttered and coughed.

There was a plastic bottle of lemonade on the bench. Lincoln reached over, unscrewed the top, and placed it on her lips, tipping it slightly. She drank, then coughed again.

"Easy," said Lincoln. He eased back, waited until she had stopped, then tilted it again. She drank greedily.

"You're thirsty." He replaced the bottle on the bench. "I'm looking forward to meeting Adam. I think we might have a lot in common."

Tricia stared at him with glazed eyes, but said nothing.

"I know a lot about him. The people I work for are very clever. They can acquire information about anyone. They found out about your little holiday home here. Imagine that. And they found out all about Adam. He was in the army. For most of his adult life, in fact. You probably know that. But did you know he was a captain in the SAS? I'll wager he didn't tell you. He keeps his secrets, does Captain Black. More lemonade?"

"Please let me go," she mumbled.

"He was awarded the Military Cross. You get that for bravery. I'll bet Adam was a handful in the battlefield."

Lincoln leaned in closer, the stool creaking.

"And that's what I think we share, the captain and I. What do you think that is, Tricia? What is it you think we share?"

"Please..."

"We like to kill," he whispered. "We both have a real taste for it."

Tricia shed quiet desperate tears.

Lincoln frowned. "No need to cry, Tricia. It'll be over soon. I promise."

39

The child refused to talk. This didn't annoy Lampton in the slightest. He watched her on one of the monitors in his room. She was sitting up in her bed. He had given her a doll and had told her it was called Lucy Smiles. She held it now, close to her, and that gave Lampton pleasure. Gradually, she would grow to trust him. He was a master in the art of manipulation.

He didn't know her name. If he'd asked, Falconer would have told him. But names weren't important. If anyone told him her name it would have to be her.

He smiled. She was special.

Bath time soon. He could hardly wait. He would be gentle. He would treat her like a tiny porcelain doll, with great delicacy and care. Never rough. Not to begin with. The hurting came later, which he never intended. It just happened. Lampton put it down to a natural progression towards a final conclusion.

The telephone on his desk bleeped. It was Norman Sands. He hated Sands. Obsequious bean counter. All he cared about was money. Lampton found him disgusting. A vile creature. He didn't care about the children. It was all cash. He didn't see the children as human beings but assets to be sold for profit. Lampton had much more noble aspirations.

He loved his little ones.

He picked up.

"Lampton."

"Yes."

"There's an auction tomorrow night. Numbers 3, 5, 6 and 10. You understand?"

Lampton found talking to the man brought a bad taste to his mouth.

"Of course."

"We've got twelve bidders. From every corner. Repeat clients. So we want them looking immaculate. Get them dressed, get them doing what kids do. Just make sure they're perfect. Mr Falconer will be down to look in later. Auction begins at seven. We want them animated, Lampton. No hiding under covers, or cowering behind cushions. You understand?"

"I understand completely. There will be no fuck-ups, Sands. There never are. Mr Falconer knows I don't let him down."

"Tell that to him if your measles problem doesn't go away."

He hung up. Lampton replaced the phone back gently. He wasn't a man to give way to rages. Unless he was pushed. Or when he succumbed to one of his episodes, when a little one needed teaching a lesson, and he forgot himself.

He watched numbers 3, 5, 6 and 10 on his monitors. They were listless, as indeed they all were. The four being sold were all about six years old, as far as he could tell. He would gee them up. They had to be natural. Smiling. Or at the very least no frowns or surliness. Tomorrow night, at seven, the hidden cameras would beam their smiles to all sorts of people. Lampton didn't know how much money changed hands, nor did he care.

But he'd been told the younger they were, the greater the price. He could understand that.

Sands joined Falconer in the dining room. Falconer was eating alone, which he preferred. He sat at the head of a long broad dining table, crafted from Venetian grey marble, around which were placed sixteen matching high-backed chairs. It had arrived only the day before. Bought in specially for the Japanese billionaire and his entourage. No expense had been spared. The cost: $75,000. Pocket change to a man like Boyd Falconer. A chef specialising in Japanese cuisine would be hired for the evening, at $3,000. He'd arranged for Japanese stencils to be hung on the white walls, ten in all, each original, each costing $50,000. And so it went on. Sands knew what everything cost. It was his job to know. Over $1,000,000 had been lavished on the room. A day's earning, he estimated.

But the worst, at least in Sands' view, was the samurai armour, fastened around a mannequin, placed in one corner, complete with sword and helmet. Made from black iron lacquered plates, gold-plated chain mail and blue silk. In Sands' view, it was crass and clumsy, and could offend. The cost was offensive too, at over $450,000. He'd hinted as much, and was told in no uncertain manner by Falconer to shut the fuck up.

Falconer was eating a plate of steamed vegetables and a baked potato. He sipped from a stem glass of still mineral water, bottles of which were imported from Switzerland. On a far wall opposite was a large screen. With a flick of a remote, it could retract into a specially adapted housing, and a wooden panel would slide down, rendering it undetectable.

Falconer was gazing at it, which he did most mealtimes. There were screens in almost every room in his ranch. On the screen were numbers, names, places, flow charts. Sands was meticulous. Falconer was more so. He knew everything about each of the items. Where they came from: age; name; cost of procurement. Also, source – the name or names of those who supplied the item initially. Then the names of each individual involved in the often-complex chain of handovers between the initial abduction to the final delivery into the sub-level. And after that, the details of those who purchased. Names, addresses, everything.

Falconer kept records of all his clients. Detailed information. From billionaires to United States senators; from government officials to CEOs of multinationals; from dictators to movie stars. Falconer knew everything about everybody. Details were documented, recorded, archived. To be accessed at the press of a button. As such, he was unassailable. Untouchable. In over fifteen years, he'd stayed under the radar of the FBI and the state police. People in high places had too much to lose. The way Falconer looked at it, if the intake of merchandise ever dried up, then the next obvious step was blackmail. But the appetite for flesh never diminished. It was a business which would last forever.

"Did you speak to Lampton?"

"Of course."

"He'd better get them up to shape. A single smile gets me an extra million dollars."

"It would recoup the money spent on your samurai warrior," replied Sands, drily.

Falconer chuckled. "You don't like spending money, do you?"

Sands shrugged. "Depends on what it's spent on. What do I know after all? I'm only your accountant. I'm sure our Japanese clients would enjoy your hospitality, samurai or no samurai."

"The problem with you, Sands, is that you know how to count it, but you haven't got the first fucking clue how to make it. Like every fucking accountant and lawyer I've met. A fucking leech. Look at the sword. It's called a *katana*. Said to be the finest cutting weapon in military history. Forged from Japanese steel.

Once it's forged, it's polished. With this particular sword, the polisher spent four weeks, using special stones. To give it that mirror finish. This one has an inscription on the side of the blade. In fucking gold inlay. By a guy called Masamune. To the Japanese this guy is like God Almighty. The greatest swordsmith ever. And he's been dead the past thousand years. The blade is so fucking sharp, you don't feel any pain. You don't notice when your arm's been taken off. It's said that those condemned to die asked specifically for the *katana*. Do you know why, Sands?"

"No idea."

"Because when they got their heads sliced off, they didn't know they'd died. The cut was so clean. When our Japanese friend sees all this, I kid you not, Sands, he will cum in his fucking pants. And that's why the million dollars spent on this stuff will make me a hundred million dollars over time."

"That, and a constant supply of children."

"Get the fuck out of here, Sands. Get back to your profit and loss. And tell Lampton that if he fucks up tomorrow night, then I'll shove the fucking *katana* up his anal passage."

Sands nodded. Lampton might enjoy such an experience, he thought.

40

War is not about who is right, it is about who is left.

Anonymous

Black checked the ferry times. The man called Lincoln had been accurate with his times. A ferry left Largs harbour at eight. Black put on the clothes worn from the evening before – a dinner suit, and a bloodstained evening shirt. He skipped the bow tie. A tad conspicuous. He had no change of clothing, but how he looked was the farthest thing from his mind.

He placed the Walther in his inside pocket. The two Desert Eagles he put in his carrier bag which he slung over his shoulder.

He left his room, got to his car. He doubted his enemies would have tracked him here. Still, he was watchful. All quiet. The journey was about an hour and twenty minutes. Black drove, using satnav. He did not take in the scenery. His mind dwelt on other things – like whether Tricia, his friend and secretary, was lying dead in a ditch.

He arrived at 7.40am. He hadn't been to Largs for five years. The last time he had visited was to do precisely the same thing he was about to do now. Which was board the ferry to Millport. Only then, circumstances were different. Then, he was with his wife and daughter. Then, life had been simpler. Now, everything was complicated. Everything Black touched, ended up crushed and dead.

Millport was in fact the name of the town. More like a village. The island itself was called Great Cumbrae. Black remembered little about it. The ferry would take about ten minutes, crossing the Firth of Clyde on calm waters. The thirteen-mile road round the island was predominantly flat, hugging the coast. Hence why it was nicknamed the bicycle island. The one vivid memory Black had was hiring bicycles, his daughter safely ensconced in a trailer attached behind him. Buying lunch in a little fish and chip shop. Smiles, laughter. Beyond that, nothing much. A nice place in the summer. Barren and freezing cold in the winter. A million years ago. Another time. Another world.

The ferry arrived. Black bought a ticket, drove on. There was virtually no queue. Four other cars. A handful of keen sightseers. The morning was dull, the waters choppy. Black got out of his car and climbed steps to an upper deck, watching the island draw closer. A bus was waiting to take those foot passengers. No other vehicles, as far as he could see. The approaching dock was stuck in the middle of nowhere – a car park, and fields behind low stone walls. Little else.

Everything seemed innocent enough. The ferry rumbled to a standstill; the steel door lowered onto a concrete ramp. Black drove off, easing out the belly of the boat. There was only one road. He could have turned either left or right. Whichever, he would arrive at his destination. He checked the time. Eight fifteen. He turned right, for no particular reason other than the fact that the other vehicles turned left. He took the journey slow. He paid scant regard to the passing scenery. To his right, the shifting muddy colour of the estuary. To his left, stretches of wild grass, gorse, rocks, boulders, clumps of trees, beyond which low moss-patterned cliffs.

Black drove slowly, because he had to. He needed to think. The man Lincoln held a hostage. She could be already dead. Black had to act as if there was still a chance. But he had nowhere to go, no cards to play. He had no choice but to see it out to the end. Which at the present moment, looked gloomy. Worse. A nightmare, from which there was no reprieve.

Time passed. The scenery changed. The wild grass became gardens. Houses, holiday cabins, rows of static caravans. He passed an old hotel of red brick behind black railings set in a low stone wall, then more houses. He was approaching the centre. The road was set further back from the water, and to his right, he passed a flat grass park with swings and chutes and a yellow roundabout. The road veered right, then left. He got to the centre. Pubs, another hotel, small quaint touristy shops with fluttering buntings and bright garlands. He saw the sign – *The Oyster*. It was open. Black drove by slowly. Large windowpanes on either side of a central glass door, between narrow terraced houses. A counter on one side. On the other, tables and chairs. Some people were there already. Black pulled into a space on the side of the road a hundred yards further up. Eight thirty. He cut the engine, tried to focus. He had no plan, as such. But then he rarely did. This time, another life depended on his actions. If indeed Tricia was still alive. Black had to follow this through. He sensed however this played out, death would be sitting nearby.

But Adam Black and death were close acquaintances.

He got out. Thankfully, the road was quiet. Dressed in dinner suit and a red-stained shirt, he didn't blend in.

He made his way to the café. He went straight in. Looked about. A woman behind the counter, hunched over a sizzling frying pan, cooking up bacon and eggs. A younger girl helping her. The place was plain, needing a new lick of paint, new linoleum on the floor. The walls were dotted with forgettable paintings in cheap frames. There were three people. A couple at the window. An individual sitting in the corner at the back.

Black settled his gaze on the man. The man smiled, raising a hand. Black nodded in return but did not smile.

He made his way over and sat on a plastic chair on the other side of a Formica-topped table.

"Mr Black?"

"Mr Lincoln."

41

Black regarded the man before him. Difficult to estimate his height given he was sitting, but Black reckoned he was about six feet. Wearing a beige overcoat, a dark close-fitting pullover underneath. His features were neat, forgettable. He was thick in the neck and shoulders. Clever pale-blue eyes. His expression was calm, a secret half-smile raising the corners of his mouth.

Black, having confronted dangerous men all his life, could trust his instinct. The man exuded menace. It seeped out of his pores, it crouched behind his easy smile. At this precise moment, his instinct told him – *beware! This man is one fucking lethal individual!*

He had a mug of coffee on the table in front of him, and a folded newspaper.

He gestured to the coffee. "Can I get you one?"

"No, thank you."

"I'm glad you could make it."

"You're American?"

Lincoln's smile widened.

"How perceptive. I've been trying for years to bring the accent in, to get it just right. You know, the type your British newsreaders use, without any inflection? And I thought I'd cracked it. Then you come along. I'm impressed, Mr Black."

"Don't be. Spotting a phoney accent is the least of my talents. I have other ones, which you might not like as much."

Lincoln nodded. "And I believe you. You've had an interesting career. Spectacular. And getting a medal. You're a hero, Mr Black."

"That's very kind. I think you're wanting me to like you. But that won't work, Mr Lincoln."

Lincoln gave a look of mock indignation. "Why not?"

"Because I don't kill people I like."

"You've killed a lot of people."

Black gave the merest shrug. "I try to restrict it to scumbags. You know – sick fuckers, evil bastards. People like yourself."

Lincoln leaned several inches closer, both elbows resting on the table, hands clasped under his chin, his voice reduced to barely above a whisper. "I've killed many men. And women." He leaned in closer still. "And children."

Black met his gaze, but said nothing.

"When I read about your wife and child being shot in your own home, you know what I thought?"

"I'm dying to know."

"Professional. The hits were clean. I think they were dead even before they knew it. Which is a flaw I have. If I'd been given the contract, I'd have taken my time. Maybe ten minutes with your wife. Get to know her a little better. And I'd have given your daughter extra attention. Let her really feel it. So she knew, beyond any fraction of a doubt, that she was going to die. Make her absolutely terrified. Make her confront it, Mr Black. The whole thing becomes more... fulfilling."

Black rested back on his chair, studying Lincoln's face. He gave a thin-lipped smile.

"You know, I hadn't given it much thought. But now you mention it, I think you're right. I think fulfilment is exactly how I'll feel when I tear your fucking throat out. A sense of achievement. One less cockroach scuttling through the sewers."

"We'll see, Mr Black. We're not so dissimilar, you know."

"How's that?"

"We're both killers. And we both enjoy it. When the trigger's squeezed, when the knife slides through the throat. Don't tell me otherwise."

Black pursed his lips, as if considering the observation.

"Your problem is that you talk too much. Men, real men that is, don't discuss killing the way you do. They tend to keep quiet about these things. Which means that you're either a bullshitting coward, or a psychopath. Or maybe both. I suspect both."

"Mr Black, for a man in your position, you have great spirit. And I can't help but admire that. But time ticks on. And time is precious. Time is money. My employers pay me to solve problems. And right now, you're a problem."

"You're a problem solver. I'm one step up."

"How so?"

"I'm a problem eliminator. Where is Tricia?"

"She's safe. But if you do something stupid, she'll never be seen again. It will be one of those unsolved disappearances you can watch on Sky Television. A life for a life, I'm afraid. Yours for hers."

"I understand."

"Good. Let's go. I have a Glock in my inside coat pocket. I'd rather not use it here. We'll walk to your car. You'll drive. I'll give you directions. It's not far."

Black rose from his chair. They left together, Lincoln following a foot behind him.

"Lovely coffee," he shouted breezily to the young girl behind the counter.

"Thanks," she replied, a weary smile on her face. "Have a nice one."

42

They walked to Black's car, Lincoln remaining a step behind. The car bleeped as Black turned off the alarm. He got in first. Lincoln got in the passenger's side. He pulled the Glock from his inside coat pocket, silencer attached. He pressed it into Black's side. "I don't want to kill you here, Mr Black. It would be messy, and cause me considerable inconvenience. Also, I have plans. So please drive, and don't try anything stupid."

"Where are we going?"

"I'm taking you to Tricia."

Black started the car, pulled away. The road was still quiet. He drove, keeping the speed slow, steady. His situation was bleak. Yet he felt detached. Black knew all there was about fear. It affected men in different ways. He had seen its manifestations many times on the battlefield. For Black, his senses sharpened, his awareness expanded. He observed almost as a bystander. Picking up details, focusing on movements. Planning. Searching for weaknesses. Searching for a way out.

This time, he saw nothing. Except his dead body buried in some shallow grave in some desolate corner of Millport.

But one thing he could guarantee. He was no easy kill. Lincoln would have to work hard for his money.

He drove past sections of terraced houses, more shops, then the houses separated out – impressive rambling structures with long front gardens. Then the houses stopped, and suddenly the wild grass and gorse and rocks re-appeared. They had left the town. Back to the wildlands. The only constant was the churning waters of the Clyde estuary at his right hand.

"Who do you work for, Lincoln?" asked Black suddenly.

"It's not important."

"But they're paying you. How much are you getting?"

"A very large sum of money. Thanks to you, I'll be enjoying the warm weather and fresh lobster for a few more years."

"I have money. Over a £1,000,000. It's yours. Tell them you killed me. I'll take Tricia, and you'll never see us again. That way you get double pay. For doing nothing."

Lincoln chuckled. "Very devious, Mr Black. But you forget. I enjoy my job. I'd feel cheated if I didn't complete the task."

"Of course. Fulfilment."

"Exactly."

"You had your chance."

"I'll keep that in mind, Mr Black."

Black drove on.

Five minutes later, he saw a house to his left, set back from the road, accessed by a single lane barely better than a dirt track.

"This is it," said Lincoln. "Time for a reunion. Drive in."

Black did as he was instructed. The car bounced and lurched over ruts and furrows. He reached the side of the house and parked beside a vehicle he knew well. A red Volkswagen Beetle. Tricia's car.

Lincoln pressed the gun harder into Black's ribs. "Get out, please."

Black opened the car door, eased out. Lincoln followed suit.

He nodded towards an adjacent barn. He held the pistol straight at Black's head.

"Glock 20," said Black. "Powerful."

"You know your weapons."

"It helps." Black still carried the Walther in his inside jacket pocket. The two hand cannons – the Desert Eagles – were still in his holdall on the back seat of his Mini. Useless to him.

"In the barn, Mr Black. The door isn't locked."

Black's nerves tingled. He had no idea what to expect. He opened the door, entered. The place was in darkness. Lincoln followed, flicking a switch. A single strip light, fastened to a low beam, flickered. Details sprang into life. A work bench running down one side littered with old tools, tin boxes, rubbish. A rough concrete floor. The air was musty. The walls were corrugated metal, painted light blue. No windows. A low gambrel roof, narrow metal ceiling joists running across its length. Attached to one by a length of rope was Tricia. Naked, bleeding, hanging limp, head bowed.

Black's heart rose to his mouth. Was she alive? He couldn't be certain. He turned to Lincoln slowly, swallowing back his dread. "A life for a life, you said. Is she dead?"

"Take your jacket off, Mr Black. Put it on the bench. Make sure you don't find your fingers curling round the pistol you're carrying."

With exaggerated care, Black removed his jacket, buying time, placing it neatly across some scattered screwdrivers, mind racing.

"You've been busy," said Lincoln, referring to his blood-stained shirt. "Cut yourself shaving? Take it off as well, please."

Black nodded. His lips were dry. Seconds were ticking fast. Counting down to a grisly end.

"Take it off, I said."

Again, with the same deliberation, he took off his shirt, and placed it on top of his jacket. He turned to face Lincoln.

Lincoln cocked his head to one side. "You keep in shape."

Which Black did. He ran every day, went to a cheap gym four times a week. Plus twenty-five years serving in the most elite combat unit in the world. Black was fundamentally fit and strong.

And lethal.

"It has its advantages," replied Black, in a measured voice.

"Of course it does. It's a prerequisite of the job for men like us. Now shoes, please. Place them on the bench."

"I think you're rather enjoying this."

"I confess to being disappointed. I thought this would be much harder. But then, I counted on you being the chivalrous type. And I was right. Your downfall, Mr Black. Your Achilles heel."

"I'll need to work on that." He crouched down, untied one shoe, then the other, removed them both, turned to the bench. This was his chance. His only chance.

"I take it she's dead," he said, his back to Lincoln.

"Very soon. There was never any other way."

"There's always another way." Black placed his shoes beside his shirt and jacket. Next to a heavy spanner. He focused. He curled his hand round it. Pointless throwing it at Lincoln. He would just laugh at such an effort. And maybe kill him on the spot. But that wasn't Black's intention. "Try this, for example."

He spun round. He threw the spanner hard and fast, upwards, to the strip light. It burst into fragments on impact; a popping sound as the glass exploded. Suddenly, darkness. Another sound. A muffled cough. Black recognised it all too well. No cough. Rather the sound of the Glock spitting a bullet through its silencer. Had Black remained stationary, he'd be coping with a hole through his chest. But he had moved, the instant he'd flung the spanner, diving to the ground, rolling, springing to his feet.

Total darkness. He heard Lincoln moving, back towards the barn door, presumably to open it, to allow in some natural daylight. When that happened, Black was as good as dead.

The building was not big, with nothing but space, save the old workbench. Still crouched low, Black kept moving. Another bullet, alarmingly close to his head. It thwumped into the gambrel roof, which, unlike the walls, was constructed of timber. Lincoln was guessing. Firing randomly. A random bullet could kill as effectively as one well-aimed.

Black kept going. Sudden daylight. Lincoln had reached the door, opened it. Black saw the outline of his head, his body. Lincoln turned directly towards him, Glock held at waist height. Black charged, propelled into him, shoulder first, using his full weight, one hand grasping Lincoln's gun. They both tumbled out, on to a grassy stretch between the barn and Black's car. Lincoln rolled free. He still had the gun. He aimed. Black was on his feet. He darted around the other side of the Mini.

"Bravo!" shouted Lincoln. "Adam Black's given himself two more minutes of life."

Black had to run. He darted from the car, past Tricia's car, towards the main house. The windscreen of the Beetle suddenly shattered. Black got to a side door, turned the handle. It was unlocked. He opened it quickly, slipped through, closed it behind him. A second later, it flew open, the top shredded under the cannon power of the Glock.

Black was in a hallway. Shoes in a neat line on old newspaper on one side. A wooden coat hanger. He got to another door. Then a kitchen. Large, merging to a living room, wide patio doors at the back wall, opening to a carpeted conservatory with white table and chairs. Beyond that, a long sloping garden, cut from the wilderness and rock. A hundred yards beyond that, low cliffs crowned by stunted trees.

No sooner had Black closed the door, when it exploded open. Black had seconds. The kitchen was modern. A fleeting memory of a conversation, months back. She'd spent a fortune doing it up. A central island. On it, a modern electric hob. Drawers, cupboards. He pulled one open, another. There! Cutlery, knives. He grabbed up a large butcher's knife. Pointed, its edge sharp enough to cut a throat. He moved to one side of the door, back to the wall. And waited. Silence. Except for the drum sound in his head – his heartbeat.

43

Lincoln could hardly believe he had allowed events to spiral off course like this. He had underestimated Black's sheer audacity. Lesson learned. And Lincoln was a quick learner. His shock had lasted all of two seconds. Now down to the hard business of killing his target. Fulfil the contract. See it through. He had a gun. Black had nothing. Though he guessed he may have acquired a knife. Lincoln knew the layout of the house, having enjoyed Tricia's company the previous evening. When this little drama was over, he might enjoy her company for a little longer, before she tasted a bullet in the mouth.

The hall led directly to the kitchen. Lincoln slowed right down. He crept along the hallway, but the wooden flooring creaked with every footstep.

"Where do you think you're going, Mr Black? There's no point in running."

But of course, there was every point in running. What would he do, if the situation were reversed? A waste of effort thinking like that. Lincoln had a very different set of values from the average human being. *What would Black do?*

Escape through the back, through the conservatory? Into the

Millport countryside, hiding in bushes? Wait until the coast was clear, then hand himself into a police station? Unlikely. That wasn't Black's way. Maybe circle round, and try to rescue the woman? Possibly. Probably. Black lived by a moral code. His Achilles heel. *Like one of the fucking knights of the round table*, he thought. He cursed himself, for his negligence. He should never have had to think about this.

"Not talking to me?"

He sidled forward, pistol held up in front, shoulder height. The door he faced was half blown away, hanging off its hinges. He looked back, thinking he heard a noise from the barn. Black was probably untying the woman, while Lincoln fucked about talking to nobody. For the first time in as long as he could remember, indecision gnawed into his mind. Which was not his way. Everything was planned, structured. This was chaos.

He would go to the kitchen, check it out quickly, then head back to the barn.

He thrust forward, kicked the door open, swivelled round.

And straight into Black.

44

B lack thrust his hand up hard, catching Lincoln's wrist. The Glock fired, punching a hole in the ceiling. Black held on, trying to twist the weapon out of Lincoln's hand. Lincoln simultaneously brought his knee up into Black's groin. Black grunted, tried to stab Lincoln in his side. Lincoln hacked down, into Black's forearm, deflecting the move, then struck the side of Black's neck. Black anticipated the move, raised his shoulder to absorb the blow. It felt like he'd been hit by a sledgehammer. Lincoln struck again, same place. The top of Black's shoulder and arm went numb.

Black jerked his head back, thrust forward, butted him in the face. Lincoln gasped, involuntarily relaxing his grip on the pistol. Black yanked Lincoln's wrist. The weapon fell to the floor. Black pushed Lincoln off him, took one step back, kicked the pistol away, then took another step back. His shoulder throbbed. Lincoln pulled a knife from a sheath attached to his belt. He advanced slowly, knife held low, blood streaming from both nostrils. Black retreated, one step, two steps, the kitchen knife in his left hand, his right shoulder and arm aching.

Lincoln thrust forward; Black dodged sideways, struck with

the heel of his hand at the side of Lincoln's thick neck. Lincoln jerked away, sweeping his arm at Black's ribs. The blade sliced open six inches of skin. Black gasped, tottered back. Lincoln, seizing the moment, drove the knife up, hoping to stab Black in the throat. Black knocked Lincoln's arm to one side, stabbed with his own knife into Lincoln's stomach. Lincoln, likewise, knocked the blow to one side, Black's knife whirling out of his hand. Lincoln punched at Black's eye, then tried to stab Black in the side. Black manoeuvred a half turn, bringing his arm up, catching Lincoln's elbow, applied a lock, tripped Lincoln, and using Lincoln's momentum, broke the joint.

Lincoln grunted; the knife fell from suddenly numb fingers. He used his other functioning hand, groped on the floor, found the knife, seized it, thrust up. Black tried to avoid. The blade cut through his trousers, tearing a gash across his thigh.

Lincoln got to his feet, one arm dangling, clutching the knife in his other hand. Black stood back. He bled from two wounds, his right shoulder and arm were numb, his left eye swollen. Soon, he would become fatigued and weak. He would die from loss of blood. Or at the hands of Lincoln.

Not yet.

He picked up a crystal bowl full of white pebbles from a low set living room table, hurled it at Lincoln. Lincoln swept it aside with his good arm. The pebbles scattered, the glass smashed on the floor. Black used the moment, retrieved his knife, strode forward, hacked at Lincoln's neck in an apparently random blow. Lincoln stepped back, stabbing. Black swivelled to one side, caught his arm, attempted a lock, but was too weak. Lincoln punched him on the jaw. Black reeled back, crashing into shelving. Ornaments, books toppled to the floor. Lincoln rushed forward. Black staggered to his feet. Lincoln held the knife high, poised for a downward thrust. Black caught the upraised arm.

Again, Lincoln jerked his knee up. This time Black caught it, heaved. Lincoln tottered back.

They each stood, panting, Lincoln taking deep ragged breaths, his left arm held close to his chest, disabled. Black felt light-headed. He could not risk another attack. Lincoln, face pale, eyes wide, came staggering forward. Black had one last chance. He threw the knife. His aim was off. It plunged into Lincoln's shoulder, almost to the hilt. Lincoln croaked in dismay. Summoning his last reserves of energy, Black charged forward, kicking Lincoln hard in the groin, then following it with a short, brutal uppercut. He heard Lincoln's teeth crack together. Lincoln flipped back, landing on his back, lay still. Black sank to his knees.

Lincoln was down. But not dead.

45

Boyd Falconer sometimes jogged around the perimeter of his ranch, instead of using the treadmill. For a change of scenery. He had installed a running track. It was a two-mile circumference, skirting the boundary wall, and he jogged round twice. Early morning, when the heat wasn't so oppressive. Though he would concede running across desert was as boring as running on a treadmill. Once a rattlesnake startled him, which livened his morning. But beyond that, the journey was the same. He did it because it was habit, and he liked to keep fit and his lungs strong.

Strapped to his waist was an elastic belt. Attached was a plastic bottle of water. He didn't carry his mobile when he ran. One of those rare times. If he was needed, Sands would get him. Which is exactly what happened, as he was halfway round the second lap. He saw Sands gesturing at the main entrance.

Fuck, he thought. *It never ends*. Why should it? The industry he was in gave him an income of over a million dollars a day. If the hassle stopped, then something wasn't working.

Hassle meant money.

He changed direction, cut towards Sands. "What is it?"

"Our Japanese friend wants to bring his trip forward."

Sands handed him a towel. Falconer, wearing a long-sleeved running shirt and shorts, was drenched in sweat, which wasn't unusual.

"He does?" He took a long exhalation. "He's one difficult bastard."

"And our wealthiest investor."

"I fucking know that!" snapped Falconer. He dabbed his face. For an educated man, his accountant liked to state the obvious. But, he reflected, Sands was a necessary evil. Clever with money, a good administrator, a strategist. But one fucking major pain in the arse. While he was useful, his insolent comment and sarcastic retort would be tolerated. One day, his use would run out, and then another desert grave.

"When's he coming?"

"Tuesday."

"Fuck. Have you spoken to the doctor?"

"He says it should be okay."

"It *should* be okay?" barked Falconer. "What the hell does that mean?"

Sands licked his lips, cleared his throat.

"It wasn't the measles. A heat rash. Apparently."

Falconer shook his head, swore under his breath.

"What the fuck am I paying that quack for?"

"Because he's the only one who'll do this. And he was just being cautious."

"Cautious? He could have cost me fifteen million bucks." He rubbed away sweat from his eyes. "She's got to look fucking amazing. Get Lampton to sort it. Three days. Three fucking days. I'll have to rearrange the Japanese chef. Another $6,000. Never mind. Worth every dime."

Sands shrugged. "If you say so."

"I do fucking say so. What about the auction. Are we ready?"

"Lampton doesn't see a problem."

"There'd better not be."

"Of course."

"Now fuck off, and start working for your money." He flung the damp towel back at Sands, and resumed his run.

Sands was right. The Japanese tycoon was his wealthiest customer.

There could be no fuck-ups. Otherwise heads would roll. Literally.

46

B lack – bleeding, exhausted – found tape from a kitchen drawer, and bundled the unconscious Lincoln onto one of the chairs in the conservatory. He positioned his arms behind the back of the chair, bound his wrists and ankles tight. Lincoln's broken arm flopped like a tube of rubber. Also, for good measure, Black wrapped tape around Lincoln's mouth. It was temporary, but it would do.

Black felt light-headed. His wounds needed treating. First things first. He made his way back out the house and into the barn. He kept the door open so he could see what he was doing. Tricia was as before, but she moaned softly. He untied her, let her drop into his arms. He held her gently, and carried her back to the house.

She regained full consciousness. He lay her on a bed, covered her in a blanket. Within an hour, she was up, dressed. She didn't speak. She cleaned and treated Black's wounds. She'd worked as a staff nurse at Victoria Hospital, on the south side of Glasgow. Accident and emergency. A life before a legal secretary. She tended his wounds with a quiet, grim competence. Black said nothing. She'd given him painkillers and a change of clothes. T-shirt, pullover, jeans, her son's. He worked as an accountant in England. He had a full wardrobe of clothes for when he came up for holiday weekends. They were a shade tight on Black but better than garments soaked in other people's blood.

They dragged the chair into the centre of the living room. They had hardly spoken. Black had no idea how she'd react. She'd spent a night with a killer. He dreaded to think what he'd done to her. Her composure was remarkable. *Shock*, thought Black. She was in shock.

They both were sitting in the living room, on separate chairs, each facing the unconscious figure of Lincoln, who was slumped forward. His hands and feet were bound by rope – the same rope he'd used on Tricia. The tape had been removed from his mouth. Black had made an effort to bring the room into a little order. He'd replaced the ornaments which hadn't smashed, replaced the books. Cleared away the broken glass.

She'd made them both coffee. Now, she stared at Lincoln, pale, hollow-eyed.

She suddenly spoke. "What the hell is going on, Adam?"

Black sipped his coffee. On a table beside him was Lincoln's mobile phone. Resting beside it, the Glock, complete with silencer. A world away from legal issues and private clients and all things normal. She'd been thrust into Black's world. Where innocents died and people's lives were ruined. Where violence and carnage were the norm.

"The man before you is an assassin. He calls himself Lincoln. He was paid to kill me."

She remained motionless, wide-eyed, focused, hanging on every syllable. Black continued.

"Remember my friend who'd died? Gilbert Bartholomew? Turns out I didn't know him, but he knew me. He reached out from the grave. He bequeathed me his estate. Which turned out to be nothing. Except a video. A group of men, hidden in masks, abusing a child. Very powerful men. Bartholomew thought these same men may have orchestrated the kidnapping of his daughter. Bartholomew wanted me to take it further than he was able. He was killed for his efforts. He wanted me to finish what he'd started. Destroy the paedophile ring and try to find his daughter."

"And this man Lincoln...?"

"He works for them."

She gazed at Lincoln, fascinated.

"Who are they?"

Lincoln suddenly stirred.

"Maybe we'll find out," said Black.

"Why do they want to kill you?"

"Because they know I'm close. Because they're scared." He gave Tricia a small, sad smile. "And you got caught in the crossfire."

Black waited. Tricia did not respond.

"This can stop now," he said. "We can bring in the police. Let them deal with it."

She turned slowly to Black. "A child?"

Black nodded. "About six years old."

"What will the police do?"

"The people involved are rich and powerful. I suspect powerful enough to influence the police."

"I understand." She swivelled her gaze back to Lincoln. "Let's hear what he has to say."

Lincoln's eyes cracked open to slits; he shook his head, as if to shrug off drowsiness. He licked his lips with the tip of his tongue. He swallowed, bringing up a rumbling cough. He cleared his throat, opening his eyes wide. He examined his surroundings, flicking his gaze from Black to Tricia, then back to Black. Focusing. Calculating.

"I'm in pain," he said.

"You should be," replied Black. "I broke your arm. The bone's poking through your skin. And there's a puncture wound in your shoulder. A deep one. You'll die soon, through loss of blood. Unless we get you to a doctor."

"What you've done to me is... unsociable."

"We were never really sociable, you and I."

"True." Lincoln looked at Tricia. "And how are you? Not too traumatised, I hope."

Tricia remained motionless.

"You don't need to worry about that now," said Black. "You have more important matters to think about. Like telling us about the people you work for."

"I'm trapped. I'm at your mercy. How will you deal with me?"

"We haven't decided. We'll think about that after you've answered our questions."

"Can I have a drink of water?"

"No."

Lincoln took a deep, shuddering breath, followed by another rattling cough. Seconds passed. Eventually he spoke.

"I don't know anything. Except this. The people who hired me won't give up until you're both dead in the ground with your throats slit."

Tricia bit her bottom lip, fighting back tears.

Black nodded slowly. "I thought you might say something along those lines. It's a failure to appreciate the sheer hopelessness of your situation. And I understand that. Have you ever been tortured, Mr Lincoln?"

Lincoln tilted his head back, regarding Black with a glittering gaze. He didn't reply.

"I'll take that as a no. I have. By real experts. There's mental torture. And there's the physical side. No matter what people tell you, the physical bit is much worse."

Black turned to Tricia. "Do you want to leave the room?"

"I'll stay."

"Fair enough."

On the floor beside his chair was a set of gardening secateurs. Heavy duty. Rusty but effective. Black had discovered them in the barn. He picked them up, and made a show of displaying them before Lincoln.

"Sometimes the simple ways are the best." Black glanced at Tricia. "This might make a mess of your carpet."

Tricia remained fixed on Lincoln. If anything, her gaze had intensified. She clutched the corner of a cushion with one hand. "Do what you have to do," she said, her voice tight.

"Looks like I've got free rein. Lucky me." He stood, looming over Lincoln. "Who do you work for?"

Lincoln stared up at Black, eyes wide, shining. "You can't be serious. You're not going to do anything. It's not your nature."

"I'm afraid you've misjudged me, Mr Lincoln. I can be quite a ruthless bastard when pushed. And you've done a lot of pushing, old friend. Now here's the thing. There's an art to torturing. Normally, if we're going to partake in a little cutting, then the accepted route is to remove the digits first, then concentrate on the more vital areas. So, toes and fingers. Then ears. And so forth – the idea being, that you work up slowly to the really bad bit, hoping the victim talks before the really bad bit happens. That way, there's less chance of a quick death, more chance of information being extracted. You get the picture. But I'm not a devotee of that method. I prefer not to fuck about. I go straight to the bad bit."

Black reached down, unbuckled Lincoln's trousers, pulled them down. Then his underwear.

"If you don't start talking, I am going to cut your fucking balls off. With these rusted garden shears. They're not very sharp, but I think, with a bit of tugging and pulling, they'll do the trick. What do you say?"

The blood had drained from Lincoln's face. He stared at Black, cheekbones harsh under his skin, eyes suddenly frantic.

"You're fucking with me."

"I'm not. But these will be."

He stooped down, positioned the open blades around his testicles, and gently squeezed.

"Jesus fucking Christ!" sobbed Lincoln. "Stop! I'll tell you!"

Black stepped back.

"We're all ears."

Lincoln swallowed, taking short shallow breaths. "You're a cunt, Black."

"I've heard worse. Now talk."

"I'm given instructions via email. Password secured. A man called Norman Sands. He's my contact."

"Who's Norman Sands?"

"American. Based in Arizona. He's not the main player. He gets orders, then contacts me."

"Arizona? Why the hell would a guy from Arizona hire someone to kill me?"

Lincoln said nothing, blinking sweat from his eyes.

Black loomed forward again.

Lincoln stared at Black, ashen-faced. "There's a bigger picture," he gasped. "The whole thing is run from Arizona."

"The whole thing?"

"It's a fucking industry! A fucking conveyor belt. The items are taken there, from all over, then sold on. Auctioned out. It's big business."

Black was silent for a spell, grappling with the concept. "And what precisely are those items?"

Lincoln bowed his head, staring at the ground. "You know," he muttered.

"Tell us."

"Children."

"What's the connection?"

Lincoln raised his head, eyes glazed. "What?"

He was slipping. Black slapped him across the face.

"Concentrate. What's the connection between the paedophile ring in Scotland, and Arizona."

"I can only guess."

"Then fucking guess."

"Arizona supplies them. Fresh meat. Once tasted, it never leaves you. So I've heard."

"Give me names. The Scottish ring. Who's in it? Does the name Donald Rutherford mean anything?"

Lincoln shook his head. "Only one name I've heard of. He organises things. Liaises between the UK and Arizona."

"Who?"

"The Grey Prince."

Black produced a wallet from his pocket, took out the photograph of Natalie Bartholomew. It was a long shot, but he had to try. "Have you seen this little girl?"

Lincoln twitched his head. "I only get asked to clean up. If there's a problem, then whoever has it gives it to Arizona to deal with. Two-way arrangement. Arizona get well paid for supply, but they take care of the problems which come with it. I'm the problem solver. That's why they do so well." He gave a ghastly smile. "Each child comes with a warranty."

Black swallowed back his disgust. He needed to move fast before Lincoln passed out. "You can contact them on your mobile?"

"Of course."

"How do I email them?"

Lincoln gave him a set of digits for access to the phone, then a password. "I need a doctor." His speech was slurred. "I'm only doing a job. You of all people should understand that."

"Of course I should. But this is not my decision." He turned to Tricia. She responded with an almost imperceptible shake of her head. "No doctor today," said Black.

Lincoln's head drooped. He faded into unconsciousness. His top was soaked in blood. It was dripping onto the carpet. He was dying.

Black sat down. "What do you want to do?"

Tricia didn't answer him immediately.

Then she said, "No one saw him come here."

Black waited.

"I can bury him round the back. No one will know. Except you and me."

She turned slowly to face Black. Her eyes were far away.

"I have a son. If he'd been taken..." Her voice trailed off. Then she said, "These kids have got no one. Except you. The people that do these things, they need to pay for what they've done. Can you make them pay, Adam?"

"I can. With interest."

"Then kill them all."

"Gladly. And Lincoln?"

"He's mine. Leave him here."

"I understand. For what it's worth, I'm sorry."

She didn't reply, her attention back to the slouched figure of Lincoln.

Black took the pistol, the mobile phone, and left.

They would all pay. With interest.

47

Lampton watched from his desk. This was on him. If anything fucked up, it became his problem. He watched the monitors on the wall in front of him with rapt attention, nerves jangling. The auction was underway. He watched, aware that others watched with him. Live feed to all over the world. Concealed video cameras placed on each corner of their bedrooms. Plus, miniature cameras inserted in the eyes of some of the soft toys. The kids completely unaware. They acted as he expected. As they always acted. Diffident, unsmiling, distracted. Who could really blame them? he thought.

Falconer wanted smiles and skipping, but he was a fucking fool. It never happened, never would. What he did not want was tears. Lampton could manage that. He had warned them. His threat was clear and uncompromising – if they cried, he would carry them to his back room, chop them up, fry them in a hot pan, and eat them. Or maybe eat them while they kicked and struggled. Eat them alive.

His eyes strayed to monitor 9. His special one. The girl he was promised. She was sitting on a large beanbag, watching a cartoon on television. He allowed his mind to wander. The things he would do.

The games they would play.

~

Falconer and Sands were not watching the children. Their attention was fixed on other related matters, of a financial nature. In particular, the bidding. Their monitors were of an entirely different sort. Numbers, details, bank accounts, names. The auction had been live for a half hour. People from every corner of the globe were bidding. A new contingent from Afghanistan, with money to burn. America, Australia, Europe. Middle East, Russia. Falconer didn't care where the funds came from, provided they came to him. Ultimately, the money was transferred to an account he had in Grand Cayman. Where the bank charges were high, but no one asked questions, and secrecy was paramount.

Four items were being sold. No. 6 was causing a frenzy, as Falconer had expected. Because of her age. The younger the better.

"Fuck me," he muttered, as No. 6 reached $16,000,000. From a group based in Russia. A quartet of oligarchs. Falconer watched, mesmerised. His eyes shone, reflecting the glare of the screen. The figure changed before his eyes. In a second, it increased by a million dollars.

Falconer relaxed back on his leather couch, enjoying the moment. The bidding would stop in another half hour. The funds then transferred. The items would be double checked by the doctor, at a cost of $300,000, packed up, transported to their destination in two days' time. Never to be seen again. Falconer didn't dwell on such matters. It was just bad luck. For them. But if Falconer's bank balance increased, then he *really* didn't give a fuck. And his bank balance was increasing exponentially. Everything was rosy in Falconer's garden.

~

The auction was over. It was midnight. Altogether, allowing for expenses, there was net profit just over $35,000,000. A good evening. Sands was satisfied. Falconer was euphoric. They were in the conservatory at the rear of the building – a kidney-shaped glass construct, with indoor vines and colourful plants, spotted with thousands of tiny twinkling fairy lights. In the centre was a dining table with chairs round it. Falconer was sitting. Next to him was Sands, with a laptop, explaining the figures. Not that he needed to. Falconer knew to the dime how much profit he'd made. On the table was an opened bottle of chilled Dom Perignon, resting on a silver bucket of ice, with two champagne flutes.

A woman entered the room. Falconer had acquired her services from Yuma, the nearest city. Escort. Hired for the night. Paid by the hour. Falconer only fucked prostitutes. She'd leave early in the morning, chauffeur driven back to whichever shithole she came from. Sands could never understand Falconer's choice. Older, plain. Unremarkable. Falconer did not go for the glamorous. The opposite. His explanation? *The uglier they are, the more grateful they are, and they run that extra fucking mile.*

Bullshit, of course. They ran that extra mile for that extra buck. But Sands kept his thoughts to himself. He was in no position to judge. He left them both, retreating to the annex of the ranch which formed his own accommodation. A suite of three rooms – bedroom, study, bathroom. Unlike Falconer, he lived a simpler life. His needs were less material. The rooms were functional. The sizable salary he earned, he saved. The accommodation and food were all part of the package. He would retire a wealthy man. Maybe move to Canada. Breathe the clean, fresh air, and look at the mountains. Or maybe Australia, and sit on the beach, and gaze at the sea. Sands lived for his work. He would probably work until he dropped. Retirement was a lie he told himself.

He went to bed, and fell asleep almost instantly.

He was woken by the soft ping of his mobile phone. Email. He glanced at the clock. Seven am. It felt he'd slept for two seconds. He opened the email. It was one he was waiting for. From Lincoln.

Lincoln – *Black is terminated.*

Sands took a deep, exhilarating breath. A good start to the day, indeed. A problem solved. Before he had the chance to respond, he received a further email.

Lincoln – *You have an issue.*

Sands – *What.*

Lincoln – *Black knew about Arizona.*

Sands stared at the computer screen for several seconds.

Sands – *And?*

Lincoln – *He talked. Spoke to people. He knew everything. It could be trouble for both of us. I want to meet.*

Sands – *I'll get back to you.*

Sands closed the laptop.

Suddenly the morning had lost its sparkle.

48

It's the biggest killer you will ever face, gentlemen. Bigger than any army. Bigger than any disease or famine.
Its name?
Complacency.

Observation raised by Staff Sergeant to new recruits of the 22nd Regiment of the Special Air Service.

Saturday mid-afternoon. Black got the ferry back to Largs. As he waited in the boat, watching the approaching dock, he wondered what was happening back at Tricia's house. Perhaps Lincoln had already drifted on to his death. Perhaps Tricia had helped him on his way. Maybe she was burying him now, on some desolate patch of gorse and grass. Digging through the dirt with a shovel. Dragging his blood-soaked body. It was something she wanted to do on her own. Black shuddered. He had a knack for bringing desolation to those he loved and cared for. Tricia would never be the same. Through no fault of her own, she'd been thrust into his world. She'd survived. Barely. Now what? Probably months of nightmares and panic attacks. Depression. All down to him.

His resolve hardened. They'd tried to kill him. Tried to destroy a person he cared for. It was only fair that he should balance the account.

His shoulder ached. The wounds on his ribs and leg would leave scars. But he already had plenty, he thought grimly. Another two in the collection wouldn't make a great deal of difference.

He disembarked. The sky was dull, overcast. The air had a tinge of rain. The Scottish summer, always short lived, was ending. He'd sent the emails to the man called Sands. The demise of Adam Black. Arizona was eight hours behind. An early wake-up call. He was expecting a response.

Black chose not to return to the hotel in Livingstone. There was no need. There was nothing there for him to return to. Instead he headed for Glasgow. His flat was possibly compromised. They might still be watching, despite his message, though he suspected not. Still, better to be cautious.

He booked into the Glasgow Hilton Grosvenor, tucked away in the west end, just off Byres Road. An unobtrusive building, accessed by a single lane. One of the busiest areas in Glasgow. Students, tourists, university staff, shoppers. It was always bustling. A good place for him to blend in and disappear. Five hundred yards from the main university building. A castle-like structure straight from Camelot, with turrets, towers, high arched entrances, lofty halls. Open to the public, Black sat on a bench inside the university grounds, looking on to a grass section enclosed by ancient stone cloisters the colour of autumn leaves. It was approaching late afternoon. The place exuded a brooding quality. Black had not attended this university when he graduated. He'd gone to Edinburgh. He had done so grudgingly. His ambition was to join the army the moment he left school. The hankering had been with him since the day his older brother, a Royal Marine, was killed by a road bomb in Ireland. But his father had pushed him towards academia, and he'd acquiesced. Pushed him, because a father wouldn't want to see two sons killed. Black, on reflection, could understand. His father had died before he'd graduated. Cancer. The same bastard illness which had taken his mother when Black was a child. Perhaps, had his father lived, things would have turned out differently. It was idle to speculate.

Now Black was alone, with his grief, his guilt. Dead bodies all around. Anyone who got close ended up dead. Perhaps he should shut himself off from humanity. But then who would kill the bad guys?

A group of students walked by him, laughing. No cares. Black felt a momentary twinge of envy. He'd forgotten the last time he'd laughed like that. A lifetime ago.

Black roused himself from his reverie. These periods of melancholy were becoming more frequent. He couldn't afford such self-indulgence. He had to think. He had to function. Rutherford had said the next meeting was Monday evening. Two days away. Black had a hunch. Rutherford had no idea where the group were to rendezvous. Now that Rutherford was dead, the individual referred to as the Grey Prince would have no need to communicate with him. A hunch was all Black had. If he was wrong, then he had nothing to go on. Plus, he was waiting for communication from a man called Sands, from Arizona.

Black got up. In one pocket he had Lincoln's mobile. In the other he carried Lincoln's Glock. In his hotel room, he had placed the Walther in the safe. In his car, in the boot, was a holdall with two Desert Eagles. He wasn't a man at all, he thought ruefully. He was a walking fucking arsenal. Better to have too many guns than too little. He walked back out of the university grounds, under a broad and intricate archway. He had things to do. He had preparations to make.

If his hunch played out, it was fancy dress time.

49

Sands got the message, but was in a state of indecision. Which was unlike him. They'd had a great evening. Never better. Incredible profits. Boyd Falconer had spent the night fucking one of his hookers. This morning he would be mellow, relaxed. Sands did not relish the prospect of altering the equilibrium. Falconer had a vicious, unpredictable temper.

Sands debated – should he tell him later, and allow the tranquillity to remain a little longer? Or tell him now, and ruin his morning. The answer was simple. Tell him immediately. If Falconer discovered he'd held on to this information, then not only would Falconer be irate, but he'd blame Sands for it.

It was 7.15. Sands quickly showered, changed, made his way through to the main building. Falconer was probably up already. He was, in the gym. On the cycling machine, hunched over, tanned legs pumping up and down, towel round his neck, T-shirt soaked in sweat. Going at it hard. *Not bad for a man over sixty-five*, thought Sands.

The woman was gone, of that Sands was sure. Bundled off early. Falconer would have no desire to make small talk with her in the early morning. Sands stood, laptop in hand. Sands rarely went anywhere without it.

Falconer raised his head, allowing him a cursory glance, then dipped his head back down, concentrating on computer read outs in the screen in front of him – speed, distance, heartbeat.

"We had a fucking good night," said Falconer, between breaths.

Sands nodded.

Falconer flicked another look at him. "But... I can tell by your face there's a but. There's always a but when you're about, Sands. Especially when you've got that machine at your side, like a fucking dick up your ass."

"Good news and bad news."

"Jesus H fucking Christ. Can't you just tell me, and stop fucking about."

"The good news – Adam Black is dead. Lincoln has just sent me the confirmation."

"Hallelujah," grunted Falconer, as he suddenly increased his speed. "Vengeance is mine, saith the Lord. That's what he gets for fucking with Boyd Falconer. Make sure Mr Lincoln gets the rest of his money."

Sands cleared his throat.

"That's half the story."

Falconer didn't say anything, just kept pedalling.

"Before Black died, he talked. He said he knew about us. Apparently other people might also. Lincoln's worried. He wants to meet."

Falconer increased the speed for ten seconds, then slowed, then stopped. He was breathing heavily. Always, when he'd finished a session, his breath was tinged with a whisper of a wheeze. The curse of asthma.

Falconer dismounted from the saddle, dabbing his face with

the towel. He got an energy drink from a glass doored chiller. He turned to Sands.

"What the fuck does this mean?"

"I don't know. I don't think he wants to give details via email."

"You're a fucking genius, Sands."

He left the gym. The one thing about Falconer was that he never showered straight after a training session. He liked the smell of his own sweat. Liked to wallow in it. It made Sands feel like puking. A downside of the job, but one he tolerated. Barely.

Sands followed him into the spacious living room. Falconer sat on the leather suite, towel wrapped round his neck. The sun was bright, as it always was. The air con was on. Had to be. It was early morning, but it would be scorching outside in the desert heat.

"Am I hosting some fucking criminal's convention?" said Falconer. This, of course, was a rhetorical question. Sands took a deep breath, letting this play out.

"We have the fucking Japanese coming on Tuesday," he continued. "The biggest fucking paedophile in the eastern hemisphere. Now a fucking assassin wants to come and visit. Am I running a hotel for the freaks of this world?"

Still rhetorical.

Sands waited.

"This is not right," muttered Falconer. "I've been at this game for fifteen years. Now this." He snapped his head towards Sands. "We survive because we're secret. Otherwise we're fucked."

Sands decided to venture a comment. "Therein lies the problem." He didn't want to say this, because the mere thought of it terrified him. Life imprisonment in a state penitentiary. "Maybe it's no longer a secret. Maybe people know about your operation."

"You know, if I wanted to employ a fucking baboon to state the obvious, then I'd employ a fucking baboon."

Falconer suddenly got up, and paced up and down the room, sweat dripping on his expensive rugs. "The merchandise gets shipped out on Wednesday?"

Sands nodded. By merchandise, Falconer was of course referring to the kids sold at last night's auction. Each to their specific purchaser.

"I have to think about this," said Falconer. "How the fuck would Black know about us? It is not fucking possible."

"Someone talked?"

"No one talked. No one knows anything to talk about. Black was bluffing. Probably to buy more time." There was uncertainty in his voice.

"Maybe. Can we take the chance?" Falconer stared at the glass wall, at the expanse of desert stretching forever. "No one knows about us."

"The Japanese knows which airport he's going to get picked up at."

"So? That's all he knows. We're a 200-mile drive from there. And anyway, how the hell would Adam Black know about our Japanese billionaire?"

"What about the Grey Prince," said Sands. "He knows everything."

"It can't be him," replied Sands, his voice suddenly soft. "That's not possible."

"We can't take the risk. We should get Lincoln here, find out what Black told him. As a precaution."

"It can't be him," repeated Falconer. "Just can't be."

50

_____

Black kept the Mini in the hotel car park. He couldn't risk driving it. If it were recognised, then game over. Instead, he hired a car. The choice was important. Black had to gauge this. It had to look good, but not stand out. Expensive, but not ostentatious. Black wanted to be invisible. He chose a BMW 5 series. Dark blue, two-litre engine. Common enough not to attract attention. Suitably expensive enough to blend in with the cars driven by the people he might meet that evening.

It was Monday morning, early. Black had breakfast in the hotel. He wasn't hungry, particularly. His stomach fluttered with nerves. His hunch might not pay off. On the other hand, it might. And if he were caught, then his fate was unimaginable. He was dealing with powerful people. Men of considerable influence. They could make him disappear, as if he'd never existed. Erase him from the planet. Black had been trained not to get caught. By the very best in the world. Though he doubted even his trainers in the Special Air Service could have anticipated the scenario he might confront. Black had faced death before. On the battlefield, on the streets. But this was altogether different. This was another world. Surreal, almost. And deadly.

~

He took a swim in the hotel pool after breakfast. Then a spell in the small gymnasium, running 5k on the treadmill. He could still do it under twenty minutes. Then some weights. After that, a sauna, a shower, then back to his room, where he changed into clothes he'd bought the day before. White shirt, dark suit, fairly loose fitting. His other acquisition was a little more exotic – a nylon shoulder holster, purchased from an army surplus store at the Barras market in Gallowgate, in the opposite end of the city. Robust enough to carry the Glock, and even one of the Desert Eagles. Worn close to the body. At first glance, not too obtrusive. Black would equip himself later.

He went down to the hotel lounge, and sat at the bar. It was not large, the drinks extortionate. Black asked for a soda water and lime, and sipped it slowly. The place was quiet. A couple sitting at a table, not talking, reading newspapers. A man at the bar on his mobile phone. Black considered him. Middle-aged, portly. Hardly the assassin type. Still, one could never tell. The man tucked the phone in his jacket pocket, nodded at Black, and left. Black's paranoia was running overtime. Nothing new there. Black got a newspaper from a rack, tried to read it, but couldn't concentrate. It was 1pm. Before Black had fired a bullet in his head, Rutherford said it was an evening meeting. Black had time to kill.

He left the hotel, meandering through streets, wandered along the famous Ashton Lane, just off Byres Road. Cobbled narrow paving. Quaint, colourful buildings facing each other, housing expensive restaurants and bars. He stopped at an ultra-trendy coffee house, with a façade of black and crimson planks of wood, and sat outside under a soft blue awning. He ordered a coffee at triple the usual price. He watched people go by, paying them scant regard. Students, mostly. Some tourists. Time drifted. It was late afternoon. He took a deep breath. Time to go. The afternoon had dulled, the sun flickering behind drifts of cloud the colour of grey gauze. Rain was looming. The place was still busy. Black wondered if anyone ever worked in this part of the city. He headed back to the hotel, went up to his room, got himself organised. He'd parked the BMW a short walk away. He carried a gym bag. Not with gym equipment. Two Desert Eagles, a Walther PPK, boxes of cartridges. He packed the Glock in the holster, the silencer in his inside jacket pocket.

He had already picked his spot. He'd reconnoitred the previous evening. A street just off the main road, adjacent to the target's home. A good surveillance point, to watch the front entrance, but discreet.

He arrived at his destination. He parked the car, sipped from a polystyrene cup of hot coffee, switched the radio on, and waited. It might take a while, but Black had nothing but time.

It was a gamble. Black's hunch could be entirely wrong. But if he were right, and his guess correct, then the person he waited on would lead him into the stuff of nightmares.

Which meant one thing – Black would become a nightmare right back.

51

Lampton was expecting praise from Falconer, and got it. The auction had gone well. No tears, no obvious sulkiness. The kids were well behaved, if a little subdued. Lampton had no idea what type of money changed hands, though if Falconer was happy, then it was easy to surmise a good profit had been made. The biggest test was still to come.

Falconer had arrived down to see him. They were in Lampton's room. It was late morning. Falconer had come without the bean-counting freak, Sands. Lampton felt more at ease when it was one to one. Falconer, however, was not his irascible self. He seemed distracted. Preoccupied.

"You did well, Lampton. You got them all sitting up and looking good. Like ducks in a row. Easy pickings. You have a skill."

"Thank you, Mr Falconer. I aim to please."

"And No. 4? Our Japanese benefactor will be here tomorrow evening. I understand there's good news?"

"All good. No sign of measles. The doctor says she's fit and strong. It was just a heat rash, but he'll call out again, to make double sure."

"I'll bet he will," muttered Falconer. "For double money. I've made that man a fucking millionaire."

"Clean bill of health," continued Lampton.

"That's good."

"Without being presumptuous, I assume our Japanese gentleman will be taking No. 4 back with him, when he returns?"

"You are being fucking presumptuous," replied Falconer, without any real anger in his voice. "Yes, he's taking the merchandise with him on Wednesday morning. Which means he's staying over on Tuesday evening. Why the fuck do you care?"

Lampton was always faintly amused at Falconer referring to them as "merchandise" or by their allotted number. The word "child" never seemed to enter into his vocabulary.

"Well, if he intends to sample while he's here on the Tuesday, then I have to make preparations. Timescales are important."

"That will not be happening," snapped Falconer, genuinely angry. "He can see her. But there's no touching. No sampling. He does his business elsewhere. He takes it away, and does what he does. But not here."

Lampton nodded. "Of course. Sorry to have suggested such a thing, Mr Falconer. If he's leaving on Wednesday, I assume then I can have my little bonus?"

Falconer looked at him, brow creased in puzzlement. Then his face relaxed. "The merchandise from the UK? That was the deal, Lampton. It's all yours. But if there's any fuck-ups, then change of plan."

"There won't be."

"What you do with it is up to you. As long as I don't get to hear about it. And if you do what you did last time, then you clear up the mess. Don't lay it on my doorstep. Bury it in the desert. Just don't tell me. You understand that?"

"There won't be any mess to clear, Mr Falconer. This one's different."

"Different?" Falconer chuckled. "You in love?"

The sarcasm in his voice did not go unnoticed. Lampton looked away, at the monitors on the wall. Such a question did not merit a response. People like Falconer would never understand. His gaze strayed, inevitably to monitor 7. She was sitting at a miniature desk, staring at golden dolphins cut from painted cardboard suspended from the ceiling by golden thread. He had made them himself.

Falconer got up to leave.

"You're very kind to me, Mr Falconer. I don't know where I'd be without you."

Falconer stared back at Lampton.

"Probably the electric chair," he said.

Falconer got the elevator to the ground floor, the trip taking about three seconds. He went past the security guard, ignoring him, punched in the code, emerged into a hallway. To be met by Sands.

"How long have you been waiting here?" Falconer asked.

"Long enough. I've just received an email."

"And why the fuck are you telling me this?"

"It's from the Grey Prince."

Falconer waited.

"He wants to know if Adam Black is dead."

"Tell him, yes. Tell him Black is dead."

Sands nodded. "And Lincoln? We need to respond. If he's worried, then shouldn't we be worried?"

"You're a coward," spat Falconer. "Grow a pair of fucking balls, why don't you."

Sands spoke, a tremor in his voice. "What harm can it do? Bring him in and talk. At the very least, it would be nice to actually meet the man who murders for us. We've paid him plenty over the years."

"Maybe I'll ask him to murder you."

"What do we do?"

"Nothing. We wait." It was the only answer Falconer could give. The truth was, like Sands, he was worried.

But one good thing had come out of it.

Adam Black was dead.

52

Black waited in the BMW. The radio was on. He flicked from station to station, not listening to any of it. His plan was unstructured. His target might not turn up. Even if he did, his theory could be way off track, the whole thing a waste of effort.

At 5.30pm a car appeared, stopping briefly at the electric front gates, waiting for them to open. It entered, the gates closing behind, then drove slowly up the forty-yard white chip driveway, tyres crunching on the miniature stones. It parked at the front of the house. The driver did not get out immediately. From his viewpoint, Black could make out the outline of his head. Looked like he was texting. Ten minutes in his car. Then he got out, a slim briefcase in his hand, and disappeared through the front entrance.

Black drew a long breath. It was all or nothing. His entire hypothesis rested on a hunch. But it was a strong hunch. He waited, his senses cranked up to a heightened competence.

Seconds dragged by, minutes, one hour, two. *Where was the fucker?*

The front door opened. The man appeared, walked round to

the driver's door. He moved briskly. He had somewhere to go, thought Black grimly. He got in, manoeuvring the car round in a three-point turn, so it was facing back the way it had come. The electric gates opened. The car moved off, into the traffic. Black followed.

Fun time.

53

Black followed, two cars between them. He was reasonably confident he wouldn't be spotted. To these people, Adam Black was a dead man, courtesy of an email from Mr Lincoln, who by now was well and truly dead, whose body was probably rotting in the Millport countryside. *You don't expect to be followed by a dead man*, thought Black. Unless these people believed in resurrection, which he doubted.

Still, he remained vigilant. He kept the visor down. The car he was following was distinctive. Not easily lost. But he could get unlucky with the traffic lights. It drove at a moderate pace, keeping within the speed limits. The cars between them pulled off. Black was directly behind him. With the visor down, his face was hidden. He could see the back of the driver's head.

They were moving out of Glasgow, heading for the motor-way, south. After twenty minutes, they merged on to the M74. Black kept his distance, allowing cars in between. They stuck to the slow lane, staying just under 60mph. Thirty minutes passed, forty. They passed turn-offs for East Kilbride, Motherwell, Larkhall. Black's old stomping ground, when he was a boy. Fleeting memories flashed through his mind. Childhood friendships. He wondered occasionally about his school friends, how they turned out. None of them like him, he wagered. None of them killers.

They kept going. They approached the turn-off for Lesmahagow, west. A place somewhere between a village and a town, a couple of miles from the motorway, perched on the edge of moorland. Black slowed, keeping well back.

What the fuck is he doing here? A remote place. Isolated. Black rethought – probably a good choice, given the events about to unfold. If Black's hunch proved true.

They passed the sign for Lesmahagow. After three miles, the road narrowed, high hedgerows on either side, beyond which were fields and woods. Black kept a good distance behind, nerves stretched. On a road like this, if he were vigilant, the driver in front might sense he was being tailed. But then not everyone shared Black's paranoia.

The miles wore on, another twelve, heading further west, heading into Ayrshire. They passed a sign for Cumnock. The car in front slowed, put on its indicator, turned sharp left, up what appeared to be a single lane. Black approached a sign – Westcoates Hall. Private. Black waited a minute, then followed, turning his lights off. It was getting dark. Black drove slowly. The road was wide enough for one car, with passing places every two hundred yards. Low dry-stone walls on either side. Beyond, the gloom of woods.

After half a mile, Black slowed right down. The road led to a house, in the distance. More of a country mansion, the windows ablaze with lights. Cars were parked in a courtyard to one side. The road in was gated, the gates open, two men standing, watching. Guards. More men milling about the courtyard. Security was tight. Important people were attending, thought Black grimly.

Black stopped the car. He could go no further. He reversed,

reaching a gap in the wall, beyond which was a cluster of trees. He manoeuvred his car through the gap, onto rough grass, and into the shadows. Black got out, retrieving the gym bag, and made his way to the house.

The woods stretched along one side of the road, a long sweep of darkness, stretching down to the building, skirting along a boundary wall, then continuing on. Black made his way towards the house, hugging the wall, invisible in the shadows. A car passed – a silver Range Rover. It swept past him. Black ducked. The car drove on, stopping at the gates, one of the guards talking to the driver, then pointing to a specific space in the courtyard. The Range Rover drove through. The men talked into handsets, closed the gates. The party was to begin soon, assumed Black.

Black increased his pace, though the going was slow. The ground was uneven. Easy to suffer a twisted ankle. Black eventually reached the side of the house – the woods pressed up close to the waist-high boundary wall. The building was huge, two storeys, with a third attic level, judging by the row of dormer windows. To one side was a large glass conservatory, curtained off. There was a rear wooden door, with a Gothic arch, black iron hinges. Two men were standing at it, talking quietly, smoking. They were dressed smartly, dark suits, white shirts. Tall, well built. They were sharing a joke. Laughing. The distance between the boundary wall and the door was about thirty yards, with nothing in between except a concrete space. Suddenly the lights went out, not individually, but as one – with the exception of the conservatory, where soft light flickered behind the drapes.

Black required to gain entry. A third man appeared, sauntering round the corner from the front, walking towards them. He stopped, and struck up a conversation with the two men. Now three. Black waited, hunkered behind the stone wall, nerves taut. He looked over – the third man was walking on.

Presumably patrolling the building. There would be other men, no doubt. Black waited twenty more seconds. One of the men knocked on the door. It opened. He said something to someone, disappeared inside. Now one man.

Black had an idea. He crept further down, fifty yards, slipped over the wall, crouching low. He pulled out the Glock, clicked on the silencer. He opened the bag, took out one of the Desert Eagles, and placed it in the shoulder holster. He looked over at the man at the door. His back was turned. Black stood, and strolled towards him, one hand close at his side, holding the Glock. The man looked round, frowning. It was dark. Black raised a hand, waving. The man waved back, uncertain. Black approached, casual.

Ten yards.

"Who the fuck..." started the man, drawing a pistol from an inside pocket of his jacket. Black was first. He raised the Glock, firing as he walked. Once. Twice. A bullet in the throat, one in the chest. Hardly any sound at all. The man bounced back, on to the ground, groaning. Black ran forward – fired a third into his head. Clock was ticking. Suddenly every second was crucial. He knocked on the door. A bolt slid back. It opened. A man stared, face frozen in bewilderment as he stared into the barrel of Black's Glock. Black fired an inch above his eye. The top of his head was a sudden froth of hair, blood and bone. Another man behind him, spattered in his friend's blood. Black used the two seconds of shock. He shoved the door open, firing. The third man dropped, dead before he could think about it, brains scattered on the ceiling.

In less than ten seconds, Black had killed three men.

He dragged in the first man, bundling him on top of the others. He closed the door gently. Their absence would be noted. If there were two guards patrolling clockwise and counterclockwise, Black reckoned he might have five minutes. Maybe a couple more as they tried to figure out what was going on.

Black slid the bolt back in place. He turned. He was in a bare narrow hall – cluttered with bodies – and at the far end was a closed door. Black moved. He opened the door, emerging into a large kitchen. It was semi-dark, the light from the hall giving some illumination. A stainless-steel island worktop in the middle, ovens, microwaves, metal shelves, units, hobs. A commercial kitchen. Black guessed the building was hired out, for wedding functions, parties, special occasions. And much darker activities.

He crept through, a shadow, Glock in one hand, the hard weight of the Desert Eagle resting in its holster, pressing against his ribs, providing a modicum of reassurance. The Glock held fifteen rounds. Ten left. Enough for considerable damage. He passed through double swing doors, into another short corridor, another door. Locked. The place was well fortified. An essential requirement, given its use. Black knocked on the door, softly, heart in mouth, nerves tingling. He had no idea what to expect.

A bolt clicked, the door opened six inches. Black held the Glock waist height, fired twice into the recipient's midriff. He heard a gasp. He pushed the door wide. Another corridor, a door on either side, one at the far end. A man was on the floor, writhing, clutching his stomach. Too bad. Black shot once more, the man suddenly still. He wore a mask. More specifically a silver Venetian mask, the type perhaps used in a masquerade, covering most of the face.

Black removed it, put it on. He was approaching the inner sanctum. His mouth was dry. Music drifted from beyond the far door. Faint laughter. Black got to the door, turned the handle, pushed. This time unlocked.

And entered into hell.

54

A spacious hall, thick lush carpets, vaulted ceiling. Opposite, the main entrance at the front of the building, comprising double stained-glass doors, two men standing on either side, wearing masks similar to Black's. On Black's right, a passageway into other rooms, too dark to make out. To Black's left, a wide arched opening, the entrance to a glass walled passage, and beyond that, the conservatory.

The lights were off. Instead, illumination was served by candles. Hundreds. Placed on holders on the floor, lining the hall, the passage. Candles placed on furniture, candles flickering from brackets on the walls. Candles on an intricate candelabra above his head. Black felt like he'd stumbled into some ghostly subterranean world, devoid of daylight, inhabited by monsters. Heavy drapes covered the windows. There were five men altogether, including the two at the entrance, all with masks. A third stood close to the door through which Black had entered. Another two standing on either side of the entrance way to the conservatory. All wearing dark suits, muscular. Paid for their lethal competence, thought Black. And their silence.

One of the men nodded to Black, who nodded back. Black

stepped to one side. Now, from his position, he could see into a section of the conservatory. People sat on couches, chairs. Men. Talking quietly. Wearing long blue gowns. Wearing ornate Venetian masks, their faces hidden. Just like the video. Black waited, acutely aware time was running out. Any moment, the bodies would be discovered. Then sheer carnage. Black hardly dared to breathe, senses sharpened to a point. Music played, classical. Piano, violins. Recognisable, but Black couldn't put a name to it. Suddenly a gong chimed, a soft echo from the opposite rooms, to Black's right. The conversation stopped. The gong sounded again. Complete silence, save the guttering of a thousand candles.

A man emerged from the darkness. Wearing a soft red-velvet gown, trailing down to the ground. He walked solemnly, looking straight ahead, paying no regard to the guards on either side. He wore a full face mask delicately designed with swirling patterns of white and gold. Black froze. Behind him, heads bowed, followed two children. A boy and girl. No older than nine. Wearing white smocks down to their knees. Arms stiff, rigid at their sides. Faces pinched and pale, wraith-like in the strange shadows of the room. Behind them, another man, same trailing gown, ornate face mask.

They walked slowly past, a sinister procession. The children were trying not to cry. Black watched them go by. A sudden, powerful, raw emotion consumed him, like fire through his veins.

Pure red rage.

The procession made its slow sombre way out the hall, through the glass corridor, into the conservatory. Drapes were drawn, blocking Black's view. A silence followed, heavy, portentous. Twenty heartbeats. A scream cut the silence – the little girl.

Black moved.

55

Black had his hands clasped behind his back, holding the Glock. He brought his hand forward and up, and shot the man next to him in the side of the head, close range, almost execution style. The man slumped to the ground, blood bursting out like a geyser. The other four men saw it happen, but shock made them hesitate. It was all Black needed.

He crouched, fired twice – two clean hits into the chests of the men at the door. Not kill shots. But the torso was an easier target. The remaining two – the men at either side of the drawn drapes – wakened into action, drawing pistols from shoulder holsters under their jackets. But their jackets were tight and buttoned. They were unprepared. Black performed a forward roll into the centre of the hall, finishing on his feet in a semi-crouch, fired twice. Both men fell, still fumbling for their weapons.

Five men down. Black strode over to the front door, loomed over the two fallen men. The Glock coughed twice. The same treatment for the men at the drapes. Just to be sure. Basic training of the Special Services – when you shoot someone, make sure you kill the fucker. Nine shots, nine whispers in the night. The Glock was out of rounds. Black drew out the Desert Eagle, a motherfucker of a gun, placed the Glock back in the holster. He remained taut and still. Men's voices from behind the drapes, laughing. Black swallowed back nausea.

Time was drifting away. He swept aside the drapes.

And confronted evil.

56

A recollection, vivid beyond all others, remained with Black, to haunt him all the days of his life – a room glowing with a hundred candles; ten men, sitting on couches, chairs, divans, naked save for glittering complicated face masks; two children, kneeling in the centre of the room, bowed heads, stripped of their clothing, trembling with terror.

Ten masked faces jerked round. The children did not look up, kept their eyes fixed on the floor. Black faced the men, the formidable Desert Eagle held in both hands, moving it in a slow sweep about the room.

"Good evening, gentlemen. Hope I'm not intruding."

The men didn't move, transfixed by the dramatic change of events.

"If you please, take off your masks."

None of them moved.

Black nodded. Encouragement was required. "I understand your reticence. Let me help."

He shot the man closest to him, straight in the face. The force propelled the chair he sat on back off its legs. Without a silencer, the noise was like a cannon firing, amplified by the confines of the room. The two children screamed, jolted round to stare up at Black. If the men patrolling outside didn't know there was a problem, they knew now.

The group, almost in perfect unison, removed their masks.

"The Desert Eagle can be persuasive," said Black. He nodded at a fat, bald man, head shimmering with sweat.

"Hello, first minister. Unlucky, tonight. Kids – what are your names?"

The children stared, glassy-eyed.

"Your names!"

They snapped out of their trance.

"Alanna," stammered the girl.

"Paul," whispered the boy.

"Over here, beside me. I'm getting you out of this shithole."

They didn't move. Terrified. A noise behind him. The front door rattling. Men trying to gain entry. They'd be here in seconds, guns blazing.

"Over here! Now!"

The two children jumped to their feet, grabbing up their clothing, and scrambled over to stand next to him.

He gazed round the room, at the faces looking back. Some he recognised – there, the chief constable. And there – the man he had followed that evening. He glared at Black, lip curled in anger. No fear there. Sheer, undiluted hatred.

"It's been a pleasure, gentlemen."

He picked up a tall bronze stand holding a tray of ten candles. He flung it over to the heavy velvet drapes at the windows. In a second, they caught fire. Black knocked over a side table, laden with more candles, a seat catching fire, the carpet suddenly alive with flame. One of the men jumped up. Black shot him in the neck. He emitted a gargled scream, staggering across the floor, bumping over more tables on his path, creating fire in other pockets of the room.

Black retreated, slowly, one step at a time, the children cowering behind his legs. The room was ablaze, the drapes catching quickly, forming a wall of fire around them. If any tried to get past Black, they were only too aware he would shoot them without compunction.

"We're going to burn!" cried a man. Black recognised him vaguely. A television soap star. Or something of the sort. Black couldn't have cared less.

Black removed his own mask, tossing it into the flames. "I fucking hope so."

Black reached the glass corridor, amazed at how rapidly the fire had taken hold. The men were screaming, shouting, pleading. Some had flames licking from their hair, lurching about, human fireballs. It was either fire or Black's bullets. Another tried to rush past him. Black shot him in the gut. The screams played second fiddle to the crackle of furniture and flesh.

Black got to the hall. He'd seen enough. The children clutched either side of his jacket. The front door crashed open. Black spun round. Two men entered, one tripping over the dead bodies.

Boom! Boom! The cannon explosion of the Desert Eagle echoed through the hall. The first man was literally taken off his feet, the impact bouncing him onto the wall, half his chest eviscerated. The second was luckier, the bullet removing the lower half of his arm.

Time to go. The fire had taken hold of the drapes at the hall, spreading across the carpet. Glass panes were exploding in the heat. More men at the front door, beaten back by the flames. Also wary of more bullets.

Definitely time to go.

57

B lack went out the way he'd come in. The children followed close behind. On his way, he encountered a man heading towards him, running full pelt through the kitchen. Black didn't hesitate. He fired once, the Desert Eagle blasting. The man bounced off his feet, half somersaulting over the cooking island in the middle of the room. Black didn't stop. They reached the back door. No one was there. They're busy at the front, thought Black. Death and destruction were a welcome distraction. For a little while. He turned to the children. They were still naked, clutching the white gowns they'd been given.

"Put them on," said Black, speaking quickly. "We're going to get out of here. But we have to be fast. We're going to run to the little wall." He pointed at it. It was visible in the darkness, illuminated by the flames consuming one end of the building. "We climb over it, then we keep running. No one will see us. We'll be hidden by the trees. Your feet might hurt when you're running on the ground, but there's nothing I can do about that. Don't make a sound. You understand?"

They nodded, gazing up at Black. He attempted a half-smile.

"Quick!"

They pulled the garments over their heads. Black raised the Eagle, vigilant. The way was clear. They darted across the open space, reached the wall. Black helped them over. They were virtually invisible, hidden by the shadows and trees.

Black walked quickly, half crouching, using the wall as cover. The two children followed closely, remaining silent. A man ran past them, only yards from the wall, a rifle in his hand, speaking urgently into a mouthpiece. Black stopped. The man ran on, towards the commotion at the far end. Black motioned for the children to keep moving.

The going was slow. It was dark, the ground uneven. The path they walked was narrow, a margin of grass and bushes between the trees and the wall. Once, the boy let out a short whimper – he'd stood on a sharp stone. He began to limp. Black tucked the Eagle in the belt of his trousers, reached down, picked him up, cradling him against his chest. The boy huddled into a ball, keeping close.

Time passed. Every step meant a step further from danger. Further from death. There! A silhouette thirty yards distant. The BMW. Black gently put the boy on his feet, motioned them to stay put. He crept closer – the car may have been found, and guards posted. All clear. Black scurried back, ushered the children forward. They got to the car. For one nerve-wracking second, Black thought he'd left the car key in the holdall, abandoned at the building. The second passed. It was in an inside zip jacket pocket. Black pressed a button, the doors unlocked. The two children climbed into the rear seats. Black looked back. The fire had taken hold. With fury. The roof was ablaze, fire flickering from every window. Black saw distant shapes of men running this way and that, like frantic ants. Westcoates Hall was no more.

Amen to that, thought Black. *May they all burn in hell.*

He got in the car. Slowly, he manoeuvred out through the

gap in the wall, keeping his headlights off. He drove slowly. Soon, the image of the burning building disappeared from his rear-view mirror, swallowed up by hills and trees. He got to the main road, which would eventually take him to the motorway.

"Where are you from?" asked Black. They didn't reply. Who could blame them? He adjusted the mirror, so he could see their faces. Two pale orbs. They stared back at him in the mirror. "Are you from Scotland?"

The girl spoke. "Please don't hurt us."

Black had to grit his teeth. He hoped every last fucker in that place felt the lick of the flame.

"No more hurting. That's over now. You're safe. Where are you from?"

The boy spoke. "York. Are you taking us home?"

"You'll be home soon."

"I'm from Ireland," said Alanna. "Dublin." She paused. "We were put on a plane. To a hot place. In a room under the ground. With a monster." She began to cry.

"What's your name?" asked Paul.

Black looked at him in the mirror, and smiled. "Adam Black."

"Thank you, Mr Black."

He got to the motorway, and took a turn-off for Airdrie. The hospital there was Monklands General. A sprawling building designed by architects specialising in ugliness.

He parked the car close to the main entrance of accident and emergency. He took them in, Paul on one side, Alanna, the other. Each holding his hand. A large waiting room, with only a handful of people. Black knocked on the window of the receptionist.

"Get a doctor here now," said Black. "Two children – traumatised."

"Your name," she replied, barely looking up, her tone dismissive.

Black rapped the glass hard. She jerked her head up, met Black's cold gaze.

"Two children. Abducted and abused. They need help. Right fucking now. So, no fucking about. And call the police while you're at it."

Black knelt down, took the two children in his arms, hugged them close.

"You're safe now," he said in a soft voice. "Tell the doctor everything. You'll be going home soon."

He stood. A doctor emerged, together with a hospital orderly. A young man, in his twenties, no older.

"What's going on here?"

"This is Paul and Alanna. They were abducted by paedophiles. I managed to free them. They need medical attention. Call the police."

"And who are you?"

"A friend. I'll be back in a moment."

Black left the building. He turned briefly. They were being led away by the doctor. Alanna turned, and gave a tiny wave.

Black got to his car. He checked the mobile phone he'd left in the compartment between the front seats. Lincoln's phone. An email, just in.

We'll meet. Here. We'll send you details.

Game on.

58

The way to kill the savages? Become one.

Advice given by Staff Sergeant to new recruits of the 22nd Regiment of the Special Air Service

It would only be a matter of time before the events at Westcoates Hall hit the news. *And what fucking news*, thought Black. Doubtless, the truth would be moulded, twisted. A sanitised version for the public. Black had other things on his mind.

The instructions were clear. All by email. Once he'd told Sands he was still in Scotland, he was given a schedule. Flight from Prestwick airport to Gatwick leaving 2.30am that morning, local time. Gatwick to Phoenix Sky Harbor International, departing 4.55am. The flight was ten hours. Arrival 7am – Arizona time. He would be met at the terminal building. They would be waiting, in a black Range Rover, distinct with darkened windows. *Christ*, thought Black, *these fuckers were organised*.

Black drove back to the Hilton on Byres Road. It was

11.30pm. He was exhausted. He'd sleep on the plane. He showered, changed. His shirt was stained with the blood of his enemies. He changed into jeans, close-fitting long-sleeved vest, dark pullover, running shoes. He had left his holdall back at Westcoates Hall, with the Walther and second Desert Eagle. Plus, several boxes of cartridges. His remaining weapons were useless to him, unless airport customs had undergone a radical change of policy.

He had a visit to make, en route. His flat. To get his passport. He reckoned it was safe territory. They would no longer be watching. Adam Black was dead. Dead men don't make home visits. The weapons he did have, he would leave in his flat.

Black still had choices. He'd killed off a paedophile ring here, in Scotland. A very exclusive one. But to his mind, it was merely a tentacle. Only one snake of the hydra. What had Lincoln said? Kids are auctioned out. Arizona supplies them. One big fucking industry. A conveyor belt for the depraved.

Black considered. He really had no choice at all. Bartholomew had described him as a warrior. Black really didn't know what he was. But he knew one thing. His mind was set. He couldn't turn his back on this. He had come too far. People had to pay. Big time.

He regarded himself in the bathroom mirror. What was he? An assassin? A murderer? A vigilante? All of the above, he thought ruefully. But maybe more. Maybe, just, he was one of the good guys.

He would journey to Arizona, and take his chances. According to Lincoln, he'd never met his contact. The man called Norman Sands. Which would be logical. Lincoln would want his identity to be secret, as indeed Sands would. So maybe Black could pull it off. He would be unarmed. Not even a knife. Nothing to protect him from those who would do him harm.

Black gazed at his reflection. The man who stared back had

no choice at all. He would go, he would destroy. And if he died trying, then so be it. This was one advantage he had over all his enemies.

He wasn't scared to die. The opposite.

He hungered for it.

The visit to his flat went without incident, as he had anticipated, which reinforced his belief that they thought him dead. He dumped the guns, packed a holdall with basics. Underwear, socks, a couple of cheap T-shirts. He wasn't too concerned about fashion accessories in sunny Arizona. The flight from Prestwick was smooth and on time. He boarded the plane at Gatwick, heading for Phoenix. Economy class. Black didn't care. He'd be sleeping for most of the trip, so what the hell. He got a coffee, read a magazine, then fell asleep. The way he felt, he'd sleep anywhere. As ever, his dreams were plagued with faces, rearing up before him – Lincoln, sitting on a chair, face pale and stark; Tricia, eyes wide in fear; the two kids, Paul and Alanna, clutching his arms, terrified, shaking.

And then, as ever, his wife and daughter. Lying beside him, faces still and accusing. And Black, his hands soaked in their blood.

He woke with a start. The woman next to him was reading a newspaper. He checked his watch. They'd be landing in half an hour.

Black looked out the window. Clear skies, the great swells and contours of an American landscape stretched out beneath him. The land of the free. The land where he could end up dead.

Bring it on.

59

Falconer had made the decision to meet with the assassin, Mr Lincoln, and had instructed Sands to send the message. "We should check it out," was what he'd said. "Get it sorted."

Sands had been surprised at the sudden change. Up until that point, Falconer had been reluctant.

"I think it's prudent," Sands had replied. "What harm can it do?"

The simple fact was, suddenly it had become a matter of high priority to meet with the man called Lincoln. More than ever. Also, he had the distraction of his Japanese guest. To add to the mix, there had been a further development – a third guest. A very special one. One which did not cause Falconer any discomfort or displeasure. Such was his importance, Falconer would charter him a personal jet, the cost an irrelevance.

When he'd received the message, he responded immediately.

The Grey Prince needed his help. The Grey Prince was coming home.

60

The airport was busy. Not as claustrophobic as Gatwick. Everything seemed more spacious, where a person didn't mind if there were crowds, because the place was so big. Black had no luggage to collect. First, he headed for the toilets, where he discreetly destroyed his passport, before dumping it in a waste bin. If he were searched, and his passport was discovered, he would face a lot of hard questions. Black preferred to avoid the situation altogether. He then headed straight for the exit. Black was mildly shocked at the sudden heat, as he left the confines of the building. He could still turn back. They didn't know him; he didn't know them. Turn right back, lose himself somewhere, disappear.

That would never happen.

Close to the exit doors, exactly as arranged by Sands, was a black Range Rover. With darkened windows. A man standing by it. He was smartly dressed – dark trousers, white shirt, open-necked, He was big. Maybe six-four. And built. A body builder, or wrestler, surmised Black. He was tanned, thick, corded neck, roving dark eyes, head shaved to the bone.

Black stepped up.

"Mr Lincoln?" The man's face cracked into an easy smile.

Black smiled. "I didn't anticipate the heat."

"No one ever does." He opened a back door. "Please." He gestured Black inside. Another man was sitting in the seat next to his, as was a man in the front passenger seat. Suddenly, another black Range Rover swept up directly behind.

"Quite a welcome," said Black.

The man nodded politely. "Please," he said. "It's a long journey."

Black took a deep breath. A step forward, and he was entering a world of potential death. He could probably still turn and run. Most normal people would. But Black's smile widened.

He got in. The man closed the door behind him. The man got in the driver's seat. The central locking mechanism clicked. The car moved off; the engine virtually silent. The one behind followed.

"Buckle up," said the other man in the front seat.

Black did so. For one fucking rollercoaster ride.

61

The Japanese were coming to the ranch that evening. Number 4 had to be ready, and Lampton knew she was. He wouldn't let Falconer down. The prize was too great. He watched his prize now, on the monitor screen in front of him. She was sleeping. He liked to watch her sleep. Sometimes she would moan, and sometimes she would sob. She missed home. She missed the embrace of her father. But Lampton would sort all that. He had made a drink. Her favourite, he was sure. He decided he should wake her, so she could share his excitement.

He opened her door, softly, carrying a tray with biscuits and a tall glass of creamy hot chocolate. He approached the bed, set the tray down on a side cabinet, and sat beside her. The light was low, from a lamp in a corner. A revolving globe created rabbits gliding across the ceiling. He used his finger to brush hair from her eyes. *Such beautiful hair*, he thought. He stroked her cheek, the act causing a thrill to ripple through his chest. She woke with a start, eyes wide. She shrank back. Lampton gave one of his best reassuring smiles.

"Don't be scared," he whispered. "It's only Stanley."

She stared at Lampton. She did not speak. She hadn't

uttered one syllable since her arrival. Lampton didn't mind. He understood.

"Hot chocolate," he said. "And biscuits. Don't tell the others."

She remained still. Lampton was sure she was holding her breath. Maybe she was as excited as him.

"Tomorrow is a special day. For both of us." He leaned in closer. Did she move away? His smile faded slightly.

"Tomorrow, I can give you cuddles. Real cuddles. Close ones that will make you feel good. Make us both feel good. Tomorrow you can be Daddy's girl. And Daddy loves to cuddle."

She didn't respond. Lampton was a little disappointed. Surely such a pronouncement would deserve a smile, a glimmer of joy.

"Aren't you happy?"

Suddenly she shook her head, and hid under the covers.

Lampton straightened, back rigid. Not what he had expected. He had been tolerant thus far.

"Your chocolate is there," he said, his voice icy. "I made it specially. Drink it before it gets cold. Or else Stanley will be unhappy." His voice lowered to a gravelly whisper – a night-marish sound. "You don't want to upset Stanley."

He got up and left, without looking back. Too late, he thought. He was already upset. Tomorrow, a little punishment first, then some loving. This also excited Lampton. Punishment was just as stimulating. Especially hard punishment.

He closed the door behind him, hardly able to keep the tremble from his hands.

62

The conversation in the Range Rover was sparse. Black was in no mood for idle chat. Those accompanying him were equally disinclined to talk. The driver had switched the radio on. Country and western music. Black gazed at the passing scenery. So different from Scotland. Land stretching on endlessly under a hot sky; distant mountains; monuments of rock burnt pink and red in the sun; vast tracts of scrub and cactus. Every now and then, they'd pass a small town, sometimes consisting of a huddle of buildings, clinging on to the hard-baked ground. Frequent petrol stations. After over an hour, Black said he needed to stop. The driver nodded. "Sure thing. Ten minutes."

They stopped at a town called Ajo, a mile or so from the road they were on. The two cars pulled up beside a petrol station. The driver got out and opened Black's door. The passenger also got out. Black stretched his legs. The heat was stifling. The four doors of the other Range Rover opened, and four men emerged, all of them watching Black.

"I didn't realise I was so popular," said Black.

"There's a sign for toilets at the side, Mr Lincoln," said the

237

driver. He was wearing mirror sunglasses. Black saw his own distorted reflection. "My colleague Mr Pierrotti will see you over."

"See me over?"

The driver merely returned the question with a smile. Black headed over to an extension clamped on to the side of the main building, more of a lean-to, built of planks of black wood, with a flat tin roof. He was followed by the individual referred to as Mr Pierrotti, plus another man. Both large, capable.

Before he reached the toilet entrance, Black suddenly cut direction, heading straight to the main entrance of the petrol station, which also served as a general convenience store.

"I need a cold drink," said Black. He went in, before anyone could object, followed closely by his two chaperones. Black had swapped some British currency for dollars at Gatwick. He picked up a cold bottle of Coke from a cooler, placed it on the counter. An elderly man was serving, skin like brown parchment, wispy grey hair. The two men stood close behind him. Black noted another now stood at the entrance.

"That'll be a dollar, please." The attendant spoke in a heavy drawl.

Black fished out some cash. "This is Ajo? Nice town."

"Used to be busier," replied the man, conversationally. "But the mine dried up, and people left. But we still get tourists, like you gentlemen."

"Tourists?"

"Sure. This is the edge of the Sonoran Desert. People want to see the Old West, like it used to be. Hundreds of miles of rugged country." He chuckled. "Awesome country for young bucks like you and your friends."

"Thank you."

Black left the petrol station. The driver opened the door for him again. He rested a hand on his shoulder.

"We don't want you talking to anyone, Mr Lincoln. If you need some friendly chat, then we're good company. No need to involve strangers."

"Of course not. Are we close?"

"Not long."

Black got in, grateful for the car's air con. The Sonoran Desert. A good place to have a hideout. Virtually undetectable. Almost impossible to find. At least Black had some idea where they were going.

The cars moved off, leaving Ajo, and back on to the main road. The scenery changed – desert on either side, the colour of red brick; in the middle distance, rocky outcrops. In the far distance, a mountain range.

An hour later, the car veered off the main route, and travelled along a single lane road not much better than a dry dirt track, kicking up plumes of dust.

Another hour passed. The scenery didn't change any. Black squinted, looking ahead through the front windscreen – there, shimmering under the sun, was a group of buildings, maybe a mile away. They reached open gates, slowed down, drove through, entering a wide square courtyard, three sides of the square enclosed by glass buildings, two levels high. In the centre was a large fountain, water sprouting eight ways from the open palm of a mermaid, carved from blue marble. The entrance comprised a series of glass doors set three steps up, onto front decking the same blue marble. Simple, elegant, expensive. A paradise in the desert.

They had arrived.

63

Sands waited for them at the main entrance, at the top of the three marble stairs. Falconer had chosen not to greet Mr Lincoln at the present time. Later, he'd said. Let him settle in first. Sands was excited. He'd given instructions to this man over the years, paying him fortunes to arrange executions. A real-life professional assassin. Now they were to meet, face to face. But it was bittersweet. It was Lincoln who had wanted to meet. If Lincoln was worried, then they should all be worried.

He waited, as the two Range Rovers pulled up. They parked directly opposite the front doors. Sands watched as the driver of the first car got out, and opened one of the rear doors. The man he knew as Lincoln emerged. He stood for a second, taking in the surroundings. Two other men got out of the car, waiting. The driver beckoned Lincoln up the stairs, towards Sands. Lincoln approached. He was a big man. Six-two. Maybe taller. He wore a simple dark jumper, close fitting, accentuating the hard muscle beneath. Blue jeans, running shoes. Thick dark hair cropped short, harsh cheekbones, flat cheeks. Dark clever eyes. He moved with an easy, almost languid gait.

He was accompanied by the driver, two others following.

"Mr Lincoln, I'm Norman Sands. We've had significant dealings. It's good to meet you."

"Likewise."

"Can I tempt you to a refreshment?" Sands nodded to a man standing to one side, holding a silver tray with a single fluted glass of champagne. "It's Moet. Mr Falconer's particular favourite."

"Maybe later. Mr Falconer?"

"He's the boss." Sands gave a self-deprecating smile. "I'm merely the message bearer."

"I understand."

"You know, I've often wondered where you're from. We've never spoken. I mean, real speech. I detect an accent. Irish?"

"Scottish. People sometimes get confused."

"Of course. I don't know much about Scotland. It's cold, I hear. All year round. And the Scottish mountains of course."

"Of course. You have your desert. We have our mountains. Both lethal, for the unprepared."

"Quite so, Mr Lincoln. Please, let me show you to your room. You'll maybe want to relax a little. It's 3pm now. Mr Falconer would like you to join him for dinner at six. If that's all right?"

"Sounds perfect."

"Please, follow me."

Sands led the way. Rarely did they have guests. In fact, in all his time here, it had never happened. Now suddenly, he had to cater for Lincoln and also the Japanese, who were expected later that evening. Plus, Falconer had hinted there might be another.

At the very least, it would be an interesting evening.

64

With Sands leading, and another behind him, Black was escorted through a wide cathedral-style hall, the sun bright and streaming through an arched glass ceiling. Doors on either side. Walls white and smooth, adorned with dazzling oil paintings. The floor a subtle ivory marble. Furniture gleamed. Exquisite, delicate.

"That's made from real tortoise shell," explained Sands, pointing to an intricate cabinet – "French. Mr Falconer loves his French furniture."

They made their way through and into a curving corridor, like a tunnel of glass. The view was of desert. More doors, until reaching a short flight of stairs, leading to a single solid wooden door with ornate hinges.

"You ought to supply a map," remarked Black.

"One gets used to it," replied Sands. "This is your room. Or should I say rooms." He opened the door – a large bedroom, bright, airy, spacious, one side entirely glass. "The next room's a comfortable living room with a television, plus you have en suite and your own sauna. Enjoy your stay, Mr Lincoln. I'll be here at 6pm." Sands left. The door clicked behind him. Black noted the man who had accompanied them remained outside. Mr Falconer liked his security.

Black turned to the glass wall, considering the view, the expanse of desert sand. He was in the middle of nowhere. Surrounded by his enemies. Unarmed. Without any real plan.

He would probably die in this God-forsaken place. He'd make damn sure he didn't die alone.

There was a soft knock at his bedroom door at 4pm. Black answered. It was one of the men he'd travelled with in the Range Rover. He was carrying what appeared to be a suit and shirt, wrapped in polythene, draped over his forearm, and a pair of shoes.

"Sorry for intruding," he said. "Mr Falconer likes his guests to be well dressed for dinner. He thinks you might appreciate a change of clothes. No disrespect intended."

"None taken. I hope they fit."

"Mr Falconer is rarely wrong about such things."

"I'm sure."

"Mr Sands will be here at 6pm to escort you to the dining room."

"Thank you."

Black took the garments. He noticed the guard was still sitting at the opposite wall outside. Black nodded. The guard merely looked back, at him and through him. Black closed the door. He'd showered, watched some mindless crap on television. It hadn't escaped him he was a prisoner. Probably wise, from Falconer's point of view. If his game really was child trafficking, the less people snooped around, the better.

The curtains were electric, able to be drawn by the push of a button. Black preferred them open, less claustrophobic. He doubted anyone was looking in through the massive window forming one side of his bedroom. The sun was setting, giving the room a subtle orange cast. The landscape was flat desert, punctuated with dots of cactus and prickly scrub. He changed, regarding himself in a full-length mirror. Black had been given a dinner suit, white evening shirt, black bow tie, black shoes. A perfect fit. The last time he'd worn an outfit like this, he had killed several men.

He sat on a heavy leather chair in the living room section of his suite. There was nothing to do but wait. He picked up a magazine, idly flicking through some pages. The *National Geographic*. He tossed it to one side.

Black knew all about fear. He'd experienced it in its many manifestations. It wasn't that he was impervious to it. He merely had a knack of dealing with it differently from the norm. Or so he imagined. He had seen men collapse and cry in the heat of battle. He wasn't critical of such a reaction. He knew he was different. Perhaps it was in him. Perhaps he had been trained to think a certain way. But he possessed a state of mind that allowed him to step outside himself, and watch as a dispassionate observer. That way he could act, and react objectively, without judgement being clouded.

He did so now. He watched himself, and laughed grimly. *How the fuck do you get out of this one, Captain Black?*

He had no answer. Actually, he did. There was probably no way out. He would die, in this beautiful house, under a desert sky.

But death would be welcome. Black looked at himself again in the mirror, and acknowledged a sad and bitter fact.

He had nothing to live for.

His reverie was interrupted. Another soft, respectful knock. It was 6pm.

Time for dinner with Mr Falconer.

65

Black was taken to another section of the ranch, to the dining room. The décor changed as he passed through corridors, rooms, as did the style of furniture. The man called Norman Sands escorted him, referring to him as Mr Lincoln, which Black found somewhat surreal, if not grimly humorous. He was followed by two men, who said nothing.

The dining room had a distinctly Japanese feel. In one corner stood a human-sized samurai statue, dressed in full regalia. Black sat at one end of a long marble dining table. There were four places set. Sands sat on one side, to his right. The two men each moved discreetly to the corners of the room behind Black.

"Mr Falconer will be with us any second. There's to be another guest, though I haven't been told who it is. He likes his secrets."

"So it seems."

Black's nerves tingled. He was about to confront his enemy. There was cutlery on the table. Suddenly he had access to a knife. It would do little good. He'd be shot in a millisecond.

French doors to Black's left shoulder suddenly opened. A

man entered, followed by two others, who stationed themselves in the two opposite corners of the room. The man sat at the other end of the table. He was dressed formally, like Black. Dinner suit, bow tie.

"Good evening, Mr Lincoln," he said.

"Good evening, Mr Falconer."

Black appraised him. A man maybe mid-sixties. Tanned, very fit looking. Full head of glossy, dark hair. Lean. No excess fat. High, almost aquiline cheeks, intense blue eyes.

"I hope your room was to your satisfaction?" Falconer spoke quietly, a metallic undertone. A man keeping his emotions under check.

"No complaints. And a guard too? Prudent to be security conscious."

"I couldn't agree more. I hope you don't mind the evening suit. I always believe you should be dressed for dinner. It creates an air of elegance, where otherwise such an air would not exist."

"I agree."

"Can I offer you a drink?"

"I'm partial to a whisky. Glenfiddich?"

"Perfect choice. In fact, I'll have one myself. And one for Mr Sands. How do you take it, Mr Lincoln?"

"Neat."

"Excellent." He glanced at one of the waiting men, who seemed to derive exact information from the gesture, and left the room.

"I hope you like Japanese cuisine. I have a contingent from Japan arriving shortly, and hired a cook for the evening. Mr Sands is still in shock at the cost. Sometimes, the cost is unimportant, if the occasion merits such extravagance. Don't you think so, Mr Lincoln?"

"I suppose it depends on the occasion."

Falconer nodded, pursing his lips, as if considering Black's response.

"I think we can say this occasion is special."

"I would like to hear what Adam Black knows about us," interrupted Sands. "You said he talked before you killed him. What did he say?"

"Please," said Falconer. "Let's at least wait until after we've eaten. Let's be civilised. Our guest has travelled far."

Sands shrugged. "I just thought..."

"Stop thinking for one minute, Sands."

The man entered the room, carrying a tray, upon which were three short glasses. He placed one at each setting.

Falconer raised his glass. "A toast. To what, Mr Lincoln? New friendships?"

Black lifted his glass, nodded. "To new friendships."

They drank. Falconer beckoned one of the waiting men over, who leaned in, close to his ear. Falconer whispered something. The man left.

"Talking about new friendships," said Falconer, "a fourth will be here very shortly. Not so much a new friend. More a very old and dear friend. I think you'll like him, Mr Lincoln. You have no objection?"

"Of course not."

The hair on the back of Black's neck prickled. A sixth sense warned him – *trouble*! He had no idea where this was going. All he could do was keep cool, see it through, wait for an opportunity. If one should arise.

"How do you like my little 'abode'?"

"Impressive. You can't be more private than in the middle of a desert."

"Privacy is important. Especially in our line of work. Here, there's little prospect of people interfering. And if anyone feels brave enough to try, then we call in a professional like yourself. To clean up, so to speak."

The man entered the room again, carrying a black box, tied with a white silk ribbon, which he placed on the table before Black.

"For you, Mr Lincoln. A gift, for all the many services you have performed for us over the years."

Black looked at Sands, then to Falconer.

"Please – open it."

Black took a deep breath. Carefully, he untied the ribbon, opened the lid.

A knot of cold dread formed in his chest.

Placed upon soft, cream silk linen, was something he recognised.

A Venetian face mask.

66

The men waiting behind Black stepped forward, arms raised, pointing pistols at him.

Sands screeched his chair back, stood, confused. "What the fuck's going on?"

"Calm it down," said Falconer. "Sit. No need to panic."

Sands looked at Falconer, to Black, back to Falconer, like a bird caught between two cats. He sat, tentatively. "I don't understand."

The doors opened. A man entered, who sat at the table, at the fourth setting.

Black knew him instantly. The man he had followed to Westcoates Hall. The man he thought had died in the fire. The wife beater. But so much worse.

Lord Reith.

"We meet again," said Reith. He turned to Falconer and Sands. "Gentlemen, please let me introduce Adam Black."

Sands stared, aghast, blood drained from his face. "But where's Lincoln?"

"Good question," said Falconer. "Where *is* Mr Lincoln?"

Black sat back in his chair, finished off the whisky. By now the other two men had stepped forward from the far corners of the room. Four guns trained on his head. There wasn't really ever a plan. He just hoped he might get lucky. Looked like lady luck had run out.

"Lincoln has departed this world," he replied. "He's probably in hell, deliberating over his many adventures. No doubt you'll meet him soon." He fixed his gaze on Reith. "I thought you were dead. Shame. How's your hand?"

"The fire killed just about everybody. The glass in the conservatory warped and broke. I got out. The first thing I did was phone Boyd, to tell him you were alive. Then he emailed you, to agree to seeing you. To catch you in our little web. And now you're here, with us. Not for long, I'm afraid. How did you manage to find out about our 'gathering'?"

Black gave a crooked smile. "Gathering? Is that how you describe it? You got careless."

"Expand, please."

"It's not rocket science. We met at your chambers at the High Court. I stabbed you through the hand. I'm sure you recall. I noticed you were wearing a ring. Then I watched a video of a bunch of depraved fuckers raping a little girl. And guess what I saw. Same ring. So, I made a mad guess that you don't only abuse your wife, but also kids. Turned out not so mad after all. I followed you. You led me to your lair. The rest is history."

"Bravo!" exclaimed Falconer. "You are one clever boy! But maybe not so clever. You're here now, about to reach a sorry conclusion. What did you hope to achieve?"

Black shrugged. "To kill you. To kill you all. Why wouldn't I? They kill vermin, don't they? I felt it was a public service, to eradicate filth."

"And now you're going to lose everything," intoned Reith.

"Wrong. I have nothing to lose. That's why I make such a dangerous enemy. I won't stop." He swivelled his gaze to

Falconer. "Until every one of you is fucking dead in the ground. Like your cosy little paedophile ring in Scotland. Burnt and dead."

"Good luck with that," replied Falconer. "I think maybe you've overstretched yourself this time. Know your limitations, Black. Too late for you."

"What now?"

"Now you die," said Falconer. "Not here. We have guests shortly. Blood on the carpet would be a little uncivilised."

"And not quickly," added Reith. He gave a ghoulish grin. "I'm going to make you suffer."

"Looking forward to it," said Black. "But do it right. Because make no mistake, any chance I get, I will fucking destroy you."

"What an amazing man," said Falconer. "Truly. You have no conception of the position you're in." He flicked a glance at one of the waiting men. Black sensed a looming presence. A thunderous blow to the back of the head. His world flipped out of focus, then darkness descended.

67

The world was a blur. Shapes, images, nothing made sense. The room spun, the ground beneath him undulated. He was floating on the swells of a great ocean, body succumbing to a sweeping drift. Sounds penetrated his head, voices, or echoes of voices, muffled, stifled. Gradually, he gained focus, the sounds became distinct, the world stopped moving. Two men were talking. Sitting on chairs, both facing him.

He was in a room. An entire wall was devoted to monitors, each showing in sharp clarity the interior of a kid's bedroom. He was sitting. He tried to move. Both wrists were handcuffed to the arms of a chair; his ankles taped to its metal legs. His head ached. Worse than ached. A drum was banging between his ears, and every beat brought a fresh wave of pain. His movement brought the conversation round to him. He recognised one of the men. The lean, pale face of Reith – High Court judge. Dressed in similar style to Black – dinner suit, bow tie, white shirt. The other he did not know. Wearing what looked like hospital overalls, the type a surgeon might wear. Thin, verging on skeletal, wispy blond hair, darting eyes, chin disappearing into his neck. *A ferret*, thought Black. The comparison made him smile. Which amazed even himself, given his situation.

"What do you find so amusing?" asked the man.

"I was just thinking," said Black, licking his lips, trying to find his voice, "how much you resemble a ferret. You are one ugly fucker."

Reith laughed. "Ignore him, Stanley. Don't let him get to you."

The man called Stanley stood. He placed a set of keys on a hook on the wall above a desk, picked off another set. "I have to go and check up on things. Enjoy."

"I shall."

Reith turned his full attention to Black, sitting back in his chair, scrutinising him, as if he were assessing a painting, or a sculpture.

"You've caused me no end of trouble. Caused *us* trouble. Look where it got you. We can't have someone like you running around, like a mad berserker. You create chaos, Black. Chaos in a neat world."

"Not so neat for the kids."

"They're here for our pleasure. My pleasure. I only do what was done to me. The world has to balance."

"Your world needs to be fucking destroyed."

Reith put his hand in his pocket, and pulled out a small object, which he placed on the desktop. "Do you know what this is?"

Black gave Reith a stony stare. This had to play out. If anything, it bought him time.

"You have my attention."

"It's a Crusader Prince. The detail is exquisite. I can't remember how I got it. But I do remember playing with it when I was a little boy. I call it the Grey Prince. We played together,

Boyd and I. We go way back. We met in a children's home, over fifty-five years ago. We left, and Boyd went to America with his aunt. She married an American. I stayed in Scotland. But we stayed close. Ever so close. Bonded by our experience. It was always me they picked on. Sometimes Boyd. But I was the smallest. I was sodomised every night, passed about, gang-banged, shared by different men. Countless men. Performed fellatio. They fucked and fucked and fucked." He leaned in closer. "Now I do the same. I fuck and fuck and fuck. I am the Grey Prince, Mr Black. And I want my revenge. On you. On fucking everything."

His seat had little plastic wheels. He pushed it across the tiled floor, to the other side of the room, to a small stove, and a gas hob. One of the rings was lit with a blue flame. On it rested the blade of a knife. A large hunting knife, the point sharp, one edge serrated. The blade was red hot.

Reith picked it up, held it before him. He wheeled back to Black, and leant in close. He placed the tip of the blade on the corner of Black's eye. Black groaned. Suddenly the pain he felt in his head was overwhelmed by the searing pain on his skin. Slowly, Reith drew the knife down, across his cheek, to the side of his mouth.

Reith pushed the chair back, considering his work. He nodded, pleased with himself.

"That's an appetiser. Talking of which, I have to go upstairs and join Boyd for his dinner party. Some big client he's trying to impress. But I won't forget you. You'll be on my mind. I'll be down in a couple of hours. To keep you interested, I've got plans for you. Big plans." He wheeled the chair close again, brought his lips up close to Black's ear. "You know how much I like face masks," he whispered. "I'm going to use that knife to peel the skin off your face. I want my very own Adam Black mask. Then I'll let you look in the mirror, before I pop your eyeballs. Then after that... well, that's when the real pain begins."

He left, placing the knife back on the naked flame.

Black watched him go. He strained against the handcuffs. No good. He was trapped.

He was a dead man. Unless there was a miracle. And Black didn't believe in miracles.

68

_____

Lampton had things to check up on. Or so he'd said. The fact was, he was angry. Without a please or a thank you, his room was being used for purposes he didn't understand, nor want to. A man was hauled in and chained to a chair. The other man he did not know, but it was clear his intention was torture. Lampton had nothing against torture. He'd applied torture often, if he felt it was required. But to take possession of his room, like he was a piece of scrap, and use it for whatever they wanted. He felt taken for granted. Diminished. Humiliated. He concentrated on other things.

The Japanese had arrived. Lampton had two children to get ready. In fact, there was little to do. He'd given them both a mild soporific a short while ago. Nothing much. Just enough to keep them tranquil. The clients hated tears, or temper tantrums. Fear was acceptable, but in small doses. Respectful fear was tolerated. Lampton had the whole thing down to an art. He'd checked in on them briefly. Both sat in front of their television screens, both wearing pink pyjamas, both listless, unresponsive. Which was for the best. The whole thing required finesse and expertise. Plus, he had a very special incentive.

He was gazing at his "incentive" now. The room was half lit, the globe slowly spinning its characters across the ceiling. He sat on a chair by the bed, and watched her. She was breathing softly, steadily. The covers almost covered her head. Her blonde hair spilled out, onto the pillow. Such a delicate creature. Such pleasure they would both experience. And pain. Soon. He resisted the urge to stroke her hair, the side of her face. He sat, entranced.

A bleep made him jump. His mobile. It was Falconer, upstairs.

"He wants to see them. Both of them. Get them ready and get them up now. We're in the dining room. No fuck-ups, Lampton."

Lampton cursed under his breath. She hadn't woken. He hurried out of the room. He hadn't fucked up yet.

And he wouldn't tonight.

She sat up. She waited for the lock on the door to click. She didn't hear it. Hardly daring to breathe, she got out of bed, put on a dressing gown, crept to the door, as silent as a shadow. She turned the handle. The door opened, just a fraction. She saw him, his back to her, unlocking a door opposite. She shut the door, softly, softly. She pressed her ear up against the hard wood. She heard him talk, doors opening, shutting, his voice fading away, leaving a deep silence. Without knowing why, or without any idea of where she was going, or what she was doing, she slipped out.

But she did know something – she was terrified, and had to get away.

69

Sands listened to Falconer drone on about all sorts of crap, wondering if Mr Kaito was really as impressed as he appeared to be. He'd arrived with two men. Picked up at the airport, same routine as the man they'd picked up masquerading as Lincoln. The man called Adam Black. Sands was still shocked. A man – highly capable – had sat next to him at the dinner table. With the sole purpose of murder. Sands shuddered. So close to death. Now Black was languishing in the dungeon. At the disposal of the man called the Grey Prince. Sands couldn't give a shit what happened to Black. As long as it ended with him being dead. And then business as normal.

He tuned back into the Falconer monologue. This was the first time he'd met an actual client face to face. The man was reputed to be a billionaire. He looked nothing exceptional. Small, a trifle portly, balding. His two bodyguards stood quietly in the shadows. Falconer had stationed one of his own men in the next room. The rest – another four – were on a roster. Two patrolling the grounds, one at the main entrance, one at the back entrance.

But despite the bullshit which spouted forth from Falconer's mouth, Sands grudgingly conceded he had it right. The samurai warrior did the trick. Especially the sword. Kaito had desired to see it. It was placed on the table, still in its metal sheath. Kaito looked at the thing like a kid with a wondrous new toy. When he'd discovered its origin, that it had been fashioned by Masamune, the guy had an orgasm right there. And offered to buy it for one million dollars. Money would be transferred that evening. Falconer had the touch. He was a monster, but he knew how to make money. And that was one major turn-on for Sands.

The man called the Grey Prince, whose real name he'd discovered was George Reith, sat quietly, smiling, offering little in conversation. He seemed distracted. Sands found him boring. Over brandy, flushed with drink and the purchase of a fabulous Japanese sword, Kaito asked to see the merchandise. Falconer immediately obliged, calling Lampton. They were to be brought up. Sands took another swig of his drink. He was light-headed. It wasn't like him. But he didn't care. They'd made a ton of money, and life was good.

The man called Reith stood, excused himself. "I have important business," he explained quietly.

"Of course you have." Falconer laughed. "Make the bastard pay. I want to hear him scream his fucking lungs out." Of course, that would never happen, thought Sands. The dungeon was well sound-proofed.

Reith nodded, and left the room. Presumably downstairs. To do what he had to do, to inflict dreadful deeds on Adam Black.

Sands sat back, swirling the brandy in his glass, thinking, *While I sip my fine $500 brandy, a man will be downstairs being mutilated, pleading for his life. While I sip my drink.*

Sands smiled to himself.

Adam Black had messed with the wrong people. Now he paid the price. May the fucker rot in hell.

70

B lack surveyed the room. It was split into two parts, as far as he could make out. He was positioned in the office section. A work desk, office chair, twelve monitors on the wall, files stacked neatly, a computer and keyboard. A small kitchen unit, comprising stove, gas hob, microwave, kettle. One of the gas rings burned bright, the blade of the knife red hot, the implement of his torture and death. Black tried not to dwell on it. If he turned his neck, he saw details behind him... a bed, cupboards, wardrobes, a far door, presumably shower and toilet. All very neat. Black imagined the person who dwelt here was precise, fastidious, obsessively so.

He couldn't see a way out. His wrists were handcuffed to the arms of the chair. His ankles taped to the legs. He was going nowhere. Soon he would taste the blade. He would endure torture, then die. Black was not scared. He was resigned. He might see his wife and daughter again, in another place. And if he didn't, then at least his guilt would end. He would meet oblivion with a smile.

Black looked up. To his astonishment, a girl stood in the doorway. Maybe seven years old. She stared at Black, wide-eyed.

Scared.

Black saw a glimmer of a chance.

"What's your name?"

She didn't respond. She stared, her face blank.

"My name is Adam. Can you help me?"

She took one tentative step forward.

"Please," he said. "These men have trapped me. Like you. Help me. I can get us away from this place."

Another step forward. Black wondered how he must look; cuffed to a chair, a raw burn mark running down the length of his face. A ghoulish figure.

She didn't respond.

"There are keys hanging on the wall." He gesticulated by nodding over to where the other man had left a set of keys on a hook. Probably another vain hope. He had no idea the right key was there. But he had to try. "If you climb up onto the desk, you could get them, and see if you can unlock these handcuffs."

Another step forward.

"Please," he urged.

A response. An almost imperceptible nod. But Black saw it. He dared to hope.

She scrambled up onto the desktop, knocking over a plastic tray containing pens, paper-clips, other stuff. It fell with a clatter. Black held his breath. She reached up, retrieved the keys, lowered herself, approached Black.

"Let me see."

She spread them out between her hands. There!

"Try the little key," he said.

Suddenly a noise, from outside. The sound of a lock. A door opening, closing. A man's voice. Reith.

"Hurry," breathed Black.

She placed the key in the chamber of one handcuff, turned. The two metal arms clicked and pulled open. She concentrated on the other one. Seconds ticked by. His voice was near. The second sprung open.

The voice only seconds away.

"Hide!" he whispered. "The back room. Go!"

She understood. She scampered away, behind him. He heard her close the door, just as two men appeared. One was Reith. He was carrying a brown paper bag. The other, a guard – a holster strapped under his arm, and in the holster, a pistol. Looked like a Beretta.

"You can go, thank you," said Reith. The man nodded, giving Black a darting look, and left. Black had positioned his wrists back on the arms of the chair. At first glance, it appeared he was still cuffed. His ankles were still taped.

"Is that a present for me?" asked Black.

Reith sat on the desk chair, the brown bag on his lap, and wheeled the chair closer. Not close enough.

"More a statement," replied Reith.

"Sounds intriguing."

"Glorious, actually."

He opened the bag, and pulled out a full face mask, made of delicate white porcelain.

"When circumstances dictate, I wear this. This is my Death Doll mask."

He put it on. The image confronting Black was something from a nightmare. Reith continued, speaking through a space for his mouth, just large enough for Black to see his lips move as he spoke, the pink movement of his tongue.

"I only wear this when the pleasure evolves into pain. When the killing urge comes on. My subject sees this and knows there's no turning back. I become death, Mr Black."

He pushed away, to the knife, glowing on the gas flame. He was wearing gloves. He picked up the knife, and returned to Black.

"If you recall, I'm going to start by peeling your skin."

He thrust his arm forward, grabbing Black by the hair.

A little closer.

Reith leaned in. "Don't struggle, or the pain just gets worse." He raised the knife, angling Black's face one way, drew the blade close to his cheek. Even through the mask, Black could smell Reith's breath. It was all he needed.

Black suddenly lifted his hand, caught Reith's wrist. The white mask remained impassive. Underneath, Reith's face was doubtless a picture of profound astonishment. Reith gave a small startled scream. Black brought his other arm up and round Reith's neck, bringing him into his chest, catching him in a headlock.

Reith collapsed forward, onto his knees, the chair skittering backwards.

"You got it all wrong," hissed Black. "It's me who is death. But I don't become it. I am it."

He forced Reith's hand downwards, the blade edging closer to Reith's neck, below his ear. Reith tried to resist, push back, but his angle was all wrong, and Black was stronger. The tip scraped his neck.

Reith's voice was a husky rasp. "Please…"

"For the children, you fucking mad bastard."

Black pushed. The blade entered, red hot, a fraction behind the jawline, sliding in, through flesh, blood, through his neck. Skin sizzled. He pushed, until the blade was in, hilt deep. Reith spluttered, emitted a gargled croak, all the while the Death Doll mask stared, reflecting neither pain nor fear. Black felt Reith shudder, his body sagged. He flopped onto the tiles.

Black stretched down, pulled out the knife, used it to cut the tape round his ankles.

He went to the back of the room, opened the door. It was a

bathroom. The girl was cowering in a corner. He held out his hand.

"Come with me."

They left, passing Reith's body, huddled on the floor, shirt soaked, blood lying in a little pool on the tiles. The girl stared at it, transfixed. Black had no words. She was in a living nightmare. Nothing he could do about it, except try to get her the hell out. And on the way, inevitable images of horror. The price of freedom.

They entered into a broad, long hall. Almost like a kids' playground. Sparkling globe lights on the ceiling, reflecting silver stars. Soft toys scattered. Brightly coloured wallpaper. Doors on either side. At the end of the corridor, a single door, with a numbered keypad. The exit, assumed Black.

He knelt down to the girl.

"Did you come from one of those rooms?"

She nodded, and pointed.

"I need you to go back. Stay inside. Don't leave, until I return." He held her gaze, looking into her eyes. "And I promise I will."

She nodded again, eyes filling suddenly with tears. She turned, went to her room, looked back quickly, disappeared inside.

Black straightened. How the hell was he going to get out? He paused. An idea struck him. It was a long shot, but it might just work. He returned to the room, to Lord Reith. Even in death, he might prove useful.

71

The guard sitting at his post sipped from a can of lemonade. He was bored. Nothing happened on this particular watch. He preferred doing the patrol route round the periphery of the ranch. At least when he did that, he got to stretch his legs. And chat. Maybe even a smoke. But here, cooped up in this tiny box of a room, nothing ever happened. He'd been working for Falconer for two years. And during this time, he hadn't seen even a hint of excitement. But he got well paid for it, so he didn't make it his business to grumble. And what went on in the basement wasn't his problem. He did a job, he got paid. End of.

This evening had been a little different. Guests from Japan. A big guy in a dinner suit kept prisoner in Lampton's room. And now he'd just taken another guy in. Blood would spill, he thought. But it wasn't his problem. His job was to watch one single monitor on the desk in front of him. The view was the entrance in and out of the big hallway, where the kids sometimes played.

He took another sip. An image appeared. It startled him. A

man was there. The guy in the dinner suit. Wearing a crazy mask. He was pointing to the door. Probably forgotten the key code. *Stupid fucker*, he thought, as he pressed a button, releasing the electric locking mechanism, opening the door.

~

Black was in. He stepped through, into a room with one man sitting at a desk in front of a monitor screen. The same man who had escorted Reith.

"You forget the code?" asked the man.

Black nodded.

"Three, three, four, three. I like the mask. A bit creepy. You finished now?"

"I'm not, but you are," replied Black. The man was sitting, looking up. Black revealed the knife. It flashed in his hand. He clamped one arm round the man's face, used his other hand to stab him in the heart. The man uttered a choking gasp, slumped forward. Black rested the man's head on the desktop. If it weren't for the blood, he might have been mistaken for sleeping on the job. Black pulled the Beretta from his side holster. Checked the magazine clip. Eight cartridges. That would do just fine.

He kept the knife, wiped it clean on the dead man's shoulder, tucked it in his inside jacket pocket. It had been lucky for him so far. He might need its luck again.

Black pressed a button. A soft chime. A door slid open. He entered a lift. He pressed the internal button. The doors slid shut, he sensed movement. Going up. Seconds later, the lift stopped, the door swept open automatically.

Another small office-type room, another man, sitting in front of a desk. Before him were several screens, showing views of different parts of the building. Some interior, some external.

"Nice mask," he said.

"Thank you."

Black shot him once in the head. He bounced off his chair, onto the floor. He suspected the room was secure enough to muffle the gunshot. He retrieved his pistol. Another Beretta. Same model. He faced a door. Another keypad. He tapped in the numbers given. The lock clicked, the door opened.

Black was out.

He was in a corridor, the walls decorated in a warm orange swirl, Mediterranean style, the light muted from candle bulbs flaming on bronze brackets on the walls. He had no idea where to go. He turned to his right, along a corridor, past pieces of exotic furniture, emerging at length into a large open-plan split-level living room, dominated by a massive cream suede corner couch. An entire wall was cloaked in heavy drapes. The light was subdued, casting a strange, witchy quality.

Black hugged the shadows, moved quietly through to an adjoining study, cluttered with antique furniture, an exquisite writing bureau, a simulated log fire. He detected noise. Laughing. Not far away. He waited by the side of the door. He still wore the mask. He might just get away with it.

He strolled out through the door, and into a connecting miniature courtyard of sea-green flagstones, illuminated in soft hues of pink and amber from silken box lanterns hanging from low stick-like trees. On the other side, French doors, opening to the dining room. He could see Falconer through the glass, talking animatedly. A single guard stood on one side of the doors. The guard stepped forward. He would be unsure. Black still wore the Death Doll mask. Black caught Falconer's eye, waved. Falconer waved back, ushered him through. The guard relaxed. Black had his hands behind his back, clutching both

Berettas. He could have been walking in the park on a summer's day. He nodded to the guard. The guard nodded back. Black brought his hands forward, shot once, twice. Chest, neck. Falconer's head snapped round, all talking stopped.

Black opened the French doors and entered.

72

The worst is death, and death will have his day.

William Shakespeare. King Richard II

Several men; two little girls.

Falconer, Sands and a Japanese man, sitting at the dining table, cluttered with an array of champagne bottles, silver trays of chocolates, a percolator of coffee, cups, glasses. And a samurai sword. Two other Japanese men now honed in towards him from the far side. They'd all heard the gunshot. Falconer's face stared; tanned features frozen in a mask of shocked confusion. Refusing to believe it was happening.

The Japanese guards advanced, pulling out handguns from side holsters. Black ducked, rolled, guns blazing in each hand, firing from a half-kneeling position. Two shots, in rapid succession. One man flipped back, face torn in half. The other staggered, taking a hit on the shoulder. Black didn't hesitate, following up with a shot to his chest, then another to the top of his head. He flew back into a tall glass cabinet, the content spilling out – crystal sets, glasses, decanters, goblets, all crashing to the floor.

Black straightened, removed the mask.

"Good evening, gentlemen. Hope I'm in time for coffee."

Silence. If there were other guards, they'd be here soon.

The Japanese man grabbed the sword from the dining table, brought it round, pointing it into the chest of one of the girls standing close to him, who stood motionless, stricken.

"I'll kill her." He stood, bringing the girl closer, adjusting his arm, angling the edge of the blade across her throat. "I don't know who you are," he continued, "but this has nothing to do with me. We're leaving. If you don't let me go, I swear I'll slit her throat."

The girl stared at Black, her face still and pale.

Black looked at her, smiled, flicked his eyes back to the Japanese man. "You're going nowhere, friend." He whipped his hand up, fired one shot. The bullet caught the Japanese man in the mouth, his lower jaw and throat shattering in a small explosion of bone and body part. The impact spun him round in a mad pirouette, the sword clattering on to the tabletop. He fell to the floor, dead before he'd hit it. The girl screamed, suddenly soaked in blood and tissue.

Black turned to Falconer and Sands. They hadn't moved, sitting at the table, Falconer at one end, Sands to his side. Black still needed information. He heard sounds – men shouting.

"You're a fucking dead man," snarled Falconer. "You'll be hunted for the rest of your fucking life."

"What do you want, Black?" asked Sands, his voice rising to a whining pitch.

"Is it about money?" asked Falconer. "How much?"

Black sensed a presence. He turned – two men stood at the French doors. Another appeared at the opposite doorway. All armed, one with a sub-machine gun. Black shifted his position, aiming both pistols directly at Falconer's head.

He raised his voice. "If you shoot, two things are going to happen. One, you'll probably kill each other in the crossfire. And two, I'll blow Falconer's head from his shoulders."

"Don't shoot!" screamed Falconer.

"You heard the man." Black took two steps, standing next to Falconer, pressing the nozzle of a Beretta to the side of his head.

"What do you want, Black?"

They hadn't taken his wallet. He placed the other pistol on the table, fished the wallet out of his back pocket. He pulled out a crumpled photograph, and held it in front of Falconer.

"Do you recognise this girl?"

"How the fuck should I know?" muttered Falconer, averting his eyes. "They're all the fucking same."

"Look at her!" said Black, his voice harsh.

Falconer glanced at the picture, shook his head. "They're all the same," he repeated.

"This little girl has a name. Natalie Bartholomew."

"We don't recognise them by their names," blurted Sands. "They have numbers. But we have detailed records. Of everything. Their names, where they came from, their source, the cost. I can give you this."

"The cost?"

"The cost of getting them here."

Black darted a glance either side. The men waited, for a command, a cue, a nod of the head. Then he had no place to go. And he would die.

But not yet.

"You give them numbers?" he asked, his voice low, dead-pan. "How many children do you have?"

"Including these two," said Sands, nodding at the two girls on the other side of the room, "twelve."

"Twelve," repeated Black, his mind trying to grasp the scale of the operation. The scale of the depravity. He straightened. He was to play the biggest gamble of his life.

He positioned the nozzle of the Beretta to Falconer's temple. Falconer went rigid.

"What the fuck are you doing?"

"I've called the cops!" shouted Black. "They're coming, make no mistake. You have a choice. You either stay, or you get as far away from here as possible. And I'll make the choice easier for you!"

Black looked down, and met Falconer's upturned gaze. Falconer's face went slack.

"I can't believe you're going to do this. Please... we can work something..."

"So long, partner."

He shot Falconer through the head. Falconer thumped forward onto the dining-room table, the champagne bottles and chocolates suddenly wet from a fresh spring of blood.

Black waited. The men stood, shocked, wavering. Black saw their dilemma. Suddenly they had no employer. So, what the hell were they doing? And if the cops were on their way. They had no beef with Black. They were mercenaries, paid guards. And suddenly the pay had dried up.

They backed off, melted away. Black didn't give a damn where.

Black focused on the two girls. "You're safe. Stay here. I'll be back."

He pointed his pistol at Sands. "Show me those records."

Sands nodded vigorously. "Of course. Follow me."

He led him back through the enclosed courtyard. Black heard cars, tyres screeching, not far away. Looked like his advice had been taken. The cavalry had deserted.

They got to the split-level living room Black had passed

through earlier. One entire wall was closed off with long heavy drapes.

"Is that the front?" Black asked.

"Yes." Sands went over to a panel on a wall, pressed a button. The drapes opened. The front area was floodlit. There, the blue marble mermaid fountain, water arcing from her outstretched palm. Several Range Rovers. A Jeep was parked up hard by the side of an outbuilding.

Sands moved with a nervous energy. His hands trembled, his face twitched, blinking sweat from his eyes. No wonder, thought Black. His world had just been destroyed. Sands picked up what looked like a TV remote, tapped out a sequence of numbers. A wooden panel above the corner suite folded back, a screen levered up into the space. He tapped a button. Names, dates, addresses appeared.

"What was her name?" he asked, his voice a dry croak.

Black took a second to absorb what he was looking at. "Natalie Bartholomew," he said slowly.

Sands typed in the name. "We don't have her," he said. "But she was supposed to have been delivered. Several months ago. It's all there. Everything."

Black stepped closer, scrutinising the details. Name, age, address. A photograph. The price. £250,000. Sterling. Particulars of the abduction. Everything, from start to finish. How it ended.

And the source. A particular name. Black was stunned. His mind reeled at the implications, which were staggering. And unbelievable. "You're sure this is correct?"

"It has to be." Sands' voice diminished to barely a whisper. "We were running a business, you understand. Information was the key."

Black snapped his head away. "A business?"

Sands nodded, blinking.

"Do you have GPS co-ordinates for this shithole?"

"Yes."

"Good. Phone the cops. Give them the location."

"What do I say?" he stammered.

"You tell them the truth. That there's a whole bunch of kids, kept prisoners in a fucking basement, ready to be sold on to paedophiles. That about sums it up. Or have I missed something?"

"I'll go to prison," said Sands, words tumbling out. "Arizona still keeps the death penalty. Please let me go. I never touched any of these kids. I'm an accountant. I just kept track of the figures."

"How many children have been sold on?"

Sands swallowed. "I don't know exactly."

"Roughly. Please, humour me."

Sands raised his hands. "I don't know – over the years, maybe 800?"

Black regarded him with a measured stare.

"Okay. I get what you say. You don't want to face the authorities. I understand. You only did the accounts. The number cruncher. What are the co-ordinates?"

Sands gave a small tremulous smile. "Thank you."

He gave Black the co-ordinates. He smiled back at Sands, then shot him twice in the chest, at close range. Sands fell back on to the couch, rolled on to the floor. Black stepped forward, shot him again in the forehead, his skull bursting in a sparkle of rich red colour.

Suddenly, a noise – outside. He whirled round.

The girl from the basement, screaming, squirming in the arms of a man he'd seen before. The man in the hospital tunic. The man from the basement. Heading for the Jeep.

Black gave chase.

Lampton had the girl. The adventure was over. The devil Adam Black had ruined everything. But the girl was his. Promised to him. He had so much to teach her, to give her. He would not be denied. He'd take the Jeep, drive into the desert. To a dark place. Let her see how much he loved her, under the stars, on the desert floor. Then, he would disappear. To another state, maybe. Another country. Perhaps take the girl.

Probably not. She would awaken in the desert. And die in the desert.

73

There was a glass door directly from the living room to the front courtyard. Locked. Black blew it open with a single shot. The man turned, kept running. He gripped the girl in his two arms, close to his chest, her face on his shoulder, pale, screaming, terrified.

It was difficult for him to keep a hold, and get his keys out of his pocket. He stopped at the car door. She writhed and struggled.

"Keep fucking still!" he screamed.

Black sprinted towards him. He fired in the air, hoping it would scare him into dropping the girl. It didn't. He got the door open, bundled her inside, started the car up, swerved it round, facing him, full headlights on. Black was dazzled. He stood, legs apart, aimed. Too risky to fire at the driver. He couldn't see him in the glare, and he might miss, and hit the girl. Instead, he fired at the lights, both guns blazing, the front tyres, the front grill. The car veered to one side, careened onto the fountain, slamming into the blue marble mermaid, where it lay, one end up off the ground, balanced precariously, both wheels spinning. The driver's door opened. The man spilled out, dragging the girl with him.

He had her by the hair. Her screams cut through the desert night. He brandished a knife.

"She's mine. You can't have her."

He moved backwards, away from Black. The girl kicked and screamed. The man slapped her hard across the face. Black's heart rose to his mouth. Her body sagged. She hung limp. The man let her drop to the ground, and placed one boot on her neck.

"If you come any closer, I swear to Jesus fucking Christ, I will snap her neck like a fucking twig."

Black stopped. He was maybe six yards away.

"Drop the fucking guns."

"Of course." He dropped them on to the courtyard tiles. They were useless to him. He was out of bullets. Otherwise he would have gunned the bastard down. "What's your name?"

"Stanley Lampton. But they call me Stan."

"Sure they do. What now, Stanley?"

"Now I take this little one with me, into the desert, where no one can find us."

"In the desert? Really? Without transport? How long do you think you'll survive? Without water."

"I'm a survivor, Black. You failed. And I've won."

"Interesting point of view. I have a gift for you."

He reached into his jacket pocket, slowly, and produced the hunting knife the Grey Prince had used to slice one side of Black's face.

"That knife you're holding looks like a penknife. This one's much better."

"What's your fucking game, Black?"

"No game. You said you were a survivor? Survive this!"

He threw the knife – a strong, hard movement. Spin style. It

277

plunged, almost to the hilt, into Lampton's upper chest, near his shoulder. He staggered back, mouth open, aghast.

Black strode forward. Lampton waved his knife in a desperate effort to fend Black off. To no avail. Black rendered him a thunderous blow to the side of the head. Lampton fell back, hitting the ground hard.

Black crouched down to the girl. She was breathing. Concussed. He turned his attention back to Lampton, who was trying to regain his feet, the knife protruding from just below his shoulder joint. He was losing blood fast.

"What have you done to me?"

"Here, let me help you up."

Black hauled him to his feet, pulling the knife out. Blood was pumping, alarmingly. An artery was punctured. "You want to go – go! Hide in the desert. But first..."

Black worked the knife on Lampton's lower abdomen – a quick, deep slice. Lampton stepped back, eyes bulging. He clamped both hands on to the sudden aperture, aware that he was holding in his internal organs.

"What have you done?"

"Made sure. Now hide in the sand dunes all you want."

"I'll die."

Black loomed in close. "I know." He pushed him away.

Lampton stared at Black for a second. Then at his stomach, his trousers saturated in blood. If he let go, his insides would spill on to the ground. His face was a white skull, lips drawn back in fear, revulsion.

"Please..."

Black looked on, without emotion. Lampton saw no salvation. He croaked something inarticulate, staggered off into the night. He wouldn't last longer than two minutes. Maybe less.

Let the vultures pick his bones.

74

B lack carried the girl back into the house, and laid her on a couch. He got the two children from the dining room – both sitting huddled together in a corner – and gently gestured them through to the living room. They followed, silent, like two wraiths. He retraced his steps, reached the door with the keypad, punched in the number. He made his way past the dead sentry, took the lift down, passed the second dead sentry. Death followed him, he thought.

He reached the hall with rainbow walls and silver globes. He kicked every door down. Nine shocked, silent children followed back to ground level. *This was how the Pied Piper felt*, Black thought sardonically. He grouped them all in the living room, and called the cops, providing them with the GPS co-ordinates. Sands' body was still sprawled on the floor, but Black was too weary to drag it outside.

They waited together. Black and twelve children. Not a word was spoken.

Perhaps he really was a good guy. Perhaps.

He had one more thing to do, to see the saga to its end.

Black had to go right back.
To the beginning.

75

Leith Walk. Three months later.

A trendy section of Edinburgh, and one of its longest streets. Tourists strolled on the cobbled walkways running parallel to the Water of Leith. They might sample a pastry from a Sicilian bakery, or browse the quaint Georgian antique shops. Perhaps leaf through books at the several bespoke bookshops. Or peruse the Leith Market, perhaps pick up a bargain. Then there were the wine bars, coffee houses, restaurants. Or a person might linger on one of the many bridges, and watch the water beneath drift by. A place once frowned upon. Now a place upmarket, desirable. Like any city. Bad becomes good. Good becomes bad.

Black was in no mood to see the sights. He had other matters on his mind. He headed for a street a mere stone's throw from the waterside. It was a Saturday morning, early. A wind whipped up, tinged with hail. The forecast was snow later. Above, clouds the colour of slate made the day feel dark. The place was quiet. Too early, and too cold, for most.

Black reached the street – Victoria Crescent. Either side, a row of mid-terraced houses, each over a hundred years old. B-listed. Manicured front gardens, stone balustrades lining marble steps to entrances. High windows, still single glazed due to stiff planning laws.

An expensive place to live, thought Black.

He made his way up a pathway, rang the doorbell. The front door had glass panes styled in Charles Rennie Mackintosh designs. Black saw a silhouette approach, a vague outline. A woman opened the door.

Pamela Thompson.

She stared at Black, speechless.

"My God. It's you."

"It's nice to see you too. How are you keeping?"

"I'm fine." She frowned, uncertain, searching for the right words. "Please, come in."

"Thank you."

Black entered a hallway some might have described as old-fashioned. High ceiling, intricate coving, a silver striped wallpaper, pale cream carpet.

"It's good to see you again. Please, come through. We're having breakfast."

Black followed her, through a door into a large kitchen. One side comprised a breakfast bar, three red cushioned high stools on either side. On one sat a man, drinking coffee, eating toast, a newspaper stretched out before him.

"Adam, this is my husband, David."

David stopped in mid-chew. Like his wife, he stared at Black for several seconds. He placed the coffee mug carefully down on the worktop, swallowed then stretched out his hand. "Nice to meet you."

Black shook his hand, smiled.

"Would you like a coffee?" asked Pamela.

"Yes, please."

She filled another mug from a percolator. "We like our coffee strong, if that's okay."

"Perfect. No milk. Just as it is."

Black took a sip. Pamela gestured that he sit, but Black said he preferred to stand. He would not be long.

"How have you been?" she asked.

"Good. How's life at Raeburn Collins and Co.?"

Pamela shrugged. "I don't work there anymore." She lowered her voice. "I changed jobs. After Donald Rutherford was killed. It didn't feel right. Did it, David?"

Her husband hadn't taken his eyes off Black. He shook his head.

"I understand that," replied Black. Then to David Thompson, "I have a message for you."

Thompson remained still.

"The Grey Prince is dead."

Pamela looked to her husband, to Black. "Who's the Grey Prince?"

Black kept a steady gaze on Thompson. "But you probably already knew that." Another sip of coffee. Black turned to Pamela.

"The afternoon we met in my hotel room. I told you not to tell anyone. Later that evening, men were waiting for me there. Killers. Only you knew, Pamela. How would they know where I was?"

Pamela's face creased in puzzlement. "But I didn't tell anyone, I swear. Except..."

"Except your husband," finished Black.

Pamela turned to look at him. Thompson didn't move. He stared straight at Black. Black stared right back.

"Little Natalie was taken. You left the window open, and somebody took her. That's what you said."

Another sip of coffee.

"What happened, David? The money was never paid. According to Boyd Falconer's records, the price was to be £250,000. But the money wasn't paid, because she wasn't delivered. So, what happened?"

Pamela turned slowly to face her husband. Still puzzled. But slowly, slowly, it was dawning on her. Something was terribly wrong. Perhaps a suspicion she'd harboured all those sleepless nights. "What's he talking about, David?"

He blinked, as if he'd come out of a trance. "I don't know what he's talking about." The words were a whisper.

"Maybe this will help." Black pulled out the photograph of Natalie, and placed it on the breakfast bar.

"Tell your wife what happened. She's owed the truth. Let go of the burden, David. Look at all the deaths. Natalie's mother, overdosed. Her father, murdered. Pamela's sister, dead. And little Natalie. What happened to her, David?"

Thompson lowered his head, staring at the open newspaper. He snapped his head up, his face white, lips stretched back, defiant. "It was the fucking money!"

Pamela gasped. "What are you saying?"

"I'm saying, my business was going down the fucking shitter. I saw a chance. It could have put us back again. Back where we belonged. How the fuck do you think I pay for all this? This fucking house. Your fucking gym. The fucking cars. How do you think I do this?"

Pamela looked stricken. "I don't understand..."

"Because you don't understand anything. I was heading for bankruptcy. I knew the Grey Prince. He made a proposal."

"How would you know the Grey Prince?" asked Black. "How could such a proposal ever come up in conversation."

"You're a bastard, Black." Thompson's voice was hoarse, ragged.

Pamela spoke, her voice suddenly cold. "Answer the question."

"I don't need to answer anything. This is all bullshit. I need some air."

He got up to go. Black pulled out a pistol and pointed it inches from his right eye.

"It would be ill-mannered to leave, especially when you have a guest. I think you know I'll use this. It will bring me pleasure to spread your fucking brains across these nice kitchen units. So, please. Answer the lady."

Thompson took a deep shuddering breath. He started to cry. He stretched his arms out to Pamela. "Please..."

Pamela took a small step back. When she spoke, her voice was tight, strained. "Answer the question, David."

Thompson sat back down, put his head in his hands. "I went to some parties." He sobbed.

Black waited. He had all day.

"Parties with children."

Pamela staggered back, clutching her chest.

Thompson continued. "Only one man knew our identities. He knew all about me. He knew who I was. He knew about my business. He made a proposal. He called himself the Grey Prince."

"And the proposal?" asked Black.

"If I could procure a child, a young child, then in return I would get £250,000." He looked up, at his wife. "We had Natalie for the night. It was planned. She was taken. I opened the window. I gave her to two men."

"And?"

"She didn't make it."

"What the fuck does that mean?" screamed Pamela.

"They put her in the boot of a car. She suffocated. She died."

Black regarded the man before him. Disgust, contempt? He couldn't describe his emotion. "What did they do with her?"

"Buried, I think. Somewhere on the Eaglesham moors. Where no one will find her." He sobbed into his hands, then collapsed on to the kitchen tiles, scrunched up, crying.

Black laid the pistol on the breakfast bar.

"There's a bullet in the chamber," he said to Pamela. "Just one. I'll leave it here. If your husband has a shred of courage, he'll use it. Or you can. Or you can call the police. The choice is yours. I'm sorry, Pamela."

Black left the house, made his way down the manicured front garden. He turned. From within the building, a sound had emanated. An echo. A gunshot? Perhaps. Or perhaps it was his imagination, playing tricks, hoping for such a sound.

He walked on, past the row of terraced houses, down to the riverside, to the Water of Leith.

He took a deep breath. He felt the rain on his face, the chill wind on his cheeks. Suddenly he was deflated, hollow. Bone weary.

The affair was over.

76

Black had never visited Dublin. It was his final destination on the list. He arrived at a tower block, one of three standing next to each other, and took the elevator to the tenth floor. He got to the door with the nameplate, *Clancy*. There was no doorbell. He knocked gently.

A man answered. Mid-forties, glasses, balding. Tired-looking. Lines etched the corner of his eyes, his mouth. He looked older than he probably was. Black got that.

"Can I help you?"

"I'm wondering if I could see Alanna?"

"Alanna. My daughter?" The lines on his face hardened. "And you are?"

"I'm Adam Black."

The man removed his glasses, took a step forward, face breaking into a sudden broad smile.

"Adam Black." He gazed at Black, eyes bright, alive. "She talks about you. All the time. She's been waiting for you. We all have."

Black returned the smile, embarrassed.

The man stretched forward, embraced him, held him close. "Her guardian angel."

Maybe he wasn't all bad.

Maybe he really was a good guy.

Maybe.

77

Tricia told Black she would not be returning, at least not in the near future and Black understood. She needed to clear her head, to think, to rationalise.

Black would wait. He didn't get a replacement. He could answer the phones and do his own filing.

Back to basics.

It was a chill February morning, and the snow had turned to a grey sleet, when a man knocked on the door to his office.

Black was looking over a lease document for a new occupant directly downstairs from him.

"May I come in?"

Black looked up, and gestured him to the chair on the other side of his desk.

"Of course."

The man sat. Black put the document to one side. The man before him was small, compact, wearing a long herringbone greatcoat. Smart. Dark hair flecked with grey, shaved above the ears. Salt-and-pepper moustache. Slight tan. Sharp, inquisitive eyes.

"Can I help you?"

"That was an impressive performance. Both in America and at Westcoates Hall."

Black tensed.

"Yes?"

"You destroyed the biggest and most sophisticated child trafficking organisation we've ever come up against. And you're just one man. How did you do that?"

"Lucky, I suppose. Who are you?"

"Someone interested in Adam Black's career."

"I don't understand."

"I'm part of a department that works closely with the government. The secret part of the government, that is."

"I still don't understand."

"Why do you think our American friends let you leave for Britain so quickly. You killed what... ten men? Even the Americans aren't that liberal."

Black said nothing.

"We told the Americans we wanted you back."

"What do you want from me?"

The man gave a wintry grin. "Isn't it obvious? We want you to work for us, Captain Black."

THE END

Printed in Great Britain
by Amazon

50663177R00167